Praise for *The Family Next Door*

"Fans of *Big Little Lies* should pick up *The Family Next Door*, stat."
—PureWow.com

"With jaw-dropping discoveries, and realistic consequences, this novel is not to be missed. Perfect for lovers of *Big Little Lies*."
—*Library Journal*, starred review

"Expertly done . . . the nuanced layers of domesticity and the psychological dimensions explored will make this novel the next great book-club read!"
—*RT Book Reviews*

"A book Liane Moriarty fans will love."
—*Marie Claire*

Praise for *The Mother's Promise*

"This bittersweet, emotionally intense novel is recommended for readers who appreciate issue-driven stories by Jodi Picoult and Lisa Genova."
—*Library Journal*, starred review

"Conveys with sympathy and depth the stories of four Northern California women who face important issues not typically found in fiction."
—*New York Journal of Books*

"Hepworth intertwines these women's stories, taking the notion that it takes a village to raise a child another step: it takes a village to raise each women up over her own tribulations."
—*Kirkus Reviews*

The Family
Next Door

Sally Hepworth

St. Martin's Griffin

New York

THE FAMILY NEXT DOOR. Copyright © 2018 by Sally Hepworth. All rights reserved. Printed in the United States of America. For information address St. Martin's Press, 175 Fifth Avenue, New York, N.Y. 10010.

www.stmartins.com

Excerpt from *The Mother-in-Law* copyright © 2019 by Sally Hepworth

The Library of Congress has cataloged the hardcover edition as follows:

Names: Hepworth, Sally, author.
Title: The family next door / Sally Hepworth.
Description: First edition. | New York : St. Martin's Press, 2018.
Identifiers: LCCN 2017043686 | ISBN 9781250120892 (hardcover) |
    ISBN 9781250185136 (international, sold outside the U.S., subject to rights
    availability) | ISBN 9781250120915 (ebook)
Subjects: LCSH: Domestic fiction. | GSAFD: Suspense fiction.
Classification: LCC PR9619.4.H48 F36 2018 | DDC 823/.92—dc23
LC record available at https://lccn.loc.gov/2017043686

ISBN 978-1-250-12090-8 (trade paperback)

Our books may be purchased in bulk for promotional, educational, or business use. Please contact your local bookseller or the Macmillan Corporate and Premium Sales Department at 1-800-221-7945, extension 5442, or by email at MacmillanSpecialMarkets@macmillan.com.

First St. Martin's Griffin Edition: February 2019

10 9 8 7 6 5 4 3 2

For Oscar
Sorry for not writing
a book about dinosaurs

Acknowledgments

It takes a lot of people to bring a story to life. You wouldn't be reading this one if it weren't for my gifted editor, Jennifer Enderlin. It gives me tremendous comfort to know that every time I write myself into a corner—and I *do* do it every time—you are there to help me out. Thank you also to the rest of the team at St. Martin's—the assistants, the copy editors, the designers, the marketing and sales people—for the invaluable roles you play in bringing books to the shelves.

I am also indebted to my publishers around the world, with special thanks to Alex Lloyd, Cate Paterson, Julia Stiles, and the rest of the team at PanMacmillan Australia.

To my agent, Rob Weisbach: Thank you for your guidance and your belief in me. I couldn't do any of this without you, and I refuse to try.

To my first readers—Angela Langford, Dagmar Logan, Emily Makiv, Kena Roach, Inna Spitzkaia, and Jane Wharton—thank you for your wonderful suggestions and words of encouragement.

To my writerly friends, especially Jane Cockram, Anna George, Meredith Jaeger, and Fran Wang-Ward—thank you for reading my drafts and for talking writer-talk with me after the rest of my friends have tuned out.

To Oscar, Eloise, and Clementine, thank you for staying alive while I'm in the writing cave. Some might call it subpar parenting, but I prefer to think of it as "building resilience."

Finally, thank you to Christian for doing the laundry and the taxes. Also for everything else. But I really hate laundry and taxes.

I've spent my whole life wanting you. As a toddler, I was forever toting around a plastic doll—wrapping it and feeding it and changing its diaper. As a child, my favorite pastime was making up baby names. As a teenager, I babysat every chance I could, imagining you nestled against my hip instead of the stranger's child I carried. There were times in my early twenties when wanting you felt shameful. After all, women were supposed to want careers, travel, success—we were capable of anything. Aspiring to be a mother wasn't original or brave or interesting. It certainly wasn't something to strive for.

Still, I wanted you.

So it was a shock when, years later, you announced your imminent arrival with a blinding spear of pain. There was no warm-up; no easing into it. It felt like being jackhammered, hollowed out. By the time I got to the hospital I was bearing down. The nurse rushed me straight through to delivery without even asking my name. The whole thing felt like something terrible instead of something wonderful.

1

ESSIE

"Fresh air!" Essie's mother had said to her that morning. "Get that baby out in the fresh air! It will do you both the world of good!"

Now Essie stood under the dubious cover of a palm tree, while the rain slapped against the tin slide of the nearby playground. Just a few minutes ago the weather had been fine. A perfect spring day. She'd been powering along the Sandringham beach path when the sky began to darken—at the halfway point of her walk, of course, leaving her no option to turn back and bolt for home.

What was so great about fresh air anyway? Given the choice, she'd have opted for the less fresh, temperature-controlled air of the indoors any day. She wanted to be indoors now, preferably at Cuppa Cottage, drinking a cup of English Breakfast out of a vintage teacup. Better yet, she wanted to be in bed, catching up on the billion hours of sleep she'd lost in the past eight weeks. But no. She needed *fresh air*.

Mia appeared to be deeply asleep under her rain cover (Essie doubted there was anything "fresh" about the plastic fumes she was inhaling), but the moment the pram stopped moving Essie knew Mia's eyes would spring open and the crying would start. As such, since Mia's birth, Essie had become an expert in keeping the pram moving, wheeling it rhythmically from room to room as she moved about the house, not allowing it to sit idle for more than a second or two. When Essie sat—which was rare—she could keep the darn thing moving with only three toes. According to Ben, she even rocked in her sleep.

"And when, exactly, have you seen me sleep lately?" she'd demanded, her voice wavering slightly. "No, *really*. Tell me."

Suddenly Ben had had something urgent to do in the garage.

Last week, after jostling the pram for so long Essie was sure she'd developed carpal tunnel, she pushed it down to the back of the garden and left it there. Just for a little while. It was a fine day, she reasoned, and she just needed some time to herself and perhaps a cup of tea. But she was barely back inside when her neighbor—who had a baby Mia's age who never seemed to do anything but sleep and smile—appeared at the door saying she'd heard Mia crying and was everything all right.

"Fine," Essie had said. "Everything is *fine*."

The rain continued to beat down and Essie kept the pram crunching back and forth on the damp, sandy path. The sea had deepened to a dark blue and the air was sharp and salty. On the road above, the cars swished by on the damp bitumen. Maybe she should make a run for it—head to Cuppa Cottage and order that cup of English Breakfast? Then again, with her giant three-wheeler pram she'd almost certainly catch the eye of another pram-wheeling mother and fall into the predictable back and forth that she loathed—*boy or girl? how old? sleeping well?* Essie didn't think she could stand it. Of course, other mothers talked about how hard it all was—the sleep deprivation, the breastfeeding, the washing!—but they always did it with a cheerful laugh, an insistence that "it was all worth it." That was the problem. Essie wasn't sure it was.

"It doesn't come right away for all mothers," her mum had told her. "You're exhausted. Just give it time."

Essie had given it eight weeks. And still, whenever Essie looked down at Mia's red, irritated little face, all she felt was . . . flat.

Every evening Ben rushed home from work, desperate to see Mia. If she was asleep (which was rare), he was devastated.

"Can't we wake her up?" he'd plead.

"No one wakes a sleeping baby," she'd snap, when what she really wanted to say was: "Why would you *want* to?"

Maybe it was just the exhaustion. In an hour her mum would come over and assume pram-jostling duties and the world would make sense again. Her mum came by regularly, snatching up the baby and putting her over her shoulder, soothing her with a repetitive thump to the bottom that Essie could never seem to imitate. Her mum never seemed bothered by Mia's crying or fussiness—she held her as easily and naturally as if she was one of her own limbs. Usually she ordered Essie to go take a nap and Essie gratefully obliged. Problem was, the nap would always end, her mum would go home and she'd have to look after her baby once more.

Essie inhaled, dragging all that *fresh air* into her lungs. She was having that feeling again. A tingling—like angry pinpricks in her abdomen and chest—that Essie had come to understand was anxiety or guilt, or perhaps some kind of cocktail of the two.

"Oh, *that*," Ange from across the road said when Essie described it to her. "Yes. Get used to it. It's called "motherhood.""

That had been a blow. Essie had assumed the anxiety was one of those fleeting parts of early motherhood—like engorged breasts and night sweats—that were there one moment and forgotten about the next. But apparently it was one of those *other* parts of motherhood. The parts that left you fundamentally changed.

A woman around Essie's age was jogging toward her on the path, dressed in black lycra and hot-pink trainers. Her soaking wet hair was looped into a casual bun. Ben had been pestering Essie to start running. "A good long run always makes me feel better," he'd said yesterday. "You should try it." Essie would have run, if she thought it would help. She would have run to the ends of the earth. She just wasn't sure whether she would run back.

The jogger was wet through, but she didn't seem to mind. She had a bounce to her step that was reserved for the young and fit. The free. Essie remembered having a bounce to her step once.

Mia started stirring in the pram and Essie realized that she'd stopped jostling. The jogger bounded past, and in the time it took her to disappear from sight, Mia had moved from confused to irate. Her face contorted and her head tossed from side to side as if desperate for answers. *Who had the audacity to stop moving this pram? Did you not see I was having A NAP?* Her face reddened and she took a breath, sucking in enough air to make sure her protest would be loud and meaningful. Essie shoved her fingers deep into her ears.

It was strange watching Mia scream and not being able to hear it. Better, really. Her eyes shut with the effort. With the rain in the background, Essie heard nothing. She felt nothing.

After a while, Essie started for home. She stopped at Cuppa Cottage and ordered her tea, extra hot, and drank it slowly in the chair by the window. She ordered another. The rain had stopped by the time she left the café. As she walked home she felt an acute sense of being out of balance—as though she'd been roller-skating or skiing and had just put on her shoes again.

Her mum was walking up her driveway when she arrived back in Pleasant Court. She stopped when she saw Essie coming and waved cheerily. "Good to see you out and about," she said, before peering at the empty space around Essie. "Where's Mia?"

Essie pulled her wet ponytail over one shoulder. A trickle of water ran down the side of her jacket.

"Essie," her mum repeated, slower now. "Where is Mia?"

Essie shrugged. "I . . . left her. At the park."

Her mum's frown froze in place. Essie got the feeling that, for the first time in weeks, her mum actually saw her. "Which park, Essie? Which park is Mia at?"

"The beach playground."

After that her mum moved quickly. In a matter of moments they were both in the car, headed toward the beach at a speed Essie thought was unnecessary. The pram was probably exactly where she'd left it! No one would be out and about after the rain;

the playground would probably be deserted and covered in puddles. Mia would be red-faced and angry. It would take hours to calm her down. Essie wished they were driving in the opposite direction.

Her mum misinterpreted her agitation and placed a calming hand on hers. "We'll find her, Essie," she said. "We *will*."

Sure enough, they did find her. Mia *was* right where Essie had left her. But she wasn't alone. A trio of mothers in puffer jackets surrounded her, the tallest woman holding Mia tightly. Mia will hate that, Essie thought. Sure enough, Mia was howling. Another mother looked on while half-heartedly entertaining toddlers nearby. They didn't seem to notice as Essie and her mum got out of the car.

"There she is," Essie's mum cried, running over to the group. "I see her. She's fine, Essie. She's perfectly safe."

"She's ours," Essie's mum shouted to the women. When she was close enough, she held her hands out for Mia, catching her breath. "Whew. Thank you so much. She's my granddaughter. My daughter accidentally left without her."

The tall woman made no move to hand Mia over. Instead she clutched her tighter, which made Mia even more hysterical. "She left the park without her *baby*?"

"Yes, well . . . she was tired and . . ."

Essie sidled up slowly.

". . . you know how your brain can be when you have a newborn!" Her mum gave a half-hearted laugh and then petered out. What else could she say? There was no explanation that would suffice and she knew it.

"I'm sorry," the woman said curtly, "but . . . how do we *know* she's your granddaughter? We found her abandoned in a park. We can't just hand her over."

Essie sidled up slowly. She felt a scream building in her throat. She wanted all these women to go away. *She* wanted to go away. Back to a time when she was a normal, childless woman—not a crazy lady who left babies in the park.

"Her name is Mia," her mum tried again. "She's eight weeks old. Her blanket was hand-knitted by me and it has frayed on one corner. Mia has a birthmark on her right thigh—a port wine stain."

The woman exchanged a glance with her friend. "I'm sorry but I really think we should wait for the—"

"What do you want us to do?" Essie cried. "Sign an affidavit? She doesn't have any ID. Just give her to me," she said, pushing forward. "Give me my baby!"

Essie felt her mum's hand on her shoulder. "Essie—"

"Give her to me."

"Essie, you need to calm d—"

"GIVE ME MY BABY!" she screamed, and that's when the police car pulled up.

2

Three years later . . .

"Good evening, beloved family," Ben announced, flinging down his sports bag. He bounded into the kitchen to kiss Essie and Mia. "Beloved wife and daughter." He scooted a few paces to the right and put an arm around Barbara, who sat on a bar stool, doing a crossword. "Beloved mother-in-law."

Barbara pushed him off. "Ben! You're sweaty."

"As you would be, Barbie, if you'd done three back-to-back boxing sessions and then jogged home!"

He took off his cap and skimmed it across the counter. It collected a butter knife and a garlic press and all three landed with a clatter on the kitchen floor. Essie shot a glance at her mother, who rolled her eyes and looked back at her crossword.

"A little bird told me," Ben said to Mia, "that you could fly."

She looked at him skeptically. "No, I can't."

"Are you sure? Because I'm sure the bird said . . ." He grabbed Mia off the kitchen counter and flung her into the air. She shrieked in delight. He was so slick with sweat it looked like Mia may slide right through his hands.

On their wedding day, Ben's best man had likened him to a Doberman—a fair comparison, in Essie's opinion. Not only was he happy, hopeless and incredibly loyal, he was also large, clumsy and accident prone. Whenever he arrived in a room it suddenly felt full, which was both comforting . . . and a little nerve-wracking.

"See," he said, "you *can* fly." He put her down.

Ben ran a fitness studio, The Shed, a studio created to assist people's dreams of being their own bona fide Hulk outside the boardroom as well as inside. Eighteen months ago he'd also developed an app, Ten with Ben, which allowed people to download a new ten-minute workout and meal plan every day. The app had received huge media coverage and had even been endorsed by several high-profile football players. As a result his business had exploded. He now had ten full-time staff—and dozens of casuals—but as Ben couldn't possibly sit still at a desk all day, he still took the classes.

"Where is beloved daughter number two?" Ben asked.

Beloved daughter no. 2 had come along six months ago. It had taken nearly two years for Essie to convince Ben to try for another baby. ("Why not be happy with what we've got?" he said, over and over again. "Why would we risk it?") Obviously, Essie understood his concerns. It had taken months—and a stint as an inpatient in a psychiatric hospital—for her to recover after leaving Mia in the park that day, and her doctor explained that after last time, her chances of her post-partum depression recurring were significant. But Essie *did* recover. And she wanted a second chance to be the mother she'd planned to be from the get-go. It was her mother moving in next door that had finally swayed Ben (also, Essie thought, a stab at having a son). Unfortunately Ben didn't get his son but Essie *did* get her second chance. And much to everyone's relief, this time Essie had been fine.

Well, mostly fine.

"Polly's asleep," Essie said.

"In *this* heat?"

It was the fourth day of temperatures above forty degrees Celsius and it was all anyone could talk about. A heatwave like this usually happened at least once during a Melbourne summer, but that didn't stop everyone from talking about it as if it was a once-in-a-lifetime phenomenon. *(Hot enough for you? I don't remember it being this hot when I was a kid. I hear a cool change is due on Thursday.)*

"Apparently so," Essie said. "We'll see how long it lasts."

Polly had been a good sleeper to begin with, but a couple of weeks ago she'd started waking at odd intervals, sometimes as often as hourly. It felt like a cruel joke, giving her a perfect baby only to have her regress like this at six months old.

Ben leaned his elbows on the counter. "So," he said, "apparently the new neighbor has moved in."

"I heard," Essie said. The whole of Pleasant Court was at fever pitch about the new neighbor. There hadn't been anyone new in Pleasant Court since Essie's mum moved in.

"Ange gave me the inside scoop." Ange, from number 6, had

been the agent to rent the place. "She's a single woman in her late thirties who has moved down from Sydney for work."

"A single woman?" Barbara said, eyes still on her crossword. She tapped the base of the pencil against her lip. "In Sandringham? Why wouldn't she get an apartment in the city?"

"Single women can live in Sandringham! Maybe she wanted to live by the beach."

"But it's an unusual choice, wouldn't you say?" her mum said. "Especially Pleasant Court."

Essie thought about that. Pleasant Court *was* a decidedly family area, she supposed. A cul-de-sac of 1930s-style redbrick bungalows—and even those in need of a paint job or new foundations sold for well over two million thanks to the beach at the end of the road. Ben and Essie had bought their place when it was worth less than half that amount, but property had skyrocketed since then. The new neighbor, whoever she was, was renting, but even rent wouldn't have been cheap. And with three or four bedrooms and a garden to maintain, Essie had to admit it wasn't the most obvious choice for a single person.

"Maybe she has a husband and kids joining her?" Essie said, opening the fridge. She snatched up a head of iceberg lettuce, a tomato, and a cucumber and dumped all three on the bench. "Salad?"

"Sure," Ben said. "And I doubt she has a husband joining her."

"Why?"

"Ange said she talked about her 'ex-partner.' *Partner*," he repeated, when Essie looked blank. "As in she's gay."

"Because she used the word partner?"

Ben shrugged, but with a cocked head and a smile that said he was in the know.

Essie grabbed an avocado from the fruit bowl. Though she'd never admit it to Ben, she was a little intrigued. The sad fact was, Pleasant Court was very white bread. The appearance of anyone other than a straight married person with kids was interesting. Essie thought back to her days working as a copywriter for *Architectural Digest,* when she had numerous gay and mixed-nationality friends. It felt like another lifetime. "Well . . . so what? I didn't realize we cared so much about people's sexuality."

"We don't," Ben said, holding up his hands. "Unless . . . hang on, did you say . . . sexuality?"

Ben slipped a brawny arm around her waist. After eight years of marriage Ben still wanted sex constantly. Essie would have blamed the excessive exercise if he didn't insist he'd always been this way. "If I was a kid these days," he was fond of saying, "I'd have been diagnosed with ADHD and put on Ritalin. Instead, my parents took me to the park every day to run me like a dog." Some days that's what Essie felt like she was doing with him in the bedroom.

"You need a shower," Essie said.

"Great idea. Meet you in there?"

Essie's mum put down her pencil. "For heaven's sake! Come on, Mia. You can stay at Gran's tonight."

Ben's eyes lit up. "Barbie! Have I ever told you how much I love you?"

"If you really loved me," she said, without missing a beat, "you wouldn't call me Barbie."

Ben put his hand on his heart. "Scout's honor."

She narrowed her eyes. "Not Babs, either. Not Babby. Not Ba-Ba."

"But those are all the good ones!" Ben cried as her mum let herself out with Mia on her hip. Then he turned to Essie. "Ready for that shower?"

One good thing about Ben, he rarely lasted more than ten minutes (Ten with Ben) and tonight Essie spent eight of them thinking about Polly. At first she'd simply been listening out for her in case she woke up, but then her thoughts had drifted to what she would do if she did wake up and then to *why on earth* she'd been waking so often these past few weeks.

It's a phase, everyone said. The most irritating of all findings. *A phase* wasn't a diagnosis, it wasn't a treatment. It was, at best, something to say when you had no idea what the problem was. But Essie wasn't going to take it lying down.

"I thought you could give Polly a dream-feed tonight," she said to Ben when he was spread-eagled and panting beside her. She lifted her head and propped her chin in her palm. "A dream feed is when you give the baby a bottle of formula at ten P.M. to get her to sleep for a long stretch. Apparently it's better for the dad to do it, because otherwise the baby can smell the mother's milk."

It was Fran, from number 10, who'd suggested the dreamfeed. Fran had a daughter Mia's age and another one a few months younger than Polly, but unlike Essie's children, Fran's children *slept* and generally did everything they were supposed to do. As such, she seemed like a good person to take advice from.

Ben stared at her. "Are you actually talking about our infant daughter? *Now?*"

Essie winced. "Faux pas?"

"*Fatal* faux pas."

Essie dropped her head back onto his chest. She lay there for a few seconds before Ben grabbed her chin and turned it so she was looking at him. Essie smiled. He did this every now and again. They'd be standing in the kitchen or out for a walk and suddenly his eyes would go all soft. He never said anything, he didn't need to. The look said it all.

She let her fingertips flutter over Ben's taut stomach, which was bare and smooth apart from the dark strip of hair heading south from his navel. His heartbeat was hard and loud under her ear. He'd been jogging down the street (of course) the first time she'd seen him. At six foot five he was hard to miss. She'd been about to drive past him in her car when the traffic lights changed. Essie had been so busy looking at Ben that she nearly didn't stop in time. The car in front *didn't* stop, continuing into the intersection at full speed. The smash was magnificent. Essie leapt from the car, as did a lot of drivers and pedestrians, but it was Ben who ran directly for the collision, peeling off his hoodie and pressing it to the head wound of one of the drivers to staunch the blood. Essie joined him after a few moments, offering her own cardigan while everyone else stood around the edges, gasping and whispering. There was so much blood, she remembered. And not enough clothes.

By the time the ambulance arrived, Ben was standing there in his underwear and trainers. Essie offered him a ride home, as a) he was in his undies, and b) he had just saved someone's life, so she figured he was unlikely to be a serial killer. Also, because c) she'd seen him in his underwear and, frankly, his body was enough reason for anyone to give him a lift home.

She'd had a nice body then too, she recalled. Slim but curvy. She had auburn hair that she'd spend ages trying to make look casually tousled. Ten years later, her auburn hair was in a permanent ponytail and she had a spare tire around her middle that she couldn't seem to shift. Ben was forever telling her to come down to The Shed and train, but whenever she did find a moment to herself, she wanted to curl up and sleep. And whenever she *did* take a moment to curl up and sleep . . . well, there was Polly.

Right on cue, Polly squawked.

"I'll go," Ben said. Clearly he'd just had sex. After sex, Ben always seemed to think he was a superhero—offering to do all sorts of things, from DIY projects to teaching Mia to ride a bike. Either he was very grateful or he had a burst of adrenaline he needed to work off. Essie was happy to let him go to Polly, even if she wasn't optimistic. He'd read stories, make silly noises, pace the floor with her. (He'd probably not think to do the obvious things like give her a bottle or change her diaper.) Once he'd exhausted his box of tricks, she'd be called in. But at least it'd give her a chance to finish making dinner while he tried.

"Thanks, babe."

She grabbed her robe and headed out to the kitchen, keeping an ear out for Polly. Every time she dared to think she might have gone off to sleep, she'd hear a coo or gurgle. She was about to go in there when there was a knock at the door.

Essie threw a tea towel over her shoulder and swung the door open. She looked up at the woman standing there. At five foot nine, it wasn't often Essie looked *up* at someone, but this woman must have been close to six foot. She had blunt-cut dark-brown hair with thick bangs. Her lipstick was bloodred and she wore heavy black-rimmed glasses. She reminded Essie of an artist or an interior designer or something.

"Can I help you?"

"I hope I'm not interrupting anything," she said. "I'm Isabelle Heatherington. I've just moved in next door."

"Oh." Essie couldn't keep the surprise from her voice. This was the single, possibly gay woman who'd moved in next door? Essie wasn't sure what she'd been expecting, but this wasn't it. People from Pleasant Court didn't look like this. They wore jeans or maxi-dresses. Lipstick was nude and hair was in a ponytail. Essie's own ponytail had started sprouting grays a few years back and she hadn't found time to go to the hairdresser to cover them. Hadn't found time in *years*. "Sorry, I'm Essie Walker."

"It's nice to meet you, Essie. I'm just making the rounds of the neighbors, introducing myself." Her voice, Essie noticed, had a faint husk to it.

"Oh . . . that's nice." Essie smiled stupidly at her for a minute, before realizing she was dressed in her bathrobe. "Oh, look at me! I was just—"

"—relaxing in your own house at night?" Isabelle smiled. "How dare you!"

Essie laughed. "Well, I'm sorry I haven't popped by to see *you* yet. I've been meaning to but I have two little kids and things can get a bit frantic."

"Yes, I saw your little ones today as you loaded them into the car. They're very cute."

"Oh God. I hope I wasn't yelling at them or anything."

"No. Actually, you looked like the perfect mother."

Essie nodded. The perfect mother. How deceiving appearances could be.

She leaned against the doorframe. "So I hear you've moved from Sydney? For work?"

"Yes."

Isabelle didn't elaborate. If Ben were here he'd have pushed her to disclose more—Ben was a dreadful gossip—but Essie figured if Isabelle was going to be living next door, they'd find out eventually.

"My mum's from Sydney," Essie said. "Well, originally. We moved here while I was quite young. I've never been there, unfortunately. I'd like to go."

You're babbling, thought Essie. *Just stop it. Stop babbling.* Essie had never been great at meeting new people or managing the small talk that was invariably required. It was frustrating, as, like most people, she wanted to have friends. But she didn't have Ben's friendliness or her mother's nurturing—or any particular charm, at least not one that was immediately evident. Essie suspected new people found her "perfectly nice" (aka dull), but for as long as she could remember she'd harbored an implausible, narcissistic belief that there was more to her personality than people saw. That there was a gregarious person inside her trying to get out.

"Well, I'll keep making the rounds," Isabelle said finally, pushing a folded piece of paper into Essie's hand. "My number, in case you need it. Though you won't need to worry about late-night parties since I don't know a soul in Melbourne." Isabelle talked over her shoulder as she turned back to the street. "And even if I did, I'm an early-to-bed type."

"You're in fine company then, on Pleasant Court!'" Essie called after her, more confident now Isabelle was leaving. "The lights are all off here by ten P.M. around here. And that's on New Year's Eve!"

Isabelle had a sway to her walk, Essie noticed. If she turned out not to be gay, Ange would be nervous when she showed up on their doorsteps. (Ange's husband was movie-star handsome and she was convinced most women were after him.) But Essie wasn't nervous. If anything, she was oddly excited at the prospect of a potential new friend, not to mention a little *life* in Pleasant Court.

She closed the door and returned to the kitchen. She was just finishing up the salad when Ben appeared. "Am I the best husband in the world or what?"

Essie frowned at him. "What?"

"Polly," he announced proudly, "is fast asleep. Go on, call me the baby whisperer . . ."

That's when Essie realized a miracle had occurred. For the past few minutes, She hadn't been obsessing about Polly and whether she'd gone back to sleep. She wasn't wondering if she was going to have to go in there, or if Polly was going to wake another fifteen times during the night. She wasn't thinking about Polly *at all*.

She was too busy thinking about Isabelle Heatherington, the new neighbor.

3

"Essie!"

Essie was hunting for the new Aldi catalogue in her letter box when she heard Ange call out from across the street. "Morning, Ange," she said, without looking up. The catalogue was stuck and Essie was determined to get it out without tearing it. With two little children at home, flipping through catalogues was one of the few pleasures in her day.

"What are you up to this afternoon?" Ange said, standing behind her now. "I thought we could get together."

It was barely eight A.M. but the day's heat hung around Essie like a cloak. She wore the same linen sundress she'd worn for days, with bare feet—in this heat even flip-flops made her feet sweaty. Polly, on her hip, wore only a diaper.

"What are you up to there? Can I help?" Ange reached down

and gave the catalogue a sharp tug. There was an audible rip of paper and then it came free in her hand. Essie stood, cursing silently.

As usual, Ange looked crisp and put-together. Her white-blond hair was blow-dried to hairdresser standards and she wore white capri pants with a navy shell-top. How did she manage it in this heat? Essie wondered. Ange's makeup was done and her expression, as usual, was gently startled thanks to the perfect amount of Botox.

"There you go," Ange said, handing her the torn catalogue. "So, what do you say? This afternoon?'

Essie readjusted Polly on her hip and frowned at Ange. *Get together?* That was unusual. Everyone in Pleasant Court was friendly, certainly. They popped around to each other's houses for Christmas or New Year's Eve drinks, they watered each other's plants while they were away. They waved brightly when they saw one another in the street . . . but they stopped just shy of being friends. For a while, Essie had hoped the relationships would develop—particularly her relationship with Fran, who had children similar ages to her own—but in nearly five years, that had never eventuated. Essie wondered, suddenly, why it hadn't.

Ange leaned in conspiratorially. "Have you met the new neighbor yet?'

Ah, Essie thought. *So that's what this is about.*

"She's moved in, you know."

"Yes," Essie said. "I know."

Essie never ceased to be amazed by Ange's capacity for interest in stuff that didn't involve her. Most days Essie could barely take in the goings-on of her own family, let alone information about others, but here was Ange, somewhere between thirty-eight and forty-two, with two sons, a husband, and her own real estate agency, and still she had room for the minutiae of other people's lives. Generally it just seemed exhausting to Essie, but today, Essie found herself mimicking Ange's conspiratorial tone and saying: "Why doesn't everyone come to my place?"

Fran, as it turned out, had been roped in as well and that afternoon, the three of them were holed up in Essie's hot living room when Ange leapt from her chair.

"There she is!"

"Who?" Fran said.

"The *neighbor*. Looks like she's getting her mail."

Essie edged forward in her chair but Ange was blocking the window. Polly, in her lap, also sat up, interested.

"Oh, Isabelle. She dropped in last night," Fran said from the armchair. She was stretched out on the ottoman and her six-week-old daugher, Ava, was wedged in the crook of her arm.

Ange snapped her head around. "Really?" she whispered. "She came to my place too!"

"Why are we whispering?" Essie asked, but Ange was already looking back at the window.

"Attractive, isn't she?" Ange tipped her head back and squinted as if to see better. "Her bangs are a little thick though. Quite severe looking."

"They're probably to hide her forehead wrinkles," Fran said, folding a fan out of a piece of newspaper. "Which, I might add, is quite a practical idea."

Fran thrived on practical ideas. Her clothes were fashionable but low-key, her shoes were flat. She wore the same nude lipstick and mascara every day, and her hair was always in the same glossy dark-brown ponytail. At the street party last year she'd revealed that she only bought a single style of beige bra and knickers so she never had to worry about hunting around for a matching set. Thankfully she stopped short of being one of those insufferable types who shoved practical ideas down your throat ('You know what really works a treat on carpet stains? Let me tell you."). The best thing about Fran was that she never seemed to care a fig what anyone thought of her, which was, in Essie's opinion, a tremendously underrated quality.

"Probably," Ange agreed. "She looks like she's approaching forty. Did she stop by your place too, Essie?'

"She did," Essie said. "To introduce herself. It was neighborly."

Ange made a face that suggested she wasn't so sure. "I don't get it," she said. "Who moves to Pleasant Court without kids?"

"*You* rented her the place," Essie pointed out. "Besides, the Larritts don't have young kids." The Larritts, admittedly, were in their early seventies. "Neither does my mum."

"The Larritts had young kids when they moved here. All three of their children went to school in the area. And your mum moved to the street to be close to you!"

Ange gave her a look to say *So there*, then patted down her white pants that somehow—despite her "beastly boys"—were pristine. It wasn't hard to understand why people bought houses from Ange. She had everything together. She was married to a sickeningly handsome man; she seemed to be making a heap of money in her business. Essie had held out hope that she was hiding some great flaw on the domestic front, but when she'd popped around recently to borrow a Pack 'n Play, Essie had followed her into the garage and it was impossibly orderly in there. The *garage*! Essie would have been happy just to have some order to her pantry. Despite having children, Ange didn't have LEGOs in her purse or McDonald's wrappers on the floor of her car. That was the thing about Ange. She didn't just sell houses. She sold the life you wanted to lead.

"What does Isabelle do for a job?" Fran asked. Ava had fallen asleep with her cheek squished comfortably against Fran's forearm. "Did you get the scoop from her application form?'

"Apparently she works for a not-for-profit," Ange said. "I've always thought that was an odd way to describe a business—a not-for-profit. Why not say what you *actually do*?"

"Which not-for-profit?" Fran asked.

Ange waved her hand. "Oh, I can't remember. They're all the same, aren't they?"

Fran was on maternity leave from her job at a law firm, but Essie knew she'd worked as in-house counsel for Save the Children for several years before that. Her expression said they were not all the same. Fran may have been about to say as much, but Ava chose that moment to open her eyes and spit up on Fran's white shorts.

"And this is why I wear white," she said.

If Ange was the image of the life you wanted to lead, Fran was the image of the person you want to be. She and her husband, Nigel, were intellectuals, the type who sat around discussing highbrow topics like religion and politics and art. At least that's what they'd done during Christmas drinks last year. Poor Ben had been so out of his depth he had spent the whole night nodding and saying, "What an interesting thought," and "Gee, I never thought of it like that."

"So I guess she went around to the whole street last night, introducing herself," Ange said.

"I guess she did," Essie said.

Fran pulled a packet of baby wipes out of a navy quilted diaper bag. "I read an article recently that said that people who knew their neighbors were sixty-seven percent less likely to be the victims of crime."

Ange rolled her eyes. "There's no crime in Sandringham."

"Um, hello?" Fran said, wiping at her shorts. "Emily Lynch?"

Emily Lynch was the baby taken from her grandmother's porch last year. Her gran had taken the pram outside as it was stuffy in the house and she wanted to give her some fresh air. She'd sat out there with her for an hour, reading her novel, before ducking inside to go to the bathroom. The phone had rung while she was inside; she'd been gone for a maximum of ten minutes. That was eight months ago. The initial horror at the baby's disappearance had died down to the odd news report of a lead that never came to anything. Now people mentioned it occasionally with somber faces, her name a reminder of what could happen if you didn't watch your kids. (*I never let my kids outside alone, not for a second*, people said now. *Remember Emily Lynch?*)

"I blame the grandma," Fran continued. "Who would leave a baby alone like that? It's no wonder she was taken."

A funny silence permeated the room. Essie kept her eyes down, burying her lips in the back of Polly's head.

Finally, Fran inhaled sharply. "Oh, no no . . . I didn't mean—"

The neighbors all knew what had happened that day, even though they never ever talked about it. It was one of those baffling things about adult relationships. The way you needed to pretend. In any case, Fran was right. Mia *could* have been taken that day. Essie had been lucky.

"But Emily Lynch was taken from *Chelsea*," Ange said quickly. "That's half an hour from here."

But it was too late; everyone's eyes had gone far away. Fran held Ava close, rocking her unnecessarily. Essie watched the two little girls playing in the corner of the room.

Ange's eyes darted back and forth, clearly unhappy with the change of mood. She wouldn't like people feeling unsafe in Sandringham, and certainly not in Pleasant Court. It would almost feel like a slight on Ange *herself*. She fidgeted for a moment, then a light came on in her eyes.

"I have an idea!" she cried. "We'll start a neighborhood watch."

4

FRAN

Even before she got inside, Fran heard it. The tiny, insistent cry. She'd just been for a quick after-dinner run but she felt a sudden pulse of shame, as if she'd gone to the casino or headed out in search of a quick hit of something when she should have been caring for her baby. She didn't remember feeling like this when Rosie was a newborn. Perhaps it was just another of those things she'd forgotten—like how small they are, and how complete the exhaustion is.

She threw open the front door. A fan rotated in the corner, blowing hot air back and forth in a way that reminded Fran of a small-town murder film. They had air-conditioning but Nigel didn't like to use it—terrible for the environment, he said. (Every day, after he went to work, Fran turned it on full blast.)

Nigel was already heaving himself out of his chair. He was

still in his work clothes, but his shirtsleeves were rolled up and his cheeks were flushed. He and Rosie sat in front of a thousand-piece puzzle that they'd been working on for a week. Fran had told Nigel it was far too advanced for a three-year-old, but it was hard to argue when Rosie was currently too engrossed in it to even notice Fran was home.

"Sit, sit," she said. "I'll deal with Ava."

"I don't mind—"

"It's fine. She'll want me anyway."

Nigel leveled his gaze at her. His thick, dark eyelashes curled up under his glasses. (*How does a man end up with eyelashes like that?* Ange always said when she saw him. *It's not fair and it's not right!*) There was a question in his eyes.

In the past six weeks Fran had barely let him near Ava, which perhaps wasn't so unusual. Breastfeeding mothers typically stayed close to their babies, and most new dads were grateful for that. But it was more than that and Nigel knew it. He remembered how she'd let him share the load when Rosie was a baby. (She had one clear memory of threatening to withhold sex for a year unless he "picked up that baby and took her out of earshot for at least an hour.") So it was only a matter of time before he asked her what was going on. She met his gaze and waited. But after giving her a long look, he just shrugged and dropped back into his chair.

It wouldn't be today.

Fran jogged to Ava's room.

It was true, Ava would want her. There were, after all, certain things only Fran could do. She knew the exact way to jiggle her to bring up wind. She knew that Ava liked the cradle hold best, with her head tucked into Fran's chest. That stroking the top part of her nose, the part between the eyebrows, could put her to sleep almost instantaneously. She could have told Nigel how to do these things, but then, of course, he'd *do* them. And for now it was better if she did things herself.

Ava was wrapped in a thin muslin cloth and Fran unbundled her, sweeping through a checklist in her mind. She shouldn't be hungry yet. She wasn't wet. She lifted her bottom to her nose. Not dirty either.

"What is it, little one?'

The answers, of course, were endless. Fran found it perplexing how baffled new mothers became when they couldn't identify a problem with their babies. *She's not hot or cold, her diaper is clean, she's been fed!* they'd cry. *What could it possibly be? For goodness sake,* Fran always thought. It could be anything! Maybe she had a headache? She might have had a bad dream or recalled a distressing incident. Maybe she didn't like the terry-cloth onesie she'd been dressed in. (Fran always found terry cloth irritating.) Perhaps she had a sore toe.

"Do you have a sore toe?" she asked Ava, pressing her fragile little head into the crook of her neck. She let out a few sobs. "Shhh," Fran said into her ear. "Mummy's here."

She was a bad mother, that was the problem. What was she thinking leaving her baby so she could jog the streets like a lunatic? For one thing, her doctor had said she should wait eight weeks before resuming normal exercise, and Ava was only six weeks old. Then again, Fran wasn't resuming "normal" exercise—there was nothing normal about what she was doing. Every day she ran until her chest burned, until her legs ached, until blisters lined her feet. It hurt, oh God it hurt. And she deserved every bit of it.

"Are you hot?" she asked. It was a stupid question because really, who wasn't? Ava's neck was damp and she smelled sweetly of sweat—there was a little spot just behind her ear that was particularly fragrant. She peeled off her onesie and immediately she calmed down.

In the living room Rosie whooped—clearly she'd placed a tricky piece of the puzzle. Fran pictured her pumping her little fists in the air while Nigel gave her a moderated smile or a word of encouragement. Nigel wasn't the dad who talked in baby voices or pretended to be impressed with something unimpressive. He was logical and literal and matter-of-fact. But he had other qualities. He was endlessly patient, for one thing. He researched preschools and primary schools and read books about parenting. He did thousand-piece puzzles. And Rosie adored him.

Ava let out a long sigh. *There you go,* Fran thought. *You were hot. The great mystery is solved.* Fran rebundled her loosely in the muslin, quickly checking her toes (not squashed or tangled) and popped her back in her crib. Her breathing had steadied and her eyelids were three-quarters closed and Fran had one of those powerful waves of love reserved for parents of children who are asleep.

She and Nigel had always planned to have two children, two years apart. So when Rosie was a year old, Fran hadn't expected resistance from Nigel when she suggested it was time to try again.

"It's just . . . I'm not sure it's such a good idea after all," he'd said.

That had been a surprise. The Nigel Fran knew didn't deviate from what had been planned. Then again, he hadn't been the Nigel she knew for months.

"It's postnatal mapression," Ange had told her when she'd complained about it one day. "Man-depression. A lot of men get it when they have young children. They lose an income, gain a mouth, and all of a sudden it feels like everyone has more money than they do. Add to this that their wives usually stop wanting to have sex with them, and you've got a recipe for an miserable bloke."

"Maybe," she'd said, but she had a feeling it was more than that.

And as it turned out, she was right.

Nigel had lost a large chunk of their savings last year in a bad investment. They weren't in dire straits—they wouldn't have to sell the house or anything—but it had put them back a good ten years in terms of their financial position.

"Well," she'd said, when he told her. "What's done is done. It's not the end of the world."

But to Nigel it was. He wallowed and wallowed. Once a self-professed morning person, he started sleeping late, and at night when he'd come home from work he flopped onto the couch and remained there for the entire evening. When Fran tried speaking with him about it, he hadn't wanted to talk—about anything. Especially not about having another child.

Fran kissed Ava's forehead and left the room. Nigel and Rosie had abandoned their puzzle and now they sat on the floor of her bedroom, staring at a children's atlas together. This was Rosie's favorite bedtime story.

"Need any help?" she asked, popping her head around the corner.

Nigel and Rosie both looked up, their mannerisms so in sync and identical it took Fran's breath away.

"We're good," Nigel said. His glasses had fallen down his nose and he pushed them up with his index finger. Under their magnification, his eyelashes looked even longer and thicker. Rosie had those lashes too. In fact, from her serious blue eyes to her jet-black hair, Rosie was every inch her father's daughter.

"We're good," Rosie repeated.

"I'll go take a shower then," she said to the tops of their heads.

Fran showered and slipped on a cotton nightie. She checked her phone—there was a message from Ange about needing her help to distribute flyers for the neighborhood watch. After leaving Essie's, she must have gone straight home, designed flyers, then headed directly to Staples to have them printed. Fran replied that she'd help, only because if she didn't, Ange would just give her some other job to do and, on the whole, handing out flyers seemed fairly innocuous. She might even do it while running.

The house was quiet by the time she left her bedroom—all Fran could hear was the hum of the rotating fan. Rosie's light was off. Fran peeked into Ava's room and was startled to see Nigel, bent over the crib, his face hovering inches from Ava's.

"What are you doing?" she asked, louder than she meant to.

Nigel looked up and frowned. "Kissing my daughter good-night." He crept out of the room, horseshoeing around her into the hallway. "Are you all right?'

Fran wondered if she was all right. For months she'd lived with this feeling of dread in the pit of her stomach, a feeling that any moment her whole world could unravel. Usually it hovered around the edges of her consciousness, where she could run it away—if she ran fast enough—but every now and then it came to the surface, where it was impossible to ignore. She felt tears begin to well, which was not like her. She'd never been a crier.

"I'm fine," she said.

"Are you sure?"

Through his glasses Nigel's eyes looked larger and more knowing. It scared her. But what could she say? *There's something I have to tell you. And it's big. It's really, really big.*

"I'm sure." She shut Ava's door firmly. "Come on, let's make dinner."

5

"Morning, Fran!" Isabelle called out from across the street.

One of the worst things about Pleasant Court was that it seemed to be inhabited entirely by *morning people*. Admittedly Fran got up early too, but it was out of necessity rather than choice—not to mention it was with considerably less cheer than everyone else on the street. The fact was, as a mother of two, if she wanted to exercise she was forced to get up with the birds. She thought she'd perfected the art of avoiding the incessant calling-out of "Morning!" by scuttling out at 6:10 A.M.—eyes down, hoodie up, earplugs in. Until now.

"Hi, Isabelle," she called without breaking stride. She lifted her hand, keeping her eyes in front. Isabelle seemed nice enough, but it was important to set clear boundaries from the start. (Nigel was fond of telling her she had social phobias, but it wasn't true.

It wasn't that she was afraid of people. She just didn't like them before 7 A.M.)

"You must be one of those morning people," Isabelle called.

Fran glanced from the footpath to Isabelle and back again, biting back an urge to scream. Would it be rude to keep jogging now? She could pretend she hadn't heard, or that she thought Isabelle had been talking to someone else. Or she could just be the rude neighbor who didn't talk to people. Fran could live with being that neighbor, she decided.

The funny thing was, Fran would never have picked Isabelle to be a morning person. Or the type to engage in neighborly banter, for that matter. Fran had her pegged as the inner-city apartment type who rode a pushbike in an ironic way and befriended the local homeless man rather than her actual neighbors. The type who took her coffee very seriously and frequented vegan cafes where you paid what you thought your food was worth. But perhaps Fran had her all wrong.

"I guess you have to be a morning person when you have kids," Isabelle said, walking over. Fran realized she'd hesitated too long. "Too much to do, not enough time, am I right?" She stopped in front of Fran, resting her elbow against the Larritts' letter box. She had this cool, casual thing going on that seemed out of step with Pleasant Court. It made Fran feel suddenly uptight. "I don't know how you fit everything in. You're a lawyer, aren't you?'

Suddenly Fran understood. Isabelle was looking for free legal advice. At least now she understood. She'd got herself involved in something—a fence dispute, a sexual harassment complaint, some problem with her rental that hadn't been resolved swiftly enough by the landlord. Everyone always had a legal issue, it seemed. And they were always so confused when Fran suggested they get advice from a lawyer specialising in that particular field. (*But* you're *a lawyer,* they always said, baffled.)

"I'm a mergers and acquisitions lawyer," Fran said, cutting her off at the pass. "Pretty specialized stuff. And I'm on maternity leave right now so . . .'

"Yes, I noticed you had a newborn." Isabelle smiled. "Congratulations. Where is she this morning?'

Fran paused. So, perhaps not the legal advice then. "She's . . . still asleep. Her dad is home."

"And her name's Ava?"

"Er . . . yes."

Fran felt off-kilter. It was too early. She couldn't figure out if she was having a lovely chat with the new neighbor or being very pleasantly interrogated. Usually she prided herself on being able to judge people's intentions.

But it was 6:10 A.M.

"Morning, ladies."

Fran glanced over at Ange's place where Lucas stood on the front lawn, pushing a garbage bag into an over-full bin. "Up and about early, today I see," he said.

Fran waved vaguely at Lucas, who didn't appear to be waiting for a response. "Well, I'd better keep moving," she said to Isabelle, aware that any minute now Ange would be outside wanting to chat about the neighborhood watch or some such horror. Fran turned her back and started walking.

"It feels like every time I see you, you've been running," Isabelle called after her. "It's very impressive."

"Well," Fran said over her shoulder, "I need to lose the baby weight, so—"

"But you aren't carrying any baby weight," Isabelle said. Her voice wasn't loud but it carried in the quiet of the early morning. Fran reached for her earplugs and was about to bury them in her ears when Isabelle added: "In fact, you don't look like you've had a baby at all."

Nigel's depression lasted a year. It felt to Fran like a betrayal. As ridiculous as it sounded, she'd always believed Nigel was too sensible to get depressed. She had assumed that if he started to feel down he'd simply go see his family doctor about addressing the chemical imbalance in his brain. He'd have been given a list of instructions to follow—take antidepressants, exercise, and stop drinking alcohol.

Instead, alcohol became the worst part.

Nigel had never been much of a drinker. In the old days he'd had only one drink a week, on a Friday, and it was for the ritual more than anything else. He'd come home from work, open a beer and sit in his chair with a soft "Ah" noise. Often he didn't even finish the beer.

At first it was just the frequency of his drinking that increased. His Friday night beer became an *every night* beer. Then the beer became Scotch. Or wine, if that was what they had in the house. And it became more than one. Each night, he sat in his chair from seven until midnight, only getting up to go to the fridge. The "Ah" noise disappeared.

He got fat. Properly fat. While Nigel had never been much of an athlete, he'd always been health conscious . . . until suddenly he wasn't. He developed a taste for cheap, student-type food—instant noodles, bags of Doritos, mac and cheese. His stomach became hard and round, the kind of stomach that screamed "early heart attack happening here . . . watch this space!" It was as sudden as it was astonishing. All at once, Fran felt like she was living with a stranger. And any attempts she made to get him back on track with healthy eating were greeted with hostility.

His sleep became erratic. Some days he was so tired he'd go to bed at 7 P.M., leaving her to feed and put Rosie to bed on her own. Once, she woke at 3 A.M. to find him sitting on the edge of the bed, rocking and punching the pillow repeatedly. When she asked him what was wrong, he lay back down immediately, muttering something about a cramp.

Fran begged him to see a counselor, to get medication. She researched a retreat for men who were burnt out. She forwarded him articles from men's health magazines about men who'd gone through depression and come out the other side. He wasn't interested in any of it.

Eventually she took Rosie away for a week and stayed at a hotel, hoping that might shock him into taking control of his life. It did. For a few days, Nigel was on his best behavior. Then it all started again.

Fran started to worry about what he might do if he didn't snap out of it. She started to worry about what *she* might do. He'd been in a slump for a year—what if something pushed him over the edge? Rosie wouldn't have a father. She wouldn't have a husband.

That was when she told him she was pregnant again.

6

"I love you, Daddy."

Fran was brushing her teeth when she heard it. Nigel and Rosie were in Rosie's bedroom, getting her ready for bed. They'd already brushed her teeth, read the story, and now she was getting tucked in.

Fran walked to the bathroom door to listen.

"I love you too, Rosie. Good night."

She smiled. The "I love you" wasn't a usual part of the routine, as far as Fran knew. Most of their conversations, even at bedtime, were fact based. The capital of a certain country. The number of bones in the body. An idea for an invention Rosie had had. Even this exchange, Fran realized, was matter-of-fact. They didn't bother with nonsense like "I love you to the moon and back" or "I love you more, no I love *you* more." Not Nigel and Rosie. It struck Fran that a different kind of daughter could have thrown Nigel completely. A daughter who demanded Barbies and fairies and silliness. But Rosie was a perfect fit.

Was Ava?

After a minute or two Fran heard the snap of the light switch. She put her toothbrush back in the holder. She felt a jittery feeling in her chest, behind her sternum. That had been happening to her quite a bit lately. Generalized anxiety disorder, perhaps. Or was it something else?

Her conversation with Isabelle this morning had been bugging Fran all day. ("I noticed you had a newborn" she'd said. "And her name's Ava?") What was *that* about? Fran doubted that when she was single and childless she'd *ever* noticed someone else's newborn. If she had, she certainly wouldn't have mentioned it to them. Like most normal people, she had a hearty fear of being labeled a stalker. Which begged the question . . . why didn't Isabelle have that fear?

Fran washed her face, slathered on some face cream, and headed down the hall. Rosie lay on her side in bed, clutching the travel-sized telescope Nigel had brought back from a business trip to China, like it was soft toy. She crossed the hall and peeked into Ava's room. Her head moved back and forth like she was on the verge of waking, but then she gave a huge, shuddery sigh and settled right back to sleep again.

Sweet girl.

Fran wondered where they would be if Ava hadn't come along. Would Nigel still be depressed? Would *she* be? There was no doubt she had been heading in that direction, before announcing her pregnancy. Nothing she had tried had worked and . . . he didn't seem to care. If something hadn't happened to break the circuit, who knew where they'd be. Ava had saved them. And also, broken them.

When she got to the bedroom Nigel was already in bed. He'd kicked off the quilt, with only the bare sheet covering him. It was far too hot to sleep under anything else. He frowned up at the wall, where a family portrait hung of the two of them and Rosie.

"We need to get some new family portraits done," he said, pushing his glasses up his nose. "With Ava in them."

Fran stared at him.

Before they had children, Nigel would have been appalled at the concept of a professional family photo. "They're all a lie anyway," he would have said. Propaganda created to project an image of happiness that doesn't actually exist. A false laugh at a stupid joke the photographer made, a stern word to the child who refused to look at the camera, a bribe of ice cream afterward. All lies. The only reason they'd had the first one taken was because Ange and Lucas had given them a photo shoot as a gift after Rosie was born. Fran glanced up at it. Lucas had taken it when Rosie was two or three weeks old. They were in the park next to his photography studio, nestled next to a pile of leaves. Fran had put a lot of thought into Rosie's outfit, as she recalled, but a moment before the photo had been taken she had annihilated it with one of those newborn poops that traveled up her back as far as her neck. In the picture, Nigel was holding a newborn Rosie up and as far away from him as possible, while Fran lay back in the leaves, laughing. Lucas captured it perfectly. It was a brilliant shot. It was that shot that had changed her own mind about professional family photos. And for that reason she said: "Sure. Why not?"

Fran generally saw eye to eye with Nigel about most things. She'd always prided herself on the fact that they were a great match. For their first date Nigel invited her to a trivia night at a pub in South Melbourne. Fran decided not to tell him about her wicked trivia skills and instead let them reveal themselves, but as it turned out, her trivia knowledge paled in comparison to Nigel's.

"Four countries in Africa starting with B?" the quizmaster called out.

"Benin, Botswana, Burkina Faso, and Burundi," Nigel answered immediately.

"Name the two letters that don't appear in the periodic table."

"J and Q," he said without even a pause, "although Q is occasionally used as a placeholder for the artificially created, super-heavy elements until a suitable name has been adopted."

"What is the most common blood type?"

"O," Fran cried, desperate to get an answer in before Nigel. "Everyone is O."

"Actually the most common is O positive," Nigel said. "O negative is quite rare."

"Really?" Fran said. "I'm O negative."

"So am I."

They smiled at each other.

"Is it true," she said, "that two negatives make a positive?"

She'd meant it as a throwaway, cheesy line, but Nigel's brow furrowed. "Well, not always. For example, negative ten plus negative ten doesn't equal positive twenty, does it?"

That was the moment she fell in love with him.

By the end of the night Fran had to physically restrain herself from jumping him, right then and there. Intelligence, she'd always thought, was the most powerful aphrodisiac. And if there was one thing that could be said about geeks, it was that they were very eager to please.

She looked at him now. He had no book, no phone in his hand. He was looking at her in that familiar way. Her heart rate quickened a little.

It had been a while.

While Nigel was depressed, he'd lost interest in sex almost entirely. It had become so bad that Fran had even bought a book called *Rekindling the Spark in Your Marriage* and started trying new things like turning up at his office unannounced and telling him she'd booked a hotel room, or joining him in the shower while Rosie was watching cartoons. Nigel usually managed to perform, but it was always lackluster, and only ever when Fran initiated it. She couldn't remember the last time he'd looked at her like this.

He crawled across the bed toward her, and kissed her. Fran's knees weakened. It felt so good, being pressed against him. And they hadn't kissed like this in years. She pulled him closer.

And something inside her cracked.

"What is it, Fran?" he said, pulling back. "You're crying."

She wiped her face. "Am I? Sorry."

"You're not yourself." He sat up. "Tell me what's going on. Please. Maybe I can help."

The concern in his face was undeniable. Nigel had always been the person she could turn to when things were bad. He was always so calm and ready to formulate a plan. She had always found him a tremendous comfort in difficult times.

Fran felt the tears begin to flow in earnest.

That's the problem, she thought. *You can't.*

7

ANGE

When Lucas came to bed, Ange was going to have sex with him. She lay there, listening to him clattering about in the kitchen, thinking all sorts of amorous thoughts. There was truly nothing sexier than a man who did the dishes. The first time she and Lucas had hosted a dinner party together, Ange had collapsed happily into bed at the end of the night, thoroughly drunk, leaving all the dishes and pots on the counter and the half-drunk glasses of wine on the dining room table. (Ange liked things to be meticulously clean when her guests arrived but once they'd left she could happily ignore the mess until morning.) But the morning after, when she woke and crawled out into the living room for coffee, she'd found the place sparkling.

"I enjoy doing clearing up," Lucas had said. "It helps me wind down at the end of the night."

It was the moment she knew she was going to marry him.

Ange rolled herself onto one side. She was naked because it was far too hot for lingerie. Besides, a few nights ago she'd fastened herself into a complicated garter belt–type arrangement only to wake up in the early hours of the morning with Lucas snoring beside her—the lingerie still fastened. Apparently since reaching forty her window between horny and asleep was ever shrinking. But tonight, she was determined. They were going to have sex, and not mundane sex. Hot sex. Decidedly unmarried-person sex. She was going to be the wife every man wanted . . . if she was able to stay awake.

The funny thing was, Lucas probably wouldn't have minded mundane sex. Lucas had an odd affection for mundane things. Replacing light globes the moment they fizzed. Writing important events on their family calendar in the kitchen so things couldn't be forgotten. Ensuring there were batteries in their battery drawer. It occurred to Ange that, without Lucas, their family would come to a crashing halt. Sometimes she even had shameful thoughts about what would happen if he suddenly dropped dead. She imagined herself going to the battery drawer and finding it empty, then sliding down the wall of the kitchen, sobbing. The kids would find her there at the end of the day screaming, "Batteries! There are no batteries in the battery drawer!"

She could hear Lucas now, in the kitchen, hand-washing the hand-washables. She willed him to hurry up. *Come on, Lucas!* Her eyelids were starting to droop. The two glasses of wine she'd had with dinner didn't help matters. It was just so exhausting, being an adult.

Ange wondered if Will and Ollie were asleep. It was possible they were, but it was equally possible they'd located an iPad and were watching random people play video games on YouTube. She didn't get it. Why would you watch someone else play a video game, for goodness sake! ('It's a guy thing," Lucas had told her when she'd lamented about ridiculous it was. A guy thing! She loved her boys but sometimes she thought that Y chromosome had a lot to answer for. Sometimes she yearned for a daughter so badly she could almost reach out and touch her.)

Ange sat up. Through the window she could see a few lights on in the street. Fran and Essie were probably having sex with their husbands, she decided. Essie's muscleman of a husband probably had a Cirque du Soleil lineup of moves, and Fran and Nigel were so straightlaced you could just tell they liked it dirty. (They were coy, of course, when Ange asked them about their sex lives, but that only proved it. It was the quiet ones you had to watch.)

Isabelle's light was on too. What was *she* up to? It irked Ange that she couldn't even hazard a guess. When she'd showed her around Mrs. Harrap's old place, Isabelle had mentioned an ex-partner, which had been telling. If it had been a man, surely she would have said ex-boyfriend or ex-husband? Add to that the fact that she was unmarried without kids at forty and, well, it made sense. Not that it mattered—Ange couldn't have cared less if she was gay, straight, bisexual, or any of the other preferences encompassed by LGBTQIA—but she liked to have a handle on these sorts of things. It would be embarrassing to ask her if she had a boyfriend for example, when she was interested in women. And if she did happen to like men, well, Ange knew some single men at the office who were great catches.

At some point Ange had designated herself the architect of Pleasant Court, determined to make it the most desirable street in Bayside, if not the whole of Melbourne. She'd done a good job too. They had families with young children. One grandmother. An older couple, one an ex-doctor. Her own family, of course—a happy family of four living in the prettiest bungalow that sat on a slight hill so every other house in the street seemed to pay homage to it. If you turned right at the end of the street, you'd be at the beach within two minutes, and if you turned left, Sandringham Village, a miniature hub of cafes, shops and AMOS hair, the only hairdresser in Melbourne that Ange trusted with her platinum blond tresses. Yes, Pleasant Court lived up to its name. Pleasant Court hosted Christmas parties and street parties. Kids rode their bikes and skateboards in the street. Soon they'd have a neighborhood watch. There was no opportunity for scandal anywhere. Whenever Ange posted photos of the street on Instagram she tagged it #pleasantcourt #whereeverythingispleasant. But Isabelle Heatherington was an unknown quantity. It was irritating.

Ange yawned. She listened for Lucas—the telltale clang of a pot or pan being washed, or the dishwasher being stacked. Instead she heard something else. He was on the phone, she realized. His voice hushed and urgent.

Ange rolled over and switched off the light. Sleep was already calling her, a siren, and all at once she was happy to answer its call. Things were far better watched from a distance, Ange thought as she drifted off. When you watched too closely, you saw things you didn't want to see.

8

"Look at *meeeeee!*"

Ange was watching Ollie skateboard—in body, if not in mind. She leaned against her low brick fence, which was still warm from the day's heat. It had been yet another scorcher. The air was sticky and salty-sweet, a mixture of ocean and ice cream, and the scream of cicadas pierced the early-evening air. A procession of children, families, and dog walkers trailed past the opening of the street, following the peach sunset down to the beach. Usually on nights like this, she and Lucas and the boys would also head down to the beach and they'd all swim until dark, but Ollie had been pestering her to watch him do tricks on his skateboard and she'd run out of excuses.

"Watch this!" he cried, doing some sort of midair spin. He

was far too focused on whether she was looking and not nearly focused enough on landing safely, in her humble opinion.

"Fantastic!" Ange concealed a yawn. "Tremendous!"

"Did you see that?" Ollie cried. "I *nailed* it."

"You sure did. You're amazing."

Ange resisted the urge to check her iPhone, which was in the pocket of her sundress. It was tough going. Sometimes Ange wondered if she had a phone addiction. With each minute that passed without checking her phone, the more uncomfortable she became. Isn't that what happened to junkies when deprived from their drug? And then, when she finally got to check it—total euphoria. Seventeen new emails. Five new Instagram comments. Twenty-seven new Facebook likes?

Nirvana. She'd got her hit.

Occasionally at work Ange even ate lunch in her car so she could scroll through her phone in peace without fear of anyone interrupting her. She always found an hour alone with her phone to be as soothing as a cold glass of pinot gris. But not now, she reminded herself with a little shake. Now she was watching Ollie try to kill himself on a small board with wheels. It was what any good mother would do.

"Mind if I join you, Ange?'

It was Isabelle. She was headed over, by the looks of it, *to chat*. Not that there was a problem with that. It was just that, in general, they tended to do a lot more waving than chatting in Pleasant Court.

"I had to get some fresh air," Isabelle said. She wore a white tank and a long black skirt covered in red flowers and her feet were bare. Her chest and neck were shiny with sweat. "My house is like an oven. I don't know how I'm going to sleep!"

"Oh. Well . . . we only get a handful of these heatwaves each summer in Melbourne," Ange said. "It's not like Sydney."

"Thank heavens for that. I'm really looking forward to four seasons."

"You'll get them," Ange said. "Probably in the one day."

Isabelle joined Ange on the fence and hitched her long skirt up to her knees. Her legs were smooth and creamy white. Ange was forever going to get spray tans to avoid this sort of pallor, but on Isabelle it looked exotic, like she belonged to another era.

Ollie zoomed by them, leaping off his board and landing (with luck rather than skill) back on it again. Isabelle cheered.

"Woohoo," she cried. "Check you out, Ollie!"

Ollie glanced over, puffing out his chest at the unexpected praise.

Ollie. Ange. Isabelle certainly liked using people's names. Ange was one to use names herself—in real estate, you had to—but she'd always been suspicious of others who did the same. When she did it, her motivation was to assert a false sense of friendship to help sell a house. The question was, what was Isabelle's motivation?

"So tell me," Ange started, "what brought you to Melbourne? You said it was work, but is that all it was?"

It may have been Ange's imagination, but Isabelle's spine seemed to straighten. "Yes," she said. "Mostly."

Ange jumped on that. "Mostly? So, there was more?"

"Let's call it . . . a personal project."

"Sounds intriguing." Ange leaned in and touched her elbow to Isabelle's, as if they were close girlfriends. "What is his name? Or . . . hers?"

Mr. Larritt's car pulled into the street and honked the horn. Ange cursed at his timing.

"Ollie," she called out. "Off the road." She kept her eyes on Isabelle, trying to think of a way to casually bring conversation back.

'"Does he look like his dad?" Isabelle asked before Ange could speak. "Ollie, I mean."

"Oh." Ange waved her hand dismissively. "He doesn't look like either of us, really. We assume he's a throwback. Anyway, tell me more about—"

Before Ange could finish, she heard a thump followed by the sickening crack of bone. By the time she looked, Ollie was lying on the ground. Before she even got her thoughts together enough to move, Isabelle was sprinting toward him.

9

In the hospital waiting room, Ollie was asleep with his head on Ange's lap. She was certain this gave her the look of a caring, concerned mother—which was lovely, if entirely inaccurate. In fact, she was highly irritated with Ollie. Sure, his wrist was in a terrible state, but he was happily doped up on morphine and passed out, stretched across three seats. *She* could've used a little morphine, just quietly. Instead, she was pinned to a sticky seat by her drugged eight-year-old, unable to move or even to reach her iPhone.

Ollie gave a long, sleepy sigh. Ange knew, of course, that she was lucky. Things could have gone very differently. She remembered that split second after she heard the crunch of bone. Her fear had been ice cold, paralyzing. By the time she'd got her legs to move, Isabelle was already by his side, gently assessing his injuries while speaking to him in a low reassuring voice. *The voice of a mother*, Ange remembered thinking.

Mr. Larritt had braked in time, thank goodness, but Ollie had panicked and landed with all his weight on his wrist. Clearly it was broken, and quite badly—but as he was in no danger of death, Ange's mind had immediately moved to practical matters. She knew they'd likely have to wait in the emergency room for hours before Ollie was fitted with a cast. There'd be paperwork, a visit to the chemist for painkillers. Lucas had come along for moral support, but of course he was currently nowhere to be seen.

Lucas had a habit of wandering off. Sometimes Ange felt like she was married to an elderly man with Alzheimer's. Any minute he'd probably come back with someone he'd met whose job it was to . . . peel oranges at the juice bar. Lucas would be genuinely fascinated. ("She peels the oranges! Bet you never thought about who did that, did you? You just drank your juice and didn't give it a second thought!")

Lucas found everyone and everything amazing. It was the way they'd met, in fact, in the local coffee shop. ("You're a real estate agent? You have your own business! Did you hear that, random guy reading the newspaper? She's a real estate agent!") Ange had been charmed, of course. Who wouldn't be? A gorgeous man who found *her* fascinating! Unfortunately it was a trait that got old after a few years of marriage—particularly when he was impressed so easily.

Ange looked at the clock on the wall. They'd arrived an hour and a half ago and every minute since had crawled. Ange hadn't been in Emergency very often, but each time she had, she found herself wishing her ailment (or more often, her child's) was just a little bit worse. Not life-threatening, obviously. But worrying enough to get seen quickly. (Chest pain, apparently, was the meal ticket. If you said you had chest pain you always went straight to the front of the queue.)

Did eight-year-olds have heart attacks? she wondered.

Ten minutes later Lucas finally appeared, carrying a packet of Twisties and a bottle of water. He winked at her and Ange sagged in relief. Both her legs had gone to sleep and she was desperate for the toilet. Ollie was so doped up he probably wouldn't even notice if she shimmied out from under him and let Lucas take her place. (It would make a nice pic for Instagram actually. She'd hashtag it #fatherandson #brokenarm #boyswillbeboys.) But as Lucas approached, a pretty thirty-something woman with a blond toddler on her lap waved at him. He stopped. *For heaven's sake.* Ange gestured at him impatiently and he sped up again.

"Where have you been, I am about to wet my pants!"

"Sorry. I was just—"

"It doesn't matter. Just . . . switch places with me, would you?"

But before Ange could get up, the waving woman appeared behind Lucas, the toddler in her arms. The child was dressed in blue but had shoulder-length white-blond hair. The mother was probably one of those hippies who wanted to raise her children as "genderless."

"Lucas," the woman said, frowning. "Is that you?"

Lucas turned. For a moment he didn't speak. And then. . . . "Erin. How are you?"

She gestured to the child's foot, which was wrapped in a green bandage, and made a face that said she'd been better.

"What happened?" Lucas asked.

"Charlie burned her foot in the bath. She turned on the hot tap when Mummy wasn't looking."

"Ouch," Ange murmured. So she was a girl. With a boy's name. How very *hip*.

Lucas half turned back to Ange, perhaps just remembering she was there. She remained half under Ollie, supporting the weight of his (surprisingly heavy) head in two hands while he snoozed on, oblivious. Ange wanted to say to *Erin* that while she was very sorry to hear about her genderless child's foot, in fact they were having their own family emergency right so it might be best if they saved their catch-up for another time. But, of course, that would have been impolite.

"Ange," Lucas said, "this is Erin, a client of mine. I took some photos of Charlie a little while back. Erin, this is my wife, Ange."

Erin gave Ange the once-over and Ange did her best to smile. She knew a lot of people were disappointed to learn of her existence. Lucas had a way of making people fall in love with him, with his genuine interest in them, not to mention his aching good looks. How could she blame Erin for hating her?

Ange glanced at the sleepy toddler starting to drift off in Erin's arms. She was a pretty little thing. Had the most beautiful jade-green eyes, she noticed. Ange had a weird sense of deja vu.

"Charlie looks tired," she said.

"Yes," Erin said. "I'd better get her home."

Good, Ange thought. Ollie's head was getting heavy and her bladder was now dangerously full.

"Do you need a hand out to the car?" Lucas said.

Ange held in a curse.

Erin readjusted the child in her arms. *Say no,* Ange willed her. *Just fucking say no.*

"Actually, that would be great."

Erin had a handbag and a child—what on earth did she need help with? Or did she think that given the privilege of holding her bag, Lucas would forget about his wife's existence and fall in love with her?

Ange was used to people lusting after her husband, but that didn't mean she liked it. For one thing, it was an insult to Lucas, who was so much more than his looks. Lucas was kind. Adventurous. Calm. When the boys asked for the hundred and fifty-seventh time for ice cream for breakfast and she was ready to throttle them, Lucas would sit down with them and ask them to break down the activities for the day ahead and then ponder whether sugar and fat would be sufficient fuel to help them achieve their goals. (It sounded ridiculous, but bizarrely the kids always went for it. It may have been the fact that he was genuinely engaged with them, rather than giving them a lecture.) He was also a much-needed injection of creativity in their family. If it were up to Ange, most weekends would be spent driving the kids from activity to activity, then sitting on the couch. But Lucas wouldn't stand for it. Every weekend they had a family adventure. To the beach, to the country. Even to the local park. (One of Ange's favorite adventures was when the kids were toddlers and they went to the park with no toys, no technology and they avoided the playground area. They spent hours following the kids around as they picked up sticks, scratched bark off trees, and collected stones.

Ange never would have done that in a million years if Lucas didn't force it.)

And yes, he was stunning. Tall and broad and golden-skinned, at forty-three, he still turned heads. He was buff (he worked out regularly with Ben Walker at The Shed) and he wore V-neck T-shirts and jeans rather than the short-sleeved button-down shirts and chinos most men his age sported. His sandy hair was just starting to be streaked with gray, which only made him more handsome.

Of course, Ange wasn't bad herself—she made sure of that. With regular Pilates, hair appointments, and facials, she wasn't going to be the frumpy wife of the gorgeous man. Recently she'd also started getting "Baby Botox," which involved receiving smaller than average dosages of Botox to soften wrinkles but still allow natural facial movement. Ange figured if she kept things looking good on the home front, Lucas would have no need to stray.

She watched him now, walking this strange woman toward the sliding doors. Lucas had the handbag (which actually seemed to be more of a diaper bag, now that she looked at it) flung over his shoulder, and Erin held the child. As they reached the doors, a gurney came rushing through, surrounded by four paramedics and Lucas touched Erin's forearm. They both stood back out of the way. His hand remained there for several seconds until the doorway cleared and they continued through the double doors to the parking lot.

"Oliver Fenway?'

Ange glanced around. A woman in green scrubs and matching green booties pulled over her shoes glanced at her clipboard and then back around the room. "Oliver Fenway?'

"Yes," Ange said. "Here!"

She still desperately needed to pee.

She tapped Ollie. He opened his eyes, then immediately closed them again. On her third try, she managed to haul him into a standing position and lead him toward the doctor. Before she proceeded through the doors into the ER, she glanced back at the doors out to the parking lot. Lucas was nowhere to be seen.

10

BARBARA

Barbara kept patting Mia long after she'd fallen asleep. It was official: that little girl had her wrapped around her little finger. Whether she wanted an extra bedtime story or a second biscuit, Barbara was utterly powerless to say no to her. A few months earlier, over dinner, Barbara had asked Essie and Ben: "How long do you pat Mia's back at bedtime?" They'd both fallen about laughing.

"Pat her back?" Essie had cried. "Let's see, approximately zero minutes."

"I'd say it's definitely a grandma thing," Ben had said, grinning.

Kids had a knack, Barbara knew, for finding a weak link, and grandmothers were nothing if not weak links. In spite of what Essie and Ben said, whenever Barbara had her granddaughters for a sleepover, she still rubbed their backs until her wrists ached, and there was nothing she'd have rather done.

One thing you didn't realize until you were a grandparent was that little children were a tiny glimpse of magic in a dreadfully difficult world. They had to be disciplined, sure, but they also had to be enjoyed. Parents worked so hard these days that often they didn't make time to enjoy them, but grandparents knew better. *The days were long and years were short*, that was what everyone said these days. But as far as Barbara was concerned, the days were short too. And she was perfectly happy to spend them patting her granddaughters to sleep.

When Mia was snoring, Barbara moved to Polly's crib and gazed down at her. She'd wrapped her in a white cotton sheet, but Polly's hands had come free and now they were stretched out on either side of her head as though she was reaching for something. Darling child. She was, in many ways, the polar opposite to Mia. Chubby where Mia was petite, dark-haired where Mia was ginger. Brown-eyed where Mia was blue. And—thank goodness—easy where Mia had been challenging.

Barbara reached out and swept a damp curl off Polly's forehead. Essie had bonded so quickly and easily with Polly. At first she'd even declined all offers from Barbara to babysit because she just couldn't bear to be away from her. It would have been reassuring, if Barbara didn't worry that she was burning herself out. Barbara knew, on some level, that Essie was trying to prove that this time she could do it.

"But you don't have to do it alone," Barbara kept telling her. She knew, better than anyone, how hard it was to do it alone. Essie's father had run off while she was still pregnant with Essie. He'd promised all the right things—financial support, a role in the child's life—but of course, he'd produced none of them. Barbara had been forced to move to Melbourne for family support. Her great-aunt Esther wasn't exactly a lot of family, but back then, she was all Barbara had. So, yes, she knew about doing it alone. And she was determined her daughter wouldn't have to do the same.

Essie had spent two weeks as an inpatient at the Summit Oaks—a psychiatric unit attached to the hospital—after she'd left Mia in the park that day. When she'd been released, she'd returned home with a psychologist's card in her pocket and a prescription for Zoloft and had been expected to get on with her life. It wasn't enough in Barbara's opinion.

"You're always worried," Essie had told her.

"I'm your mother," she'd replied. "It's my job."

But Essie may have been right. Now that Essie *was* asking her to babysit more often, Barbara was still worried. Call it a mother's instinct, but these past few weeks Essie had seemed a little . . . off. Barbara hoped it wasn't the beginning of something.

She snuck out of the spare room, leaving the door ajar, and made herself a cup of tea. She'd been trying to stay off the tea and drink more water lately, but she had a feeling she was coming down with a cold and she needed the comfort.

"Drink the damn tea," her friend Lois had told her when they'd discussed it recently. "Everyone is always denying themselves these days. No sugar, no gluten. No dairy! For Pete's sake, what is more natural than dairy?"

So Barbara made the tea, then slipped on her glasses to check her phone messages. Lois had sent her a text—a cartoon of two people with a smaller person between them. Barbara squinted at it. What on earth was that supposed to be?

Barbara hated texting. She much preferred speaking to people on the phone, but when she said it out loud, it made her sound so appallingly old that she just pretended to be happy with texting. She put up with texts from Essie and Ben, but why did Lois have to do it, for goodness sake? She punched in her number and called her. This was always her silent protest.

"Did you get my text?" Lois said. No 'hello.'"

"I did. But I have no idea what it means."

"Teresa is having a baby!"

"Oh!" she cried. "Lo, that's fantastic. Congratulations to you all."

Barbara felt a thrill that was perhaps disproportionate to the occasion, considering that Teresa wasn't even a relative. But Barbara loved nothing more than a newborn. Besides, Lois's daughter had been trying to get pregnant for two years. For the last year Lois had kept Barbara so well informed about Teresa's fertile dates, ovulation cycles, and vaginal mucus that Barbara had felt positively shy around Teresa. According to Lois, they'd been about to try IVF. Now they wouldn't have to.

"Yes, she's thrilled, of course. I would never have said any-thing but I was worried she was getting too long in the tooth."

Lois *had* said that to Barbara, several times.

"When is she due?" Barbara asked.

"Don't know. I should've asked that, of course. I actually have no details whatsoever. She just texted me a few minutes before I texted you."

Barbara took a moment to digest that. Lois's only daughter had *texted* to say that she was pregnant (she didn't call?) and then Lois's response was to text *Barbara*!

Stop being so judgmental, Barbara chided herself.

"Actually I should probably go, as she might be trying to call."

"Yes, go. Great news, Lo. Give Teresa my best."

Barbara put down the phone just as a sneeze came on. She pulled a tissue from her sleeve, then picked up her tea again and took a sip. A new baby. Was there anything more precious? It was particularly special, as it hadn't come easily to Teresa. It hadn't come easily to Barbara either, but back when she'd been trying for a baby they didn't have IVF or support groups or fertility specialists. If anyone asked whether she wanted children, she was expected to smile and say, "Maybe one day." As if wanting a child was a shameful secret.

Barbara's phone rang.

"Barbie," Ben said when she picked up.

"Hello, Ben."

"I just left work. How is everything?"

By "everything," of course, Ben meant *Essie.* She and Ben checked in with each other like this every week or two ever since . . . last time. Barbara had expected that as the months and years went on, Ben would stop checking in, but he didn't.

For all his foibles, there was no doubt Ben loved his wife.

"Essie said you're having the girls for a sleepover."

"Yes," she said. "Essie was tired."

"Ah," he said. He was panting, clearly running home. "And she . . . seems okay to you?"

Barbara put down her tea. "Does she seem okay to *you?*"

Ben's breathing had softened. He must have slowed to a walk. "More or less. I mean, she's obsessed with Polly's sleep patterns at the moment and is constantly on Google looking for solutions. But that's normal, right, for a mum of a new baby?'

Barbara had no idea what was normal these days. When Essie was a baby there was no Google, no sleep trainers. If you had a baby that was crying, you just had to deal with it.

"I don't know, Ben."

He was silent for a moment. It occurred to Barbara that it was one of the only times Ben was serious—when he was talking about Essie.

"Spend some more time with her," Barbara said finally, decisively. "Come home earlier and help out with the girls as much as you can. I'll do the same. If anything changes, let me know."

"Okay," he said. "Good plan. Talk to you later."

"Talk to you later," Barbara replied and hung up.

It wasn't exactly worrying, what Ben had said, yet Barbara had a bad feeling. Things had gone downhill quickly last time, and this time she needed to pay attention. She was a mother, after all.

It was a mother's duty to worry.

11

ESSIE

In Pleasant Court, mornings were busy. People going to work, doing the school run. Kids riding bikes, adults jogging. Essie raced by them all as she ran out of the house with Polly on her hip, a box of muffins under her arm, and Mia's lunch box in her hand. It wasn't even 8 A.M., and you could feel the day's heat building.

"Ben," Essie called, flagging him down in the bulb of the cul-de-sac. "Mia's lunch box!"

She handed it to him through the open car window while Mia waved from the backseat. She went to kindergarten for three-year-olds two and a half days a week, and Ben dropped her off (something he dropped into conversation to anyone who'd listen). It would have been wonderful if only he didn't always forget *everything* Mia needed. Most days Essie found herself driving up to the kindergarten later in the day to drop off her hat, her blanket, her water bottle. When she told Ben about it he always looked suitably chastened, but that didn't make her life any easier.

"Essie." Ange was slowly navigating her front steps in very high beige wedges. "Essie! Do you have a minute?"

"Sure." Essie hitched Polly up on her hip.

"I spoke to the people at Neighborhood Watch, Victoria," Ange said, panting. "They said that once we have recruited as many members as we can, the next step is to schedule a meeting with the local police. We can have it at my place. I was thinking a weeknight. So, we need to ring around the neighbors and . . . Oh there's Fran . . ."

Fran was coming down the front steps in her running gear.

"Another run," Ange muttered. "I swear I saw her head out for a run two hours ago."

Fran *did* seem to have been running a lot. Essie remembered because every time she saw her she felt guilty about *not* going for a run. Maybe she had an exercise addiction. Or an eating disorder. Maybe she binged on cake and then punished herself by running for hours. She didn't seem the type, but who really knew? The truth was, despite appearances, she didn't know much about her neighbors at all.

"Anyway," Ange said, "can I count on you to come to the meeting?"

"Sure," Essie said.

"Great. Well, excuse me then, I'll go ask Fran. Fran!"

Essie headed up Isabelle's path. Last night while nursing Polly back to sleep for the fifty-seventh time, Essie had decided she should do something nice to welcome Isabelle to the neighborhood, so first thing this morning she'd baked muffins. What could be more welcoming than muffins? She held the Tupperware container under one arm and Polly in the other as she approached her front door.

It was a brand-new door, she noticed, with a shiny knocker that seemed too modern for the house. Essie hadn't been inside since the fire, nearly four months ago. Electrical fire, apparently, started in the roof. The flames had woken Ben. By the time they'd gotten out into the street, half the neighbors were standing outside in their bathrobes. Mrs. Harrap, the previous tenant, was visiting her daughter in Queensland (they knew this for sure because everyone had taken turns watering her plants and collecting her mail) so the neighbors were free to enjoy the drama without fear for human life. It had been exciting actually. Film crews had come down and most of the neighbors had spoken to them, but Essie, for some reason, had gotten major camera time on the six o'clock news (Ange had been devastated). Mrs. Harrap moved in with her daughter after that, and the landlord repaired the damage. A few weeks later, Isabelle moved in.

Essie was just lifting her hand to knock when the door peeled open.

"I didn't even knock!" Essie exclaimed.

Isabelle smiled. She was makeup-free, dressed in a burgundy oriental robe. Her feet were bare and her toenails were painted a deep purplish-red. "I saw you coming up the path and it looked like you had your hands full. Here, let me help." She opened her arms and to Essie's surprise, reached for Polly.

"Thanks," Essie said. "Sorry, did I wake you? I wanted to drop these off early because I thought you'd be headed off to work."

"I'm not working today. I still have unpacking to do." Isabelle kept her eyes on Polly, who placed her chubby little hand on Isabelle's chin. Isabelle flickered her eyes toward the container in Essie's hands. "What have you got there?"

"Raspberry and white-chocolate muffins. To welcome you to the neighborhood."

"Wow." Isabelle finally tore her eyes off Polly and reached for the container. "These are still warm. You must have gotten up early this morning to bake these."

Essie shrugged. "Well . . . I have children so I'm always up early."

Isabelle's robe had come undone slightly, she noticed, revealing a narrow line of bare flesh down as far as her belly button. Essie quickly looked away, but she needn't have bothered because Isabelle had turned her attention back to Polly.

"She's sweet," Isabelle said, clasping one of Polly's toes between her fingers. Polly rewarded her with a huge gummy smile, which Isabelle returned. Essie watched the interaction, feeling like an outsider. When was the last time Polly had smiled at her like that? Did *she* ever squeeze Polly's toes? "I love kids," Isabelle said. "If you ever need a babysitter, just let me know."

"Thanks," Essie said, though she was surprised. Isabelle didn't seem the type to go ga-ga over babies. "I'll tell Ange and Fran. We're always looking for babysitters around here."

"Well, I suppose I should give you your baby back," Isabelle said, handing Polly back. Her gaze lingered on Essie for a moment. "Your eyes," she said.

"Oh," Essie said. "Yeah. They're strange."

"One blue, one brown?"

"Both blue." Essie pointed at her left eye with her free hand. "But this one has a birthmark over it, that's why it looks brown."

Isabelle's eyes were also blue, Essie noticed, a rich deep color even bluer than her own.

"I'll bet you get lots of comments about them."

"Some," Essie said, though in actual fact it was rare that anyone noticed. The odd guy had when she was younger and dating. But since she'd drifted into the married-with-kids "tickbox," people didn't tend to notice her at all. It felt nice that Isabelle was noticing now.

"Well, I guess I'd better keep moving," Essie said after a long silence. She'd been hoping Isabelle would invite her in. Her own house felt so lonely during the days when Mia was at kindergarten, and Polly always seemed especially grumpy on those days. The neighbors were rarely around on weekdays—Ange worked full time and Fran, as Ange had pointed out, was constantly jogging. Essie's mum often dropped by to keep her company, but it wasn't the same as a friend. Essie found herself imagining them making cups of tea together, perhaps even helping Isabelle unpack a few boxes. But Isabelle just hugged the door, three-quarters closed.

"Thank you for the muffins," Isabelle said. She reached again for Polly, this time grasping her little hand. "Bye, Polly."

Isabelle closed the door and Essie headed back down the path toward the street. But with her hand on her front door-knob, something occurred to her.

She'd never told Isabelle her daughter's name was Polly.

12

ISABELLE

Isabelle sat at her dining room table and peered out the front window. She was still in her bathrobe even though it was early afternoon—it was too damn hot to get dressed and go outside. And so she sat in her front room, doing some people watching.

There was plenty to see. An hour earlier Ange had pulled up outside her house and run inside carrying a Red Rooster bag, presumably lunch for Ollie, who was home from school with a bright green cast on his arm. Fran had been out for a run twice—twice!—with her kids in the double jogging pram. And ten minutes ago Essie had piled Polly into her car seat and driven off, waving to her mother who was weeding her front garden in a wide-brimmed hat with a floral band.

So this was what suburbia was like, she thought. Close-knit. *Pleasant.* People talking to one another, keeping an eye on everyone else's business (in fact, Isabelle had received a flyer in her letter box about a neighborhood watch meeting tonight at Ange's house). It was a hard place, you'd imagine, to keep a secret.

Her phone began to ring.

Jules, she thought. Isabelle had been thinking about Jules a lot today.

"Do what you have to do," Jules had said when Isabelle had explained she was moving to Melbourne. *Do what you have to do.* She hadn't given a reason, or any notice. She couldn't. And Jules let her go anyway, no questions asked.

On the surface it seemed like a dismissive response, as if Jules didn't care what she did one way or another. But in fact the opposite was true. Jules cared enough *not* to ask. It was the reason their relationship worked when so many before had failed. It occurred to Isabelle how lovely that was . . . and how sad.

Isabelle glanced at the screen. It wasn't Jules, it was her father. "Dad."

"You picked up!" came his booming voice. "I thought I was going to have to file a missing person's report. Then I hear you've up and moved to Melbourne!"

Isabelle fought the urge to fake a bad connection and hang up. She needed to speak to him sometime or he *would* file a missing person's report. "Look, I'm sorry I haven't gotten in touch with you. I just . . . needed a change."

"Well, I don't like it," he said. His voice may have been loud, but she knew he'd be hurt that she'd moved without telling him. She imagined his large, craggy face lined with concern. "I don't like you being so far away."

It was a nice comment, even if she hadn't seen her father in nearly a year in Sydney. She thought back to Easter last year, when she'd spent the day at his house with her two teenage half-sisters. Her dad had bought them all novelty Easter eggs, which none of them had eaten—her sisters because they were on some sort of diet, and Isabelle because she simply couldn't stomach watching him beam around the table, saying how marvelous it was to have all his kids together in one room. Isabelle had to remind him that her brother Freddy was spending the holiday with his wife's family and he didn't even have the good grace to look sheepish. Her father wasn't a bad man, but he'd been as good as useless to her and her brother for years.

"Listen, I just wanted to—" he said, then suddenly, his voice went far away and Isabelle heard Rachel, her sixteen-year-old half-sister, talking in the background. "What is it? Oh. Izzy, hang on a sec, would you? What is it, honey?"

Isabelle closed her eyes and banged her head softly against the table.

"The iPad's not working," Rachel said in a whiney, obnoxious voice.

Isabelle tried to remember whether she'd spoken to her dad like that when she was sixteen. It was unlikely since when Isabelle was sixteen her parents were divorced and she was a guest in her dad's home.

"I'll be there in a minute," he said to Rachel. "I'm talking to Isabelle. Do you want to say hi?"

Isabelle heard the phone being passed through air and pictured Rachel wildly shaking her hands, mouthing "Noooo!" while her dad, oblivious, smiled.

"Hi, Rach," Isabelle said.

"Hi." She sounded sullen and unenthused. "Now can you fix it, Dad?"

Isabelle sighed. She knew how this would end. Her dad wanted to be there for Isabelle, but his new family was his priority. He'd made that perfectly clear every time he rang to wish Isabelle a happy birthday a few days late, while the same day posting a Facebook photo of him and her half-sisters on some kind of day trip—to a lake, a mountain, a zoo. Isabelle knew she was far too old to care about being her father's top priority—for God's sake, she was nearly forty—but it still managed to irk her. She wondered if the fact that she'd mysteriously moved to Melbourne would make a difference. Maybe this time he'd tell Rachel, *Sorry, but the iPad will have to wait. I'm talking to Isabelle.*

"Have you tried turning it off and on again?" he asked her.

Isabelle glanced at the window. Fran was out there again, putting Ava and Rosie into the jogging stroller. Surely she wasn't running again?

Through the phone, Isabelle heard her sister let out a high-pitched noise that sounded more animal than human. "Dad!!!!!"

"Izzy, do you mind if I call you back later? I'll call from work tomorrow and then we'll have no interruptions."

"Sure," she murmured. Fran *did* appear to be running for the third time today. Crazy lady. Essie pulled into the street and gave her a wave. Did no one else notice that that woman had some sort of exercise addiction?

"But Izzy?"

"Yes, Dad?"

A pause. "You're all right, aren't you? You'd tell me if you weren't all right . . ."

It was so typical of her dad, waiting until the last moment to tell her why he was really phoning. He always did that when he didn't really want to know the answer. As such, she didn't see the point of telling him the truth.

"I'm fine," she said. "Thanks for calling."

She hung up, still looking out the window. Essie was attempting to unstrap Polly from her car seat while Mia stood by her side, clutching a pair of binoculars made from toilet rolls. This could have been her life, Isabelle realized. It could have been her jogging obsessively or wrangling kids or bringing her kid lunch when he had a broken arm. Instead she was a spectator—a strange woman in a bathrobe, watching through the window.

But she was going to get her life back. That was exactly what she'd come to Pleasant Court to do.

"The baby is definitely coming?" I asked the nurse.

"There's no stopping it now," she said, handing me a clipboard. "I just need you to fill in this paperwork so we can admit yo—"

The next contraction was already here. I'd barely caught my breath from the last one. The nurse put the paperwork on a side table.

"Are you sure you don't want someone to contact your husband?" she said.

My husband. A few weeks back, he'd told me I was acting unhinged. When had he started saying things like that to me? Once, while we were still dating, he'd told me my passion was one of his favorite things about me.

Now I was unhinged.

I shook my head.

"This will all be worth it," I said a few minutes later, ostensibly to the nurse but really to myself. "Once I have my baby, everything will be all right."

The nurse looked at me. I expected a smile, perhaps a reassurance of some description. Instead she gave me a look I'll never forget.

13

ESSIE

"Can I have ketchup, Mummy?"

"Sure," Essie said, squirting a generous dollop onto her plate. "Knock yourself out."

It was 6 P.M. and the neighborhood watch meeting at Ange's place was starting any moment. Essie had cooked dinner, stacked the dishwasher, tidied the house somewhat, and now she just needed Ben to get home. Normally Essie's mum would come over to look after the girls, but tonight she was in bed with a cold so Ben had agreed to come home early and take over. Essie had to admit, she was excited. There was something torturous about the dinner, bath, and bed routine—not least because it had to be done every single day. It had been bad enough with one child, but with two it was relentless.

Ange and Fran got it, at least.

"I am suicidal and homicidal every day between five and seven P.M.," Fran always said, straight-faced. "I *wish* I was kidding."

"Alcohol," Ange told her sagely. "It's the only way."

Essie suspected Ange was right. She had to admit, the prospect of a glass of wine and a chat was one of the reasons she was looking forward to the neighborhood watch meeting so much. Apart from Ben and her mother (on the phone), Essie hadn't spoken to another adult all day. And after the impromptu gathering at her house the other day, who knew? Maybe catching up socially would become a regular thing.

"I'm home," Ben called from the door. Mia scrambled off her chair and a mere second later Ben had a three-year-old wrapped around his head. "Who turned out the lights?" he cried, flailing about. "Where's Mia? Why can't I see anything?"

He walked into the hall table, knocked over a picture frame and stepped into a basket of clean laundry, leaving a dirty footmark on top of a clean white sheet.

"Ben!"

"Sorry." He winced.

She picked up the basket and headed for the laundry. Might as well put the wash on so it would be ready to put in the dryer when she got home.

"I'll do it," Ben said. "Really. Just go." He unwrapped Mia from his head and looked at her earnestly. "I promise, I've got this."

"Polly's in the bouncy chair," she said finally. "I won't be late."

Ange's house beamed out light from every window. She and Lucas had added a second floor to their bungalow a few years ago, and now a skylight window peeked out of the roofline

(Ollie's room). The garden was perfectly manicured, with green lawn and ornamental pear trees and symmetrical kumquat trees on either side of the front door in terra-cotta pots. Often when she went to Ange's place, Essie felt like she had arrived in Wisteria Lane.

Only one other house in the street beamed out light: Isabelle's. Essie had hoped to see Isabelle there tonight—she knew Ange had invited her. Perhaps neighborhood watches weren't her thing. Essie couldn't help feeling a little disappointed. Although she hadn't processed this thought until right that very second, Essie realized she'd been harboring a childish hope that Isabelle might become her first proper Pleasant Court friend.

She hesitated in front of Isabelle's house. Perhaps Isabelle *wanted* to go to the meeting but felt self-conscious as the newest person on the street? Perhaps if Essie came by and offered to walk her there, she might decide to come? It was, after all, the neighborly thing to do.

With unusual decisiveness, Essie spun around, walked up Isabelle's driveway, and knocked on the door. Quicker than she expected, it swung open. Isabelle was dressed in a red tunic with a matching scarf around her hair. Her legs were bare and her toenails, today, were teal green. "Hey, Essie. I was just getting ready for the neighborhood watch meeting."

"Oh good," Essie said, feeling relieved and also suddenly very suburban housewife in her jeans, button-down shirt, and ballet flats. "That's why I was coming by. I thought I could walk you there."

"Sounds great." Isabelle smiled.

She had, Essie noticed, a spectacular smile. A familiar smile.

She was trying to figure out why it was familiar when suddenly, a smell hit her. "Uh . . . is something burning?"

Isabelle cursed. "The pasta!"

Isabelle spun and bolted back into the house. Essie stood there uncertainly for a moment, then slowly trailed after her.

From some reason, perhaps the fact that Isabelle hadn't invited her in the last time she visited, Essie had assumed the place would be a terrible mess—filled with boxes and unpacked suitcases. Instead she found it pristine. Brightly colored, oversize art hung on the walls, and the surfaces were dotted with eclectic designer-looking knickknacks. A headless mirrored mannequin stood in one corner. Essie peeked into an adjoining room that appeared to be a study, also spotless. Looking at it, Essie felt a stab of envy. This was how she would have liked to have lived.

Alas, Essie had *children*.

"Damn," she heard Isabelle say from the next room. "There goes dinner."

Essie followed the voice to a steam-filled kitchen, where Isabelle was emptying a congealed slab of pasta into the garbage.

"You haven't eaten yet?"

She shook her head. "It's okay. There'll be nibbles at the meeting, right?"

Right on cue, Isabelle's stomach gave a little whine.

"You need to eat," Essie said. "There's a great Thai place just around the corner."

"But what about the meeting?"

Essie shrugged with a nonchalance she didn't feel. She imagined she looked like an easygoing go-with-the-flow type who didn't care that she was already running seventeen minutes late for the meeting. She *liked* looking like that type of person.

"All right. I'm assuming you'll join me then?"

Essie felt a twist of unease. She'd RSVP'd to the meeting; it wasn't like her to be a no-show. She pictured all the residents sitting around Ange's plush couches eating cheese and crackers, Ange glancing at her watch.

"Sure," she said. "Why not?"

Two hours later, Essie sat at one end of Isabelle's couch, happily pinching the stem of a wineglass. It was rare for her to drink alcohol during the week. With two small children and a fitness junkie for a husband, it just wasn't something that occurred to her. But as she sat on Isabelle's couch, it felt surprisingly *right*.

"That chicken cashew stir-fry," Isabelle said, resting her pale, bare legs on the coffee table. Next to Isabelle's feet were two empty plastic containers where their dinner used to be, and a wine bottle—the contents of which had been emptied into their bellies. "Best I've ever had."

"Mmm," Essie agreed. The neighborhood watch meeting would be well under way by now. Essie imagined the empty spot on Ange's couch where she should be. For the first time in her life, Essie was a *rebel*.

"So," Isabelle said, "was this better or worse than a neighborhood watch meeting?"

"I'm not sure yet," Essie said. "It depends on how much grief Ange gives me for not showing up."

Isabelle laughed, even though Essie wasn't joking. Isabelle's lips made Essie understand what people meant when they described a "heart-shaped" mouth.

Isabelle clutched a cushion to her chest. It was white silk with hand-painted fuchsia and aqua flowers across the front. It was the kind of item that Essie would have picked up in a store or at a market, but then put down again because she wasn't brave enough to own it. Isabelle's couch was teal velvet, and her coffee table had steel legs and a surface made of black and white mosaic tiles. A deep red Persian rug lay beneath Essie's feet.

Essie thought of all the times she'd stood in boutique art galleries admiring a piece of modern art or an unusual sculpture. There was no doubt she was attracted to unusual art. Several times she'd even managed to justify the price tag (a birthday or anniversary present from Ben). But when push came to shove, Essie always settled for the muted, Pottery Barn–type wares that filled every suburban living room. She had a sudden urge to run home and throw out every piece of Pottery Barn furniture. This was the home she was supposed to have, she thought irrationally.

"So," Essie said. "Tell me about yourself. I hear you work for a nonprofit. Which one?"

Isabelle lifted her glass to her lips, then put down it down again without taking a sip. There was a slight change to her eyes. "I work for the Abigail Ferris Foundation."

"The Abigail . . ." Essie tried to think why that name sounded familiar. "Wait, Abigail Ferris? Wasn't she the little girl who disappeared while riding her bike to school? Years ago, when I was a kid?"

Isabelle nodded. "The foundation was created by friends and family members of Abigail's. It's dedicated to the safety of all children, and the recovery of missing children."

Essie sucked in a breath. The recovery of missing children. It felt so immediate, so terrifying. Something that could happen to you, rather than something that happened to other people.

"And," she said, clearing her throat, "what do you for the foundation?"

"Our goal, of course, is reunification of families. I do everything I can to facilitate that."

Essie she wasn't entirely clear whether Isabelle had answered her question, but she nodded anyway. Isabelle seemed to have gone into work mode at this talk of work, even sitting straighter in her chair. Or maybe Essie was just imagining it.

"Does that happen often?" Essie asked. "Reunification?"

"It depends. In a lot of cases a parent or relative is involved and it's just matter of finding them. In other cases, sex traffickers or pedophiles are involved."

Essie winced.

"And then there are the baby snatchers," Isabelle continued. "Women who steal a baby and raise it as their own. Those are the hardest cases for reunification, because the child itself doesn't know it has been stolen."

Essie felt a twist of unease. Isabelle had become so serious all of a sudden. But then, how could you *not* be serious when talking about missing children?

"So . . . how do you find these children?" Essie asked.

"The best leads we get are from the community. You'd be

surprised by how many children have been recovered because someone follows their instincts and asks questions when something doesn't feel right."

"Did you come to this area for a particular case?" Essie asked.

"Yes."

"You think one of your missing children might be in *Sandringham*?"

"Yes."

Isabelle watched her steadily. Essie shifted in her seat. Talking about lost children reminded her about what she'd done that day, leaving Mia in the park. She thought of what might have happened if Mia hadn't been there when she returned—how much worse it could have been.

"Well, I'd better get going," Essie said, standing.

"I hope I didn't scare you away."

"No . . ." Essie fumbled for her bag which had become wedged under the couch. "I just want to get away before the meeting is out. If anyone spots me leaving your place and tells Ange I'll be in all sorts of trouble." With a heave, her bag came free.

Isabelle smiled. "Well, we don't want that."

"Thank you for tonight," Essie said, babbling now. The wine had clearly gone to her head. She headed for the door. "It was much more fun than a neighborhood watch meeting."

"It was," Isabelle said, following Essie. "I really wasn't expecting to make any friends in Pleasant Court."

Friends. They stepped outside into the warm night air. Essie couldn't help feeling a thrill at that word. At the same time, she suddenly found it hard to meet Isabelle's eye. It was such an unfamiliar scenario to her. What was the protocol for two grown women saying good-bye after an evening together? A wave? A handshake? A hug?

"We should do this again," Isabelle said as Ange's door opened and the gentle hum of chatter carried across the road. The silhouettes had disappeared from the window and presumably everyone was about to spill out onto the street.

"Uh-oh," Essie said, "I'd better make a run for it."

Isabelle chuckled, leaning back against the wall. "Go on, then. Run!"

Essie took a step toward her house. But at the last minute she quickly turned back and planted a kiss on her new friend's cheek.

Essie's house looked like it had been ransacked. Peas were all over the floor, dirty dishes were in the sink, and toy trains lay on their sides alongside the longest continuous train track that Ben and Mia had made to date. The laundry basket was in the exact spot she'd left it, footprint and all.

Essie put down her bag, sighing. She swept the floor, put the trains away, put the laundry into the machine ready to turn on in the morning. Then she took a minute to fluff the cushions and set the throw rug before heading for the bedroom. Ben was a large mound in the bed, surrounded by the cushions he constantly bemoaned. (Cushions, Ange had recently proclaimed, were responsible for more divorces in America than infidelity or alcoholism. Funny, Essie thought it would be *sheets*.)

"How was the neighborhood watch meeting?" Ben murmured as she climbed into bed. His eyes were still closed, his face still collapsed against the pillow. "Is Pleasant Court the safest place in the world?"

Essie opened her mouth to tell him she'd been to Isabelle's instead. That they'd had takeout and wine and spent the night chatting. But then Polly started to cry.

"Safest in the universe," she said, and headed to Polly's room as Ben drifted back to sleep.

14

ISABELLE

The street was silent. Everyone had waved good night and finished up their conversations after the neighborhood watch meeting and were now safely back inside their homes, probably tucked up in bed. Isabelle's was the only light left on in the street, despite the fact it was just after 11 P.M. Pleasant Court really was a sleepy suburban street. So very quaint. So very *ominous*.

She lay in bed, wide awake. The anonymity of a new city, as it turned out, was an unexpected gift. Essie, clearly, had no idea who she was—even after she'd mentioned missing children. If that didn't tip her off, nothing would. In Sydney it was fairly common for people to recognize her name. When they did, they practically fell over themselves to run away (people really did believe bad luck was catching) or to give her their sympathies. Isabelle didn't mind the running away, or the sympathies, but she hated the stories. Everyone, it seemed, had a story. It had almost happened to their friend, their neighbor, their cousin.

Almost.

Almost isn't the same, she always wanted to tell them. Almost isn't even *almost* the same.

The worst was the breathless exhilaration with which people recounted their tales. People found it thrilling being so close to something so terrible—and they always seemed desperate to tell her all about it. Like the woman who told her that after hearing her story, her daughter had insisted on keeping her newborn twins within arm's length the entire time she was in the hospital. Or the man who'd seen someone suspicious when he was at the playground with his kids, and after hearing her story he decided to call the police because "you could never be too careful." Once, an elderly woman at a grocery store had told her, "If you really think about it, that child did the world a favor. Think of the children who are safe because of what happened!"

Isabelle never knew what to say. You're welcome? Sorry? Lucky you? What she really wanted to say was *Fuck off.*

Beside her, her phone sprang to life. She glanced at the screen.

Should I be expecting you home anytime soon?

It was Jules, reminding her that, outside of Pleasant Court at least, people stayed awake after eleven.

The message was classic Jules. Minimal words. No *x*'s or emojis. No hidden meanings for her to read into or obsess about. She would have given anything to have him here with her right now, to let him transport her away from all this for a little while so she didn't have to think.

Isabelle knew the whole street thought she was gay. She'd seen the flicker of surprise, excitement even, in Ange's face when she'd mentioned her ex-partner. Isabelle wasn't trying to be tricky, that partner *had* been a woman—a business partner in an online business that sold wristbands to music festivals. So she had, in fact, had a female partner. But sexually speaking, Isabelle liked men. One man in particular.

Julian was a high school teacher in a not-so-nice part of Sydney. He was passionate about his job and a champion of underprivileged adolescents. On the weekends he coached a basketball team of his students because none of the parents had volunteered to do it, and he spent most of the school holidays organizing activities for kids whose parents were working—because boredom and a lack of supervision were two of the most important factors sending teens into juvenile detention. He was a good man, a born father.

Before Jules, Isabelle had never had anything more than a string of sex-based relationships.

"Men must love you," people always told her, when she explained she didn't *do* boyfriends.

And it was true: men did love her. At first they loved the sex and the no-strings part of their relationships, but eventually they all loved *her* too. It wasn't because there was anything special about her, it may have even been the opposite. They'd think, how could someone so ordinary *not* want to have a relationship with them? Eventually some of the guys she dated became positively crazy with desperation, begging her to love them back. And that was invariably where the relationship came to an end.

But Jules was different. Perhaps it was because he'd made his intentions clear from the get-go. *I don't have purely sexual relationships with anyone,* he'd told her the first night. *I have too much respect for myself for that.*

Jules never made dreamy plans for the future or asked to meet her family. But without ever saying it in so many words, he commanded different treatment compared to the others. She never called him late at night or kicked him out of her bed in the wee hours of Sunday morning, the way she'd done with countless others. They made plans in advance, and though those plans always involved sex, they also often involved a takeout meal of some description and a sleepover. And over countless evenings, they'd gotten to know each other pretty well.

When Jules proposed, six months ago, Isabelle actually considered it. They didn't live together, but they spent several nights a week together, which was a big deal for Isabelle. But ultimately it turned out that was as big a commitment as she could make. When she'd declined, he said he understood. Jules often understood things without Isabelle having to explain them. He was, without doubt, the perfect guy. But Isabelle wasn't looking for the perfect guy. She was looking for someone else.

Jules knew what she was going through, and so he wouldn't pressure her to come home, or to stop doing what she was doing. He made allowances for her strange behavior, her erratic spells, her sudden disappearances. What he didn't know was that she had come to Pleasant Court to find someone. And the next time she spoke to Jules it would be to tell him that she'd found what she was looking for.

15

FRAN

Fran found Nigel in Ava's room. He was in the rocker with his feet on the stool, Ava splayed across his chest, both of them out cold and snoring. Fran had been at Ange's neighborhood watch meeting, which was just as dull as she'd feared. Stories about break-ins in the neighborhood had quickly turned to complaints about people putting their rubbish in other people's bins (which, frankly, Fran had never seen the problem with—after all, it all went to the same place, didn't it?), and it had gone downhill from there. Ange had seemed unusually high-strung throughout the meeting, and Essie hadn't even shown up. Fran wished she'd given it a miss too. But Nigel had insisted.

"I'll watch the girls," he'd said. "You need a break. Go!"

His earnestness was hard to bear. He thought she had postnatal depression. And maybe she did. After all, it would explain everything. The tears, the odd behavior. Perhaps not the running, though. The other night when she'd broken down in tears in bed, she'd tried to tell him the truth, *really* tried, but she couldn't bring herself to say the words. It was too terrible.

Something no one told you about real life was that it was complicated. Sure, on your wedding day you were given cryptic words of encouragement from older, wiser women—things like "let things go," and "love is more important than being right," or "the real reward is getting to the end together." Fran believed all those things. She *did* let things go. She *did* think love was more important than being right and that getting to the end together was the real reward. Unfortunately, there were some questions even the wise women didn't have answers for.

On TV there were always two parties—the villains and the victims—but real life was more complicated than that. In real life husbands became depressed. Men invested and lost large amounts of money. Men shut out their wives. In real life wives buried themselves in work—and workmates—for comfort. Wives told themselves it was innocent—a text message with a colleague here, a coffee date there—when they knew exactly where it was headed. But no one ever explained that things weren't clear-cut like they were on TV.

There was never an excuse, but there usually was an explanation. Fran had waited until she was in her thirties to get married to make sure she was ready. She'd made sure she found someone that she loved, someone who shared her values and morals. She wasn't the kind of person who had affairs. Her parents were still married, after all, and so were her in-laws, at least they were until

Nigel's father died. Growing up, the only person Fran knew who was divorced was her aunt Frieda, and the entire family had been appalled about that.

"Marriage is a commitment," she'd heard her mother say countless times. "It's not always easy but you see it through. If it gets hard, you work harder."

To her parents, marriage was some kind of test that you passed or failed, and they took great pride in being part of the graduating class.

Mark had been a work colleague. Her "work husband," she'd jokingly called him. He was handsome-ish, in an entirely different way from Nigel. Mark was short, burly, and full of confidence, not to mention her biggest cheerleader. Nigel had been impossible to talk to back then and Fran's attempts to help had left her demoralized. Work was a release from all that. At work, when she talked, people listened. Mark listened.

Nigel had been depressed for six months when Fran called his mother. His mother was the meek, mousy type—the kind of woman who said she "didn't understand the computers" and apologized when someone bumped into *her*. But there was no doubt she loved her son. And Fran was out of ideas.

"Oh," she'd said when Fran had explained what was going on. "Oh, dear."

Her response didn't fill Fran with optimism, but she listened carefully, at least, and it was nice to be listened to. His mother had promised to call Nigel and that was the end of that.

Until Fran got home.

"How *dare you* call my mother?" he cried the moment she

walked through the door after work. It was the most animated Fran had seen him in months. "Why would you do that? This isn't her business. This isn't anyone's business."

"I . . . didn't know what else to do," Fran stammered. It wasn't like Nigel to yell. One of her favorite things about him was that he was soft-spoken, measured. "I thought she might be able to help."

"You know what would help? You staying out of it."

That was the point when something hardened inside her.

She started spending more time at work where people appreciated and respected her. If it weren't for Rosie who was a little baby, she would have stayed at work all the time. She and Mark started ordering dinner on the nights they worked late. There were a few text messages, a few personal jokes. A little flirting, and not just on Mark's end.

It started one night after a conference, during drinks in the hotel bar. Conversation got a little too personal, physical touch got a little too physical. Fran found herself thinking . . . why not? Mark was a handsome, single guy. He couldn't seem to get enough of her. It was like she'd been starving for months and he was standing there with a platter of delicious food. She couldn't say no. She didn't *want* to say no. It happened a total of seven times.

And then, Fran found out she was pregnant.

It was possible the baby was Nigel's.

It was also possible it wasn't.

So, here they were. With Fran trying desperately to keep her secret while running (quite literally, running) herself into the ground in a form of self-flagellation. She'd thought she could keep the secret. But now, with him being the perfect, supportive husband? She wasn't sure she could do it.

Nigel's glasses had fallen down his nose. His hands were clasped around Ava, holding her safe, even in his sleep. Fran knew Nigel would do anything for Ava. One day he'd read books with her and do puzzles and laugh mildly at her jokes. He might even *be* her father. Was it really fair to jeopardize that just to ease her guilt? Was it fair to destroy all of their lives because of her mistake?

She wasn't going to tell Nigel, she decided. She'd live with her guilt, for the sake of her family. It was the *least* she could do.

She touched Nigel's elbow and he jolted awake, glancing down at Ava quickly and relaxing when he found her safe. He pushed his glasses back up his nose and blinked up at Fran with his lovely thick eyelashes.

"Hey," he said sleepily.

"Come on," she whispered. "Let's go to bed."

16

ANGE

A cheer went up among the parents on the grandstand. Ange joined in even though Will was on the bench. *It's about team spirit, not individual performance,* the coach had said before the game, a nice little excuse for leaving the weaker players on the bench.

"Whatever happened to 'It's not about whether you win or lose, it's how you play the game?'" she wanted to scream. "Just give each kid a bloody turn!"

Instead she nodded and smiled and cheered other people's kids on the field.

As she sat, watching other people's kids kick the ball around, she was thinking about the neighborhood watch meeting. Even without a few of the residents, it had, by all counts, been a raging success. Afterward, she'd Instagram'd and tweeted several pictures. Ange liked the idea of a neighborhood watch. She liked the idea of making the neighborhood safer and keeping an eye on the neighbors. Tomorrow she'd put in an order for stickers and lawn signs, which would be prominently displayed on the street. YOU HAVE ENTERED A NEIGHBORHOOD WATCH ZONE. WARNING! YOU ARE BEING WATCHED. VIDEO SURVEILLANCE: ALL SUSPICIOUS ACTIVITY WILL BE RECORDED AND SENT TO RELEVANT AUTHORI-TIES. Ange was looking forward to getting those signs up. It was good for people to know they were being watched, she thought. It made everyone behave better.

"Mom, I'm bored!" Ollie whined.

Me too, Ange thought.

"Shh," she said. "We're here to support your brother."

"But he's not even playing."

"He will soon," she insisted. But honestly, who knew? Will only turned up to sports games because Saturday sport was compulsory and he was a rule follower. But he wasn't a natural athlete. He was bookish and inquisitive. When he was little, five or six, he would often wander off the field and start picking up leaves and examining them. (*Photosynthesis!* he'd said once, when Ange had chased after him to ask what he was doing. *Look! Can you believe it?*) At eleven he was tall and smart and an unequivocal geek. His saving grace was that he was exquisitely handsome, perhaps even more so than his father. And every year, as he filled out more, he became even more breathtaking.

Ollie shifted in his seat. "Please, Mum, can we go? My arm hurts."

Ange locked eyes with Ollie. He was lying, of course. Unlike Will, a classic firstborn unable to tell a lie (an annoying trait when they were on holidays in the Gold Coast and were trying to get him into Sea World for free, and he insisted on telling everyone he was four and not three), Ollie could lie so convincingly it was hard not to be impressed. Ollie was a fabulous sportsman, of about average intelligence, but when it came to looks he'd inherited a horrible assortment of genes, from Ange's pointyish chin to her mother's stocky physique. Still, the boy could lie, which was bound to serve him well at some point. He'd probably make a very good real estate agent one day. Unfortunately, right now, there was a very slim chance that he wasn't lying. And a slim chance was all it took to make a hairline crack in her resolve to laugh at his pathetic attempt to get out of watching the game.

"Where does it hurt?" she asked him.

He pointed vaguely at his arm. "Here."

"Is it a sharp pain? An ache? What?"

"An ache," he said.

Of course it was an ache. ("The arm might ache quite a bit over the next few weeks," the doctor had said. "Ibuprofen and rest are the best things. And maybe some extra TLC. It can be quite painful. If he complains, indulge him a little. Let him stay home from school or whatever he's doing." But of course, Ollie had been there when the doctor had said that. And Ollie was no fool.)

"Oww," he said, loud enough for surrounding people to hear.

"Shh," Ange said, patting his arm awkwardly.

It was one of those moments when motherhood felt like a shock. As if someone had just walked up to you with a baby and cried, "This is your child. You are a mum! You are meant to know what to do in this situation!" Fran would know what to do, Ange thought. She seemed to be equipped for any situation—whether the child needed a Band-Aid, a lollipop, a hug, or a pep talk. She was the girl guide of motherhood and she'd earned all her badges.

"How about an ice cream?" she tried.

Ollie pretended to consider that. "It might help," he said solemnly. "It *is* hot. Where's Dad? Can he take me?"

Lucas, of course, was nowhere to be seen. Ange had last seen him wandering off with another dad to fetch equipment from the storage shed. But now the other dad was back in the grandstands cheering on his son, and Lucas was MIA. She felt a wave of irritation with him. Why did he always wander off? Why did he strike up conversations with strange people and find them fascinating?

Ange called his phone, but it rang on the bench beside her. It must have fallen out of his pocket. She sighed. "I'll go check The Shed."

Ollie gave her a winning smile. "I'll wait here."

Ange climbed down from the stand and trudged across the grass. Lucas had probably bumped into someone and struck up a conversation. Or maybe he'd discovered the world's best climbing tree. Last weekend, he'd taken the boys to a treetop adventure park, where they'd been strapped into harnesses and climbed. Ange had sat that one out. She'd thought Will might have sat it out too, but he was surprisingly keen. Lucas had that effect on the boys. He had that effect on everyone. They'd all come home exhausted and drunk on adrenaline.

Ange's pocket was vibrating. Lucas's phone. She glanced at the screen as she continued toward The Shed.

"Lucas Fenway's phone," she said.

Silence. Ange waited. People were often a little thrown when an unexpected person answered the phone.

"Hello?" she repeated after a few seconds. "Who is speaking please?"

Nothing. Ange looked back at the screen. An old photo of Will and Ollie smiled back at her. The call had ended. She put the phone back in her pocket, mildly irritated. It was probably a client. A young mother who wanted a newborn shoot—a millennial. Didn't everyone say the millennials had no phone manners, because all they did was text and email? Perhaps now if they didn't get the person they were looking for, they simply hung up? It irritated Ange to no end. Why not just say, "Oh, I'm calling about a photo shoot"? Ange would have happily taken a message. Now the silly girl would have to call back and it would probably send her into a full-blown anxiety attack. A second phone call! Mortifying!

It was hard to believe these children were mothers themselves.

And then, out of nowhere, the young mother from the hospital sprang to mind. Erin, that was her name. Erin and her pretty little girl. She'd thought about them a few times since that day, and the affectionate way Lucas touched her arm. A paranoid thought occurred to her.

It wasn't Erin on the phone, was it?

No. She laughed, an unhinged-sounding giggle. Why on earth would it have been Erin?

"Ange!" Lucas jogged up behind her. Leaves stuck to the soles of his boots. "What are you laughing at?"

"Where have you been?" she exclaimed. "I was looking for you."

"These guys needed a hand setting up for Little Athletics," he said.

He turned and waved to a couple of dads who waved back and shouted, "Thanks, Lucas."

"I told them I was happy to help. Remember Little Aths?" he said, his eyes wistful. "Feels like yesterday, doesn't it?"

His eyes welled up with *actual* tears, and Ange softened. How could he make her so angry one minute and the next, make her fall completely in love with him again?

"Ollie has a sore arm," she said. "He wants ice cream."

"Where is he?"

"He's over there by the stand. He's probably faking . . ."

"Roger that. I'll take him to Dairy Bell and refuse to buy him anything until he admits he's a faker. I'll be back for you and Will in half an hour." Lucas winked at her. "See you soon."

"Wait. Your phone," she said, holding it up. "You left it on the bench."

He reached for it, but Ange didn't let go. The result was a strange little tug-of-war-with-the-iPhone game, except that neither of them were pulling.

"Someone phoned but they didn't say anything," she said. "Pretty strange, don't you think?"

They locked eyes for a moment.

Do you want to be asking this? he asked her.

I'm not sure, she replied.

Remember what happened last time? he said.

Yes. I remember.

Except they didn't say any of this. Not out loud. Because there were some questions Ange didn't want answers to.

"Well," he said. "I'm sure whoever it was will call back. Make sure you get a video if my boy gets off the bench!"

Ange nodded, and even managed a smile.

"I will," she said. "Thanks, Lucas."

17

ESSIE

Essie had always loathed people who started sentences with "I'm the kind of person who . . ." mostly because it was invariably followed by a positive quality. "I am the kind of person who does anything for her friends; I am the kind of person who says what she thinks." Well, good for you, Essie always thought, but if you were truly that certain kind of person, you wouldn't need to talk about it. Everyone would already know.

But in a way Essie knew her revulsion toward these people was tinged with jealousy. Because even if it wasn't true, at least those people had a grasp on who they *thought* they were. Essie had no such grasp. She *could* be funny, but not funny enough for it to be a defining quality. She was welcoming and generous, but fear of not being liked will do that to you. People who said "I'm the kind of person who . . ." always spoke in absolutes, *I am this* and *I do that*. Everything was black-and-white while Essie existed in shades of gray.

Essie was thinking about this as she walked over to Fran's house. Mia and Rosie had been invited to a birthday party of a girl from kindergarten and Fran had offered to take them. Essie carried Polly while Ben jogged beside her at a comically slow speed, on his way to take a Saturday body-pump class.

Essie thought about the fact that she'd lied to him about attending the neighborhood watch meeting. Why had she done that? The silly thing was, if she'd just told Ben she'd gone to Isabelle's instead of the neighborhood watch meeting, he wouldn't have cared. He'd probably have given her a high-five. ("My rule-following wife finally rebels," he'd have said. "Good for you.")

The problem was, now that she'd lied, she couldn't very well tell him. He'd think it was strange. It *was* strange. That was the thing with lies—they grew like weeds until, eventually, they strangled you.

"Essie!"

Essie heard a car door slam and saw Ange walking toward her. Her heart sank. Behind her, Will, Ollie, and Lucas tumbled out of the car and headed toward their house. Essie threw them all a wave and headed determinedly toward Fran's.

"What happened to you last night?" Ange called after her. From the click of her heels, she'd picked up the pace. "Your mother didn't make it either. We had two empty seats!"

"Didn't make it where?" Ben said.

Essie looked around helplessly. Of course, this was the *one* time Ben paid attention to her conversation with Ange.

"Oh, uh . . . Mum had a cold. She was in bed."

"Oh," Ange said. She stopped. "Well, that's a shame. Tell her I'm around if she needs anything."

"I will. Thanks." Essie kept walking.

"And what's *your* excuse?"

"Your excuse for what?" Ben said. He picked up Mia and deposited her on his shoulders. She started running her toy train through his hair. "Choo choo. Choo choo."

"Her excuse for why she wasn't at the neighborhood watch meeting last night," Ange said.

Essie wasn't sure if Ange was trying to punish her or just being obtuse. She seemed particularly forceful this morning, even for Ange. Perhaps the evening had gone late. She looked a little tired, like she hadn't slept well.

Ben was looking at her with an expression that was so *Ben* she almost smiled. He wasn't suspicious. Not angry. More . . . curious. Essie cursed silently. How had she got herself into this situation?

In her peripheral vision, Essie noticed her mum walking up the drive, mail in hand. It gave her an idea.

"I was with Mum. She was a bit feverish and I wanted to keep an eye on her. Sorry we didn't make it to the meeting."

At the word "Mum," Ben immediately disengaged, bored. "Right, then. I'll keep going."

He kissed Essie, gave Mia a fancy dismount from his shoulders, and jogged away.

"Bye," Essie called, wishing she could jog away with him.

"You could have called," Ange said.

"I'm sorry," Essie said. "I should have."

Ange nodded. "All right. Well, you'll come to the next meeting, won't you?"

Ange noticed Lucas coming out of the house and she spun around.

"Yes. Of course I will. I'll . . ."

But she was gone.

Essie walked up the driveway. Fran was already loading a second car seat into the back for Mia. (Of course, Fran had a second car seat for these types of situations.)

"Was Ange giving you a bollocking for not coming to the meeting?" Fran called, her head still inside the car.

"She was, actually. She seemed a little high-strung this morning."

"Ah well. That's Ange."

Essie was about to say something more when Rosie appeared by the car, dressed in a tutu. A present wrapped in pink and white paper was tucked under her skinny arm. Essie's heart sank. It meant they had three, maybe four seconds before Mia melted down, begging to go home and change into her tutu.

"Mia—" she started.

But it turned out Essie had underestimated Mia. It only took her a split-second before she dropped the present and bolted. Fran watched the whole thing, baffled.

"She's getting her tutu," Essie said. "Mia, wait!"

But she wasn't stopping. She continued straight across the street, toward home. Essie scanned the cul-de-sac for cars, but thankfully it was empty. Fran raised her eyebrows at Essie—*Do you need help?*—but she shook her head. "I'll get her," she said, and turned in time to see Isabelle scoop Mia into her arms.

"Got ya!" Isabelle said, tickling her. Mia squealed in delight. Mia usually didn't take well to strangers showing her affection. Normally she was a shy type. Maybe, like Essie, she'd seen something special in Isabelle.

Essie jogged over to them. "Thank you. She's quick!"

Isabelle put her down. "Perhaps," she said. "But I'm quicker."

"I've done something strange," Essie said when her mum opened her front door.

Her mum widened the door, letting Essie in. "Would you like a cup of tea?"

One of the most astonishing things about Essie's mother was her patience. If she were to say those words to anyone else the obvious response would be to scream: *What is it? Tell me now!*

Her mum made tea.

"Sure," Essie said. "Tea would be great."

Already Essie felt more relaxed. It was just something about being in her mother's home. She lay a blanket on the carpet and put Polly in the middle. Mia had changed into her tutu and headed off to the party with Fran and Rosie.

"How are you feeling, by the way?" Essie asked.

"Fine," her mum said. "Just a bit snuffly. I needed an early night."

Essie leaned against the counter while her mum filled the kettle, got out mugs, and put out mini muffins, raspberry and white chocolate. She put it all on her neat round kitchen table, next to a vase of frangipanis.

"So," she said as they sat down. "What did you do?"

"I've lied about something," Essie said, feeling immediately better. There were few things more cathartic, she decided, than confessing something to your mother. "And I've involved you."

Barbara paused, the milk jug hovering in midair, above her mug. "I assume you're going to provide details."

"Well, I planned to go to the neighborhood watch meeting last night. I *meant* to go. Ben came home early from work and I was on my way over there when I saw Isabelle's light on. I went over there to tell her to come to the meeting. Instead, I ended up staying there for dinner."

"And you don't want Ange to know because she will think you've chosen Isabelle over her?" She finished pouring the milk and took a gulp of her tea.

Essie was ashamed at how girlish this sounded. "Partly. But I also lied to Ben. I told them both I was here last night, looking after you."

Her mum choked. She coughed a couple of times, then said: "But *why?*"

"I don't know! Ben was half-asleep when I got home and he asked how the meeting was so I just said fine. Then this morning Ange confronted me while Ben was there, and I was trapped, so I said I'd come here to look after you."

Her mum put her tea down again. Neither one of them had touched the muffins. "So I suppose you want me to back up your story?"

"Well . . . not necessarily. It probably won't come up again. You know Ben, he's hardly suspicious."

Her mum looked appalled. Essie had thought a visit to her mum was just what the doctor ordered, but she seemed to have taken a misstep. She should have expected it. Her mum prided herself on her good character, her honesty, her distaste for gossip and lies. Now Essie felt horribly guilty—as though she was a schoolgirl rather than a thirty-two-year-old mother of two.

Polly squawked on the floor. "Oh, I meant to ask," Essie said. "Is there any chance you could look after Polly for me for an hour this afternoon? Mia is having a playdate with Rosie and I thought I might go to the farmer's market with Isabelle. I just bumped into her outside. What?"

"Nothing," her mum said, though it was clear she was thinking *something*. "Of course you can leave Polly with me." She was quiet a moment. "I do have to ask though . . . is everything all right?"

"Everything is fine. I just thought it would be nice to go to the market with Isabelle. It's no big deal."

Her mum watched her, her eyebrows arched skeptically. "You seem quite taken with Isabelle, Essie."

"She's a friend," Essie liked the way that sounded. "You know I don't have a lot of friends."

"Not everyone needs a lot of friends.," her mum said. "It's a silly myth they push in American teen movies to fill people with insecurities."

"But there's nothing wrong with striving to have a few more, is there?"

Her mum's expression didn't change. Her gaze dropped back to her tea. "I just worry about you, Essie."

Essie smiled. She reached over the table and patted her mum's forearm. "Well, you're my mum. That's your job, isn't it?"

"The only one I ever wanted," she replied, and she managed to smile back. A little.

18

ANGE

Ange sat on the couch flicking through Instagram and Facebook, getting irritated with people's posts. *Don't write open letters to your children/husband/parents about how much you love them,* she wanted to cry. *It's vomit inducing! Don't post about how many kilometers you've run today, it's boring, not to mention braggy. Don't rant about the traffic conditions on the way home—people don't give two hoots about your commute!*

She tossed her phone. It was getting dark outside and Ange was tired. Why did no one get it? As far as she was concerned, social media was a place for witty, satirical comments; stylistic food pics; photos of beautiful homes and children; and birth announcements. (Who didn't love a good birth announcement?) It was a place to scroll through to get an idea of where you fared in the world, and figure out whether you were winning or losing at life. Sometimes it felt like she was the only one who understood this.

With a huge sigh, she sank back against the cushions. Lucas was pottering around somewhere and the boys were asleep—she'd checked on them half an hour ago and been treated to her all-time favorite sound: their snores. Thank goodness. Ollie had been complaining about a sore stomach all day, which had Ange worried. Ollie was a champion vomiter (the kid could actually vomit on demand—no finger down the throat, nothing) and she'd pictured herself spending the long night ahead washing sheets and rubbing his tummy. Instead she found herself at an unexpected loose end. Normally she loved nothing more than an evening on the couch with her phone, but tonight she just felt agitated.

"It's the heat," Lucas had said to her earlier this evening.

The heat was the catchall excuse for everything at the moment. Mothers at the school were using it to explain their children's brattiness, Ange's employees blamed it for their not sleeping well, Ange *herself* had blamed the heat for the fact she couldn't do a thing with her hair. She almost felt sorry for the poor old heat, taking the blame for everything. Especially since it was in no way to blame for her agitation.

It was Erin.

Ange couldn't stop thinking about her. It was irritating. All day she'd been popping into her mind, out of the blue. And the image was always of Erin standing next to Lucas at the hospital, her little girl, Charlie, clasped to her hip.

Ange would have loved a little girl. When she was younger,

she'd always imagined she'd have two daughters with blond curls and old-fashioned names like Goldie and Ivy. Ange was going to dress them in navy-blue pinafores with red stockings, black Mary Janes, and red bows at their temples. Goldie and Ivy would have had fairy parties and dollhouses and tutus.

Instead Ange had Minecraft parties and football and farts.

When she had Will, she hadn't been devastated. A daughter will come next, she told herself. Maybe, when they were older, her daughter would date Will's friends and he'd keep an eye on things. A protective older brother. Yes, that would be perfect, she'd told herself. Except the younger sister hadn't come. Instead, Ollie had arrived, far too happy with himself, thankfully, to consider that he was ever anything less than coveted. Ange loved him for that confidence. It had given her the space she needed to grieve.

She knew she wasn't supposed to think these things. But then again, what were thoughts *for* if not to process the awful things you couldn't say out loud? It wasn't as if she didn't love her sons. Will was handsome and gentle and sweet, and Ollie—well, it was impossible not to adore Ollie. Today, for instance, after driving him across town to a friend's place, he'd announced: "You are the best, Mum. When you're old, I'm going to buy you a walking stick. Diamond encrusted!"

Random, she'd thought. But also lovely.

"Thank you, Ollie," she'd said. "I'll be the envy of everyone in my nursing home."

Ollie was funny and stubborn and downright charming. He could make you want to throttle him one moment and kiss him the next. Ollie understood the fragilities of relationships in a way most adults never would. He'd never get her a walking stick, but he knew what she needed to hear in that moment. He knew that lies were necessary sometimes. He got that from her.

After all, the way he'd come into their lives hadn't exactly been honest.

Ange stood up. She'd been sitting too long, she realized. Sitting lent itself to obsessing about things best left in the past. There was a message on her phone, and she turned her attention to it. It was Julia, from the office. Perfect.

"Hey, Ange, sorry to bother you. I finally got hold of Isabelle Heatherington's workplace to check her employment status . . ."

Ange groaned. The landlord had been in a hurry to rent the place as the fire had left him without rent for months, so when Isabelle applied they moved her in quickly, thinking she could check the paperwork later. Of course the first time she did this, they'd run into trouble.

". . . Isabelle listed her place of work as the Abigail Ferris Foundation, but the number she provided didn't work so I called the head office. The person I spoke to said they didn't have any record of her working for them."

Ange ran her finger along a high shelf of the built-in cabinet, bringing away a trail of dust. She wasn't worried about Isabelle. Employers had become increasingly reluctant to give out information about their employees and it was not uncommon for employers to refuse to even admit they'd *heard* of the person in question. She'd just speak to Isabelle tomorrow about getting someone to release the information.

"Anyway, let me know what you want me to do," pre-recorded Julia continued. "She's paid her first and second months' rent and her bond. Byeeeee."

Ange ended the call on the way to the laundry. Her house needed a good cleaning, she decided. She found the feather duster and returned to the front room and started dusting. When was the last time she'd dusted? Usually the cleaners did it—but clearly they weren't doing a great job of it. Dust was flying all over the place. Next, she'd have to vacuum.

"Muuuum?" Ollie called from his room.

"I'll go," Lucas called to her.

Ange kept dusting. There was something vaguely calming about it. Maybe Ange would start dusting for relaxation. It would be like yoga or meditation or adult coloring. What did they call it these days? Mindfulness, that was it. She would dust mindfully.

Once she'd had such plans for her life. She'd been *passionate* about everything. Refugees. Women's rights. Religious freedoms! She marched in marches and signed petitions. On the weekends she took a canvas outside and painted, just for fun. Now, she made lunch boxes and signed permission slips and was passionate about breaches in her social media etiquette. She made a point of not getting too up in arms about anything and whenever anyone got too passionate, she felt her eyes start to glaze over.

What had become of her?

Maybe she needed to get passionate about things again. Start volunteering for some committees, raising money for a good cause. She could start a foundation, or at least offer her time to an established foundation. Maybe she'd pick up a paintbrush again. Her children weren't babies anymore, maybe she could get some of her life back? Maybe she could get some of her *self* back. Then she'd stop obsessing about Erin and her daughter. After all, she had secrets too.

Her duster hit something and a second later a hard object fell and skittered across the floor. She had to duck to avoid it. She put down her duster and picked it up.

A brand-new iPhone.

"Ange?" Lucas called from upstairs.

"Yes?"

"Ollie just threw up."

Ange glanced in the mirror above the fireplace. She'd worked up quite a sweat. Clumps of dust sat on her head and shoulders like dandruff and her face was quite red. "I'll be right there," she said.

But instead of heading to the stairs, she sat in the armchair. She powered on the phone and waited as it sprang to life.

19

FRAN

Fran lay on her back, breathing heavily. Beside her, Nigel let out a soft groan. They'd just had sex. Not boring, married sex. New couple sex. *Interesting* sex.

"That was . . ." Nigel started.

"I know," she agreed.

She rolled onto her side and laid her head on his chest. The room glowed with peach light as the sun made its descent into the bay. If the girls hadn't been in bed, she might have suggested they run down to the beach and watch the sunset while bobbing in the ocean. She felt drunken, euphoric. Perhaps it was the fact that it had been a while? Perhaps it was because they were on the living room rug? Or maybe it was the fact that they were going to be all right. She and Nigel were moving on. Moving forward.

"Water?" Nigel asked.

"Please."

He got up and Fran slid off his chest, watching his naked bottom as he walked into the kitchen. She sighed contentedly. It was the first day of the rest of her life. She'd always loathed that saying, but today, it was perfect. She was putting the past behind her. She was going to have sex, and lots of it. She was going to be a devoted wife and mother. She would make up for her indiscretions. If it got hard, she would *work harder.*

Today had been a good start. She and Nigel had taken Rosie and Ava out for breakfast, then to the adjacent park to play. It had been one of those blue-skied mornings where it felt good to be outside and alive. By midmorning it was too hot to be outside so they all came home, piled onto the couch to watch *Frozen*, and then everyone had a lunchtime nap. It had been bliss. Perfect family bliss.

"I might make a toasted cheese sandwich," Nigel called from the kitchen. "You want some?"

"No, thanks," Fran said sleepily. "I'll just share yours."

She could feel his grin, even from the next room.

Nigel was happier too, she realized. He had been worried about her. They'd been through a rough patch, that was all. He'd made mistakes, she'd made mistakes. Keeping the secret would, in a way, be her penance. She wasn't returning to her job after maternity leave, she didn't want to risk running into Mark. She'd told Nigel that now that she had two children, she wanted to stay home with the girls for a while, and he hadn't questioned it. Probably because it was exactly what she *should* be doing. Focusing on the family.

From the kitchen, Fran heard the sizzle of bread in the pan, and Nigel started humming "Quando Quando Quando." He'd sung it that first trivia night—word for word—to get them a bonus point (after already naming Engelbert Humperdinck as the original singer), and since then, it had been "their song." Nigel didn't have a bad voice, and he only sang it when he was happy. So far, it seemed, she was doing a good job.

She pulled a cushion from the couch and rested it under her head. They'd both put the girls to bed tonight. The four of them had sat on the floor in Rosie's room while Nigel had read a story. Rosie had actually sat in Fran's lap, which was a first, while Ava lay on a cushion next to Nigel and blinked up at them all in contented puzzlement. Fran had tucked Rosie in afterward and by the time she'd gotten to Ava's room, Nigel had been sitting with her in the armchair. ("There's nothing nicer, is there," he'd said, "than a baby on your chest?")

She was so lucky, Fran realized. Those girls were even luckier.

Nigel was singing loudly enough now that Fran worried he'd wake up the girls. Rosie adored it when he sang. When she was older, she'd probably roll her eyes. *You're so tragic, Dad,* she'd say, and he'd probably pull her in and make her start dancing with him, the way he did to Fran sometimes. But then, dads were meant to be tragic. To embarrass their kids. It was part of the gig.

Would he embarrass Ava that way? Fran wondered suddenly. Yes, he loved her now, but what about later, when she started to show her personality? He'd always had such a connection with Rosie, but then Rosie was so much like him. Ava may not be. What if, as she got older, it became apparent that she was *nothing* like him? What if her eyelashes were short and pale? What if she was short and burly and full of confidence—like Mark? Would he keep her at a distance? Would he feel as though something just wasn't right?

Fran had a sudden picture of Ava on a psychologist's couch lamenting the fact that she'd never felt her dad's approval and didn't understand why. ("He's so close to my sister," she'd say. "But he doesn't *get* me. He doesn't even seem to *want* to get me.") Adolescent girls were attuned to these kinds of things. It could ruin her for life. What if Ava spent the rest of her days searching for approval in unhealthy, even abusive relationships? Was that what Fran was doing to Ava by hiding the truth?

Cupboard doors clanged as Nigel searched for plates. Clang, crash, bang. *Quando, quando, quando.*

Fran sat up. She desperately wanted it to be simple. She wanted to be able to let this go, but these kinds of things kept tripping her up. Yesterday she'd found herself staring at Ava while waiting at the supermarket checkout—analyzing her every feature. Did she have Nigel's nose? Lips? Eyes? Her eye shape did look like Nigel's but the color was such a deep blue that it often garnered comments. "Are those baby blues from her father?" people asked, after checking out Fran's own browny-green eyes. Fran always nodded, even though Nigel's eyes were pale blue. Mark's, as she recalled, were more vivid.

She had to tell Nigel, she realized. She *had* to. And she needed to know for sure who Ava's father was. If she found out she was Nigel's, then they could *really* put this behind them—providing Nigel wanted to. And if Ava wasn't Nigel's, she supposed she'd live with that too. She'd have to.

Fran heard the clank of the pan into the sink and then Nigel appeared in the sitting room with a plate and a glass of cold water, which he handed to Fran. Nigel preferred room temperature—it was better for digestion, he said—but day after day he filled the water jug and put it in the fridge so Fran could have her water chilled. He put the plate down between them and handed half the sandwich to Fran. The bigger half. It moved something in her. Fran knew that a lot of women seemed to wake up in their thirties or forties and find themselves shocked by the man they married. (*What was I thinking?* she'd heard a recently divorced woman from her work say once. *I mean . . . he wasn't even my type!*) Fran had never felt like that. She'd always felt a secret thrill to be married to Nigel, as if she'd discovered a treasure that somehow everyone else had missed. Even while he was depressed, she'd always loved him. But now, she'd ruined it.

"We should do this more often," Nigel said. "Get the kids into bed early and spend time together. Did you say the new neighbor babysits?"

He took a big bite of his sandwich, holding a hand out below to catch the crumbs. His glasses had become steamed up during cooking so he looked at her over the tops of them. Both the crumb-catching and the steamed-up glasses were so achingly familiar, she could've cried. There was no way out, she realized. She wanted to be able to leave the past in the past. Failing that, she wanted to have the courage to tell her husband what she'd done and to live with the consequences, whatever they were. The problem was, neither option seemed possible for her. Which left her trapped in a world of neither here nor there.

"Yes," Fran said. "Apparently, she does."

20

ESSIE

Polly wailed in Essie's ear as she hung up the phone and Essie jiggled her uselessly. Polly had been fussy all afternoon so she had resorted to carrying her around in the Babybjörn, which hadn't helped any. Essie laid a hand on Polly's forehead, which was warm but not hot. The child was clearly just in a bad mood. Essie understood the feeling.

"Who was on the phone?" her mum asked from the couch. She'd arrived a few hours earlier and since then she had ironed a basket of shirts, unpacked the dishwasher, sewed a new button on Mia's pinafore, and vacuumed the living area. Now she was folding laundry on the couch while Mia knelt beside her at the coffee table, coloring. Sometimes, Essie's mum was the only thing that made sense in Essie's life.

"Ben. He won't be home until late."

Essie put the chops under the broiler. The weather had dropped a few degrees today but it was still warm, and in the kitchen with the baby strapped to her Essie felt hot and bothered. She opened the fridge. ("Alcohol," she remembered Ange telling her once. "It's the only way.") Alas, Essie and Ben weren't the type to keep it in the house so she plucked out a Lindt ball instead.

"Do you need to put on all those chops then?" her mum asked.

Essie popped the chocolate into her mouth. "What?" she mumbled.

"The chops. If Ben's not coming home . . ."

"Oh. Right." She chewed and swallowed, not tasting. "No, probably not."

Essie's brain wasn't working properly today. It was the crying. Crying had a way of boring its way into your skull until there was no room for anything else, particularly patience, logic, or reason. She opened the broiler and removed two chops just as there was a knock at the door.

"Go away," Essie murmured. "Whoever you are just go away."

"Give her to me," Barbara said, appearing behind her. "You get the door."

Essie unstrapped Polly from the carrier and handed her over. She felt lighter immediately, free of her ball and chain. She took a minute to roll her shoulders and stretch out her neck.

"Essie, the door!"

"Oh. Right."

It was Isabelle. She carried a bottle of white wine and wore a preemptive smile that faded quickly. "Uh-oh. I've just done that thing childless people do when they call in during kids' dinner, bath, and bedtime, haven't I?"

Essie wasn't sure if it was Isabelle or the wine, but she felt an instant lift in her mood. "Technically you *have* done that thing. But you've brought wine. So let's call it even. Come on in."

Isabelle walked inside.

"Oh," her mum said, as they rounded the corner. It may have come out wrong, but it didn't seem like a friendly "oh."

"Hello, Barbara," Isabelle said, equally curtly. She turned to Essie. "I saw the light on and I thought maybe you could use a drink. Don't they call this time of day the witching hour?"

"They do," Essie said. "But if I had a broomstick, I have to say, I'd have been out of here long ago."

She filled two glasses, nice and full. She'd just turned to put the bottle in the fridge when she noticed smoke drifting out of the broiler.

"Shit!" she cried, wrenching out the tray. Immediately she dropped it. The burning-hot tray clanged to the floor. "Oh . . . holy . . . *owww.*"

Essie looked at her right hand, which was already pink and throbbing.

"Are you all right?" Isabelle asked.

"I'm fine."

"Are you sure?"

But Essie wasn't sure. She looked down at the tray on the floor—and then at her hand. It was already showing signs of blistering. For a long second she didn't know what to do. Apologize for her silliness? Sweep up the charred chops? Call for pizza? She'd been feeling like this a lot lately. It was as though processing a series of thoughts or reacting to a basic situation was beyond her.

Isabelle appeared beside her. She guided her over to the sink.

She turned on the cold tap and held Essie's hand underneath, letting cold water stream over the burn.

"Better?" she asked after a moment or two.

"Yes. Thank you. Sorry, I . . . don't know where my head is at today."

"Neither do I," Essie's mum said, bustling up behind them. She'd put Polly in her swing and Mia was in front of the television. "In any case, why don't you two sit down and let me clear this up?"

"No, Mum, really I—"

"I insist. We don't need any more accidents." Barbara stuffed her hands into oven mitts before Essie could protest any further. Essie felt a little like a teenager getting into trouble. She wondered what was up with her mum.

"You know what I think?" Isabelle said. "I think you need a break. Why don't you take the night off, Essie? Go and see a movie with Ben? I can babysit."

Essie felt herself sway with desire. A *movie*. For mothers of young children, going to the movies was the ultimate indulgence. The comfortable chair, the quiet, the escapism. The sugar, if she treated herself to a candy bar. The fact that no one was touching you, or talking to you. There had been nothing—including sex— that had transported her more completely since becoming a mother than seeing a movie. "Unfortunately," Essie said, "Ben has to work late. But maybe . . . you and I could see a movie? You could babysit couldn't you, Mum?"

Barbara looked up from the tray she was scrubbing: a deer in the headlights. "But what about Polly? I thought you were worried she was coming down with something?"

Essie looked over at her, gurgling happily on her mat. "She seems all right now, don't you think?"

Barbara put the tray on the draining board, her brow furrowed. Her hair, which she usually dyed herself with a box of Clairol ash brown, was threaded with gray at the temples. "I guess it's all right," she said finally, sounding like she meant the opposite.

"Thank you," Essie said, rushing to the bedroom to swipe on some lipstick and grab her bag. When she returned to the lounge room Isabelle was on her knees, talking to Mia and Polly in a funny, playful voice. They both smiled back at her, delighted at the attention.

"We'd better go," Essie said, and Mia made a pouty face. Polly started to cry again. Everyone seemed sad to see Isabelle leave.

Everyone except Essie's mum.

Essie and Isabelle had just ordered a second bottle of wine. They weren't going to make it to the movies. Essie didn't care. Dinners out with friends should be mandatory for mothers of small children, she decided. They should be *the law*.

Essie didn't usually do things like this. She and Fran and Ange met for tea and cakes, and for drinks at Christmas, but they rarely went out, and they rarely laughed. It felt sophisticated and fun, even if they were just at The Pantry in Brighton, the next suburb along.

"What looks good, ladies?" the waiter had asked when he came to take their order.

"The prospect of not cooking," Essie had said, and Isabelle had laughed.

It may have been the alcohol, but they'd spent a good portion of the evening laughing—at the waiter's desperate attempt to get Essie's name right (she'd called up and made a booking from the car) and their subsequent agreement to make the booking under the name "Jane"; at the men at the next table who kept ogling them, one of whom uncannily resembled Essie's high school P.E. teacher; at Isabelle's excellent impersonation of Jerry Seinfeld. It made Essie acutely aware that she hadn't laughed much recently.

They sat opposite each other at a small table with a single white flower and a drinks menu between them. Essie had already wolfed down her chili prawn pizza in a matter of minutes and now was watching Isabelle eat her linguini *aglio e olio* with similar gusto. Essie was relieved to find Isabelle wasn't a salad kind of girl (not that it would have been an unforgivable offense, but it would have been a shame).

"So," Essie said. "I feel like you know everything about me and you haven't told me anything about yourself."

Isabelle speared a mussel with her fork. "Sure I have."

"You haven't. Just that you're here from Sydney, looking for a missing child."

Isabelle chewed and swallowed, covering her mouth. She seemed to take longer than necessary before speaking again. "Well, that's about all there is to me. I'm not married. No kids."

Essie cocked her head. "Which is interesting since it's pretty clear you love kids. Have you ever thought about having any?'

Isabelle paused for a long second. "Of course I have," she said finally.

Essie wasn't sure why this surprised her. After all, just because she was gay didn't mean she didn't want children. Lots of gay people had children.

"Let's just say it hasn't worked out for me so far."

Isabelle lifted a napkin to her lips and wiped them. She was probably the kind of girl Essie would have gone for if she were gay, she decided. She was so sensual. The way she walked, the way she dressed, even the way she wiped oil from her lips was appealing. Essie had kissed a girl once, back in her university days. She'd been on the dance floor at a nightclub when a girl had grabbed her face and pressed it to her own. Essie had gone along with it, mostly because there were guys watching and she thought it would impress them. And the kiss hadn't been bad, exactly. The girl's skin had been soft and she'd tasted like rum and Coke. But nothing had stirred inside Essie. If she'd been experimenting, the results were clear. She wasn't gay. And yet when she looked at Isabelle, she felt . . . something. She wondered, had it been Isabelle on that dance floor instead, would the results of the experiment have been as clear?

"But I'm not one to give up easily, so . . ." Isabelle was saying.

Essie tried to regain her train of thought, but she'd drunk too much wine. "Sorry?"

"Kids. I was saying that I *am* going to have them. Sooner rather than later."

"Wonderful," Essie said. "Let's drink to that,"

Isabelle picked up her glass. "Yes," she said. "Let's drink to that."

When they arrived back in Pleasant Court, the street was almost in darkness. But Essie didn't feel tired at all. To the contrary, she felt exhilarated.

"Do you want to come in for another drink?" Essie said, once they were out of the taxi.

Isabelle paused. "What about the kids? We wouldn't want to wake them up."

Essie giggled. For a moment she'd forgotten she *had* kids. "Oh wow. I'm drunker than I thought."

Isabelle laughed. "How about I take a rain check?"

"Sure." Essie concentrated on not slurring her words. "Good idea."

Isabelle gave her an unexpectedly tender smile. She reached out and touched Essie's upper arm gently. "This was nice," she said. "I really enjoyed it."

"I did too," Essie said shyly.

They smiled at each other. Isabelle's lips parted and Essie's breath stilled. She wasn't sure if she was horrified or exhilarated. They remained like that for a heartbeat, then Isabelle's hand slipped back to her side.

"Well, good night," Isabelle said.

Essie watched Isabelle walk up her driveway, her chest alive with butterflies. Finally, once Isabelle's door had closed, she headed into her own house. Essie's mum was on the couch, her stockinged feet up on the ottoman, a novel splayed on her chest.

"Mum? Where's Ben?"

"Ben will be home any minute," she said, rubbing her eyes. Clearly she'd been dozing. As she sat up, the book slid off her chest onto her lap. "There was a problem with his app. It crashed or something. He's been talking to his technical people."

"Oh, dear," Essie said, though she wasn't really concerned. She was more concerned that she was quite drunk, and even at the age of thirty-two, she felt weird being drunk in front of her mother.

"How were the girls?" she asked.

"Precious. Perfect." Her mum located her purse on the floor by the couch and stuffed her novel inside. "How was *your* evening?"

Something was funny about the way she said it.

"It was great," Essie said. "Really, really fun." She hiccuped.

"Are you drunk?" her mum asked.

"A little."

Barbara watched her steadily. Essie got the feeling she was being scrutinized.

"*What?*" she said. It was rare that Essie had more than one drink. But just because her husband didn't drink much didn't mean that she couldn't.

"I just wonder if you should check in with your psychologist," Barbara said finally. "Just for a chat. You seem . . . a little off."

"Because I went out for a few drinks?"

"No," she said. "Because—"

Keys jangled in the door and a split-second later, Ben was inside. He flung down his sports bag. "Babs! I am so in your debt I can't even . . . Oh look! Two beautiful women. It's my lucky day!"

"What happened to your app?" Essie asked dutifully.

"Nothing you need to worry about. I got it all sorted out." He looked at Barbara. "I owe you some flowers."

"Not necessary."

Ben frowned. He looked from Essie to Barbara and back again. "Everything okay here, ladies?"

"Fine," Mum said, standing. "But at my age you turn into a pumpkin at midnight . . ."

"At my age too," Ben agreed, yawning.

Essie was glad they were doing all the talking. She felt both self-conscious about being drunk and irritated with her mother for being so judgmental. On top of all those feelings, she couldn't possibly also process *words*.

"I'll see you tomorrow," Barbara said, letting herself out. Ben followed her, standing on the porch and watching until she got into her own house.

When he returned to the house, Essie vaguely noticed Ben watching her with that soft, familiar expression. He leaned in to kiss her, but Essie was miles away. She was still thinking about that strange moment she'd shared with Isabelle.

"Shall we go to bed?" His eyebrows wiggled suggestively.

"I thought you were tired."

"Do I look tired?" Ben swaggered toward her and Essie couldn't help but laugh. The confidence. Had this man considered for even a second that he wasn't irresistible? "Just give me five minutes to convince you," he said, as his lips hit hers. She didn't protest, which Ben, of course, took as a green light. And it was a green light, at least in body. In mind, she was thinking about Isabelle arriving on her doorstep. Isabelle sipping wine over dinner. Laughing with Isabelle. And a few minutes later, as Ben led her into the bedroom, Essie found she wasn't thinking of Ben at all.

21

ANGE

Pleasant Court was starting to look quite different. A sign had been erected at the mouth of the street, warning people they were entering a NEIGHBORHOOD WATCH ZONE. Wireless cameras had been installed in front of every home (except the Larritts', who'd insisted it was overkill and they'd never had such a thing in "their day"). Whenever the camera detected movement they started recording and then emailed the footage to the person monitoring the camera. So far Ange had received an email of the Larritts' cat trying to get into their garbage, Fran speeding past on a late-night run, and Ollie standing out in front of the house jumping up and down trying to trigger it.

As she chopped the salad vegetables, Ange was wondering if she could put the cameras to better use. Particularly as it related to Erin. She'd been thinking about Erin for the best part of three days. She'd be blow-drying her hair and she'd think of Erin. She'd drop Ollie at school. Erin. She'd close a deal at work. Erin. Nail salon. Erin.

It was driving her crazy. Ange's life was usually so blissfully compartmentalized. She'd be at work and she'd get a message from one of the boys about sports practice/money/something they'd left at home, and she'd think: *That's home stuff. I'd deal with that later.* On the weekend while she was with the family, an email would come in about work and she'd ignore it. It was family time. But Erin appeared in home thoughts. She appeared in work thoughts. She appeared fucking everywhere.

"Erin!" she shouted.

Ollie and Will looked over their shoulders in perfect unison. They were watching a documentary about Africa on the TV, the only thing they could agree to watch. They both adored animals (a trait they got from her, thank you very much; Lucas was allergic to virtually every kind of animal and was the reason they had goldfish as pets).

"What did you say, Mum?" Will said. Ollie had already turned back to the television.

"Lemons," she said. "For the fish. I forgot to get them."

"There's a lemon in your hand," he said, pointing to it.

"Ah," she said. "So there is."

Will gave her a look that said "my mum is nuts" and turned back to the television. Fair enough, really.

Ange watched the screen for a moment. The lioness was bounding toward a zebra in long, lithe strokes. She was surprisingly beautiful—and apparently soundless, though perhaps that was just the editing. The poor zebra hadn't even noticed her coming.

Ange suddenly felt bad for the zebra. *You could at least give him a fighting chance, lioness. Come on zebra,* she thought. *Run, you daft thing!*

She chopped the lemon in half. The silly thing was, she didn't know for certain that Erin was *anyone*. When she'd turned on the mystery phone a few days ago, she'd found the contacts section blank. Not a single name was stored. She'd checked thoroughly, going through every section. Finally, as they were headed to bed, she'd asked Lucas about it.

"What's this?" she'd asked, holding up the phone.

Lucas looked at it and Ange watched his face closely.

"It's my new phone," he said.

"It was on a high shelf in the front room. A *very* high shelf."

"It's a brand-new phone. I wanted a few weeks with it before Ollie started filling it with games and apps. That kid can *smell* a phone or iPad from fifty feet."

He wasn't wrong. Ollie had filled every other bloody phone and tablet in the house with his ridiculous games. She had to scroll to the fourth screen on her phone now to get to Instagram. Little bugger.

And yet Ange couldn't quite accept Lucas's explanation.

The next day at work Ange went through his dialed numbers. He'd called one number—a number she didn't recognise—four times in the previous seven days. She decided it wouldn't hurt to give the number a try.

"Hello?" the voice said.

"Oh, yes, I had a missed call from this number," Ange had said jovially. "Can I ask who this is, please?"

"May *I* ask who is calling me?" she countered. Ange listened keenly to the voice. It was high-pitched and feminine, and didn't sound *un*like Erin.

"It's uh . . . Dianne. Dianne Taylor."

"I'm sorry, I think you've got the wrong number. I haven't called any Dianne Taylor."

"Are you sure? Maybe if you told me your name?"

"I'm sorry," she said. And she hung up.

So there was no evidence to say it was Erin. It may have been someone else entirely and Lucas's phone may have been hidden for the exact reasons he gave. But Ange had a feeling that wasn't the case. And Ange had a sixth sense for these things, ever since Josie.

Josie. Ange felt a knot form in her throat. It was such a nice, normal name. It was a veterinarian's name. A kindergarten teacher's name. Then again, why wouldn't she have a nice name? It wasn't as if Josie's mother would've looked down at her newborn daughter and thought *she looks like she'll become a home-wrecking harlot.*

Will had been a toddler. Ange had been a stay-at-home mum for over a year and still, she hadn't gotten used to it. Every day she got dressed, blow-dried her hair, put on lipstick. But the day offered so little. A visit to the park. Playgroup. Finger painting. It wasn't that she didn't love Will. It was just that she didn't love motherhood.

Lucas had been in his studio constantly. His business was booming, in large part because of Ange. Every banal playgroup she attended she brought along a bunch of his flyers. His photos, admittedly, were sensational. He had a gift for capturing the moments. The toddler pulling her mother's necklace and pearls spilling all over the floor. The child throwing a tantrum while the rest of the family laughed. Falling in puddles and squinting into sunshine. Somehow he made the disasters into art.

One morning, Ange was dressed, blow-dried, and lip-glossed with nowhere to go, when she had a brilliant idea. *We'll get a family photo of our family!* she decided. It seemed ridiculous, now that she thought of it, that they didn't have one already. The cobbler's child always had the worst shoes. And, aside from being something to fill the next few hours, it was the perfect advertising for Lucas. They could use it on flyers, and she could display it proudly when she hosted mothers' group at her house.

She loaded Will into his stroller and they wandered down to Lucas's studio. It was located in the center of a park—an ideal location for outdoor shoots when the weather was good. If Lucas was with a client, Ange decided, she'd let Will have a play in the playground while they waited.

The door was locked when she arrived, which meant Lucas was in the darkroom. *Good news*, she thought, *he's not with a client*. The weather was perfect for an outdoor shoot, she realized. Perhaps Lucas would be able to set a self-timer and get in the shot himself?

She knocked loudly. "Lucas!"

She wasn't concerned when it took a while—the darkroom involved lots of chemicals. It could take a few minutes before he could step away. Ange just waited. After a minute or so, she knocked again.

And waited.

It was possible he'd gone to get a sandwich, but then again Ange had made him a chicken, avocado, and mayo this morning (making a lunch that did not consist of tiny pieces of cucumber and cheese gave a tiny sense of purpose to her day). And his car was in the parking lot; she could see it from where she stood.

Finally the door swung open.

"Ange."

There was no blissful moment of confusion, no split-second of nothingness while the pieces whirled into place. She just *knew*. And that was even before she saw the woman standing behind him. There was no newborn with her. No toddler. No fiancé or husband. The overplayed looks of innocence on their faces were as good as confirmation.

"This is Josie," he said.

Josie was a brunette. Not pretty exactly, but slim and large breasted with striking Egyptian-looking eyes. She had the audacity to hold out her hand. Ange remembered staring at it. Was she meant to shake it? Slap it? In the end, she'd just looked back at Lucas, and Josie eventually let her hand drop back to her side.

That night, after Will was in bed, Ange sat cross-legged on the floor while Lucas paced the floor.

"I'll get an apartment," he said. "Not far away. I can still see Will every day."

The shock of that had been worse than discovering Josie in the darkroom. For some reason it hadn't occurred to her that he wanted to leave her. She'd been waiting for Lucas to beg for forgiveness, to swear he was going to change his ways. For a while, they'd tiptoe around each other, timid and uncomfortable, until finally they'd realize, "Wow, we got through it." *All marriages have hard times*, they'd tell Will on the eve on his wedding day. *But when you make a commitment, you work through those hard times and wind up stronger for them.* But that wasn't what was happening. Instead, Lucas was leaving her for Josie.

"No," Ange said firmly. "Stay. We'll work this out."

Lucas sighed. "I'm sorry, Ange. But I want a . . ."

Don't say it, she thought, bracing. *Don't say it.*

Ange's parents had divorced when she was eleven. Ange's father had remarried within the year and had two more children—he was still married to Deidre and they were excitedly expecting their first grandchild. Her mum, on the other hand, had spent the decade after the divorce watching *Oprah* and telling Ange she should never settle for a man who didn't appreciate her. Her mother had died of a heart attack in front of the television. Ange always hoped it happened during *Oprah*. Then, at least, she wouldn't have been completely alone.

Suddenly, Ange began to see a world without Lucas. A world of *Oprah*, and inevitable death on the couch.

"I'm pregnant," she'd blurted.

The lioness was eating the zebra now, each mouthful a great bloody massacre. Will cringed away from it, burying his face in his forearm the way he did when he found something shocking. (Lucas had the exact same tic.) Ollie, on the other hand, was enthralled. His elbows were on his knees and his chin in his hands. *Poor zebra,* Ange thought. It was so conspicuous there on the plains with its great black-and-white stripes. What hope did it have?

The front door opened and shut and a set of keys clattered into the little bowl on the hall table. The boys looked up, grunted, and looked back at the TV.

"Nice to see you too, boys," Lucas said, winking at Ange. Usually she loved that wink, but today, it bothered her. Why no kiss?

Did he smell of perfume? Had he gotten enough kisses today from Erin or someone else? She had so many questions, not least of which was: *If you're the one fooling around, why am I the one going crazy?*

"Do I have time for a shower before dinner?" he asked.

"Of course."

She looked down at the chopping board where the fish fillets lay bare. She seasoned them with a little salt and pepper and positioned a wedge of lemon to the side. Then she took a photo, which she posted it on Instagram. *Nothing better than a healthy delicious dinner with my men,* she captioned it. #fish #family #yum

It was showtime. The pillows were propped behind me, my legs were in the stirrups. The baby's head was out and I was in a bizarre reprieve from pain, waiting for the next contraction. The drugs I'd been given were spectacular. (I'd said yes to everything they'd offered me. What fool wouldn't?) They didn't take the pain away entirely, but they made it so I was flying too high to care.

"Patient's name?" the doctor muttered, after glancing at my paperwork and finding it blank. It had all happened too quickly for paperwork.

The nurse shrugged.

"Is the baby's father coming?"

They both looked at me. I dropped my gaze.

When I began to moan again, the nurse nodded. "Big push, whenever you're ready. I want you to give it all you've got."

I screwed my eyes shut, and pushed. A moment later, it was over.

They didn't hand you to me right away. They had to check you over, I guess. I didn't mind, to be honest. Birth had left me depleted and a little sick. Did I tell the doctor that? Did he prescribe something? Because I have a vague recollection of a needle in my arm and then going into a lovely, deep sleep.

When I awoke, it was with an odd, ominous feeling. I remember pushing my buzzer for the nurse.

"Can I see my baby now?" I asked when she came in.

"I don't think that's a good idea."

"Why not?" I said. "Is it a boy or a girl?"

I don't know why, but I always had a feeling you would be a girl. I'd been craving pink for nine months. Strawberries and watermelon and raspberry jam.

"A boy or girl?" I asked again.

Silence.

"For heaven's sake," I cried. "Is my baby a boy or a girl?"

"I need to speak to the doctor," the nurse said, and she shuffled off again.

A sickening feeling overcame me. Was something wrong with you? I hadn't laid eyes on you—had you been born with a defect? What if . . . you hadn't survived? I imagined going home without a baby in my arms. No. That couldn't happen.

It wouldn't happen.

The doctor came into the room. Though I was frustrated that he didn't bring you with him, I also felt relieved. Finally I'd get some answers.

"Can I see my baby?"

He pulled up a chair beside the bed and his eyes fell to the floor. "I'm very sorry to tell you this," he started.

22

FRAN

Fran had considered skipping her six-week follow-up altogether, but she forced herself to go. After Rosie was born, she'd diligently attended all these appointments so she reasoned she should do the same for Ava, even if there wasn't much to say. There was never much to say about her pregnancies, they were both more or less normal. Some morning sickness, a little heartburn. She'd never had any of those frightening periods when she couldn't feel the baby move, or any panic attacks about eating potentially harmful food. Everything had been remarkably, blessedly normal. Except, perhaps, her mental state.

Three other women sat in the waiting room, all of them big-bellied. Two of them made googly eyes at Ava, while the other one (clearly already a mother) focused on her magazine. (Fran didn't take any offense to this. When you had children at home, you didn't waste your alone-time looking at other people's babies.)

"Fran," Dr. Price said, appearing in the doorway to his office. "Come on in."

Fran gathered up her purse and the baby seat, and shuffled into the room.

"Hello," he said, sitting behind his desk. "It's good to see you."

"It's good to see you too," Fran told him.

It was the truth. There was something comforting about Dr. Price that always put her at ease. And she wanted to feel at ease, even for a few minutes. Despite her decision to leave the past in the past and move forward with Nigel, she felt like no matter what she decided, her mistakes were destined to haunt her.

Dr. Price had white hair, spectacles that perched on the end of his nose, and a fondness for short-sleeved checked shirts and chinos. In her appointments with him while pregnant with Rosie, they'd spent much of the time talking about all matters other than the pregnancy. The parking fine his nineteen-year-old daughter had been contesting, Fran's recent holiday to Bali, the outrageousness of paying five dollars for a cup of coffee ("daylight robbery," Dr. Price said). But while pregnant with Ava, Dr. Price had become more doctorly, somehow. He'd started inquiring after her health, asking if she was taking it easy, looking after herself. It was nice and at the same time, uncomfortable. As if he was seeing things she didn't want him to see.

Today, as he sat in front of her, Fran found that she was unable to meet his eye.

"So," he said. "How have the first few weeks been?"

"Fine," she said.

"Getting much sleep?"

"Does anyone ever say yes to that question?"

"Only the dads." He grinned. "How's the bleeding?"

"It's stopped."

"Good. And any issues . . . with anything?"

Yes, she thought. *My child might not belong to my husband.*

"No."

He was silent a moment. "Fran?"

"Mmm?"

"You're not looking at me."

He was right. She'd been focusing on a spot of wall to the right of his head. She forced herself to look at him now. She noticed his eyes were a striking blue.

"Has your mood been low—in general?"

"Yes," she said.

"Unexplained bouts of crying?"

"Not unexplained exactly."

"Any trouble sleeping?"

"Yes. My newborn sees to that."

"Have you got anyone supporting you? Family?"

Fran shrugged. Her mother, father, and brother were all in Sydney living their own lives, being overachievers. Her brother and his wife were both investment bankers and had opted not to have children lest it interfere with their careers. Her parents, who described themselves as "busily retired," visited Melbourne once or twice a year, usually when it coincided with an event they wanted to go to, like an exhibition or musical. Fran *could* have called them if she was really struggling and she knew they would come. But they wouldn't have understood. Overachievers didn't struggle with new babies. They didn't have marriage troubles. They certainly didn't have extramarital affairs or illegitimate children.

"Okay, Fran, this is going to sound dramatic, but I want you to be honest. Have you considered, or made any plans to commit suicide? Or had any thoughts of harming Ava?"

The question baffled her. Who had *time* to make plans to commit suicide when they had a newborn? Certainly not her. And she'd never, not for a fraction of a single second, thought about harming her child.

"No," she said. She *wished* she had postnatal depression. Then he could give her a pill and a referral to a psychologist who would make everything go away. She soared on that thought for a moment. The lovely, quiet sessions, in a clean office with a therapist, talking about her feelings. Ange would probably organize a food-roster, and the neighbors would drop around a meal every night. Essie or Barbara or Mrs. Larritt would come by sporadically and pop in a load of laundry while Fran napped. But she didn't have postnatal depression. She had a potentially illegitimate child. No one organized a food-roster for that.

"I did want to ask you something though," Fran said.

"Oh?" He removed his glasses. "What's that?"

"Is it possible to find out if your husband is the father of your baby," she said, "without him knowing about it?"

23

FRAN

Fran reached for one of Essie's banana muffins. She'd run for seven miles without stopping that morning, and she hadn't run that far since before she was pregnant with Ava. When she got home she'd breast-fed Ava and made scrambled eggs on toast for Nigel and Rosie. Somewhere in between all of that she'd forgotten to eat herself.

"I was thinking," Essie was saying, "if we are going to start catching up regularly like this, maybe we should invite Isabelle next time. After all, she does live on the street. What do you think?"

Regularly? Fran thought. When had they decided to catch up regularly?

Essie had been the one to instigate this catch-up and Fran's initial thought was to politely decline. With everything going on she couldn't feel less in the mental space to sit through coffee and pleasantry with the neighbors. But then she heard a funny note in Essie's voice. It was subtle, barely there at all. She might have decided that she'd imagined it if she hadn't noticed that Essie had seemed a little flustered lately. And, given last time, Fran decided she really should accept. She didn't know she was accepting a regular catch-up.

"Uh, sure," Fran said, dividing the muffin between Rosie and Mia, who played on the floor.

"Ange?" Essie said.

Ange blinked as if she'd just woken up. "What? Oh. Yes, fine."

Ange had been roped in to the catch-up too, and she seemed as enthusiastic as Fran had been. She picked up her own banana muffin and took a bite, which was unexpected. Ange rarely ate anything with refined sugar in it. Fran noticed that Ange's shirt was rumpled and untucked, which was also unlike her.

"Great!" Essie said, with odd enthusiasm. Essie didn't even seem bothered by the muffin crumbs that Mia and Rosie were mashing into her floor rug, and usually she was quite house-proud. But her good mood only lasted a few more seconds before Polly shrieked from the bedroom.

"Noooo!" She fell back against the cushions. "Surely not! I only put her down . . . twenty minutes ago!"

"Catnapping," Fran said sympathetically. "Ava is the same. The only place she wants to sleep is in my arms. Little devil."

Ava was sleeping in her arms as she spoke. Although Fran was exhausted from her three-hour routine, she had to admit, with everything else that was going on, Ava's basic needs were a relief. Essie, on the other hand, seemed almost *angry* that Polly had woken up. She stomped off to the bedroom to resettle her. Fran stared after her.

"Do you think Essie's all right?" Fran asked Ange.

Ange frowned in the direction Essie had just wandered, but it was clear her thoughts were elsewhere. Fran started to wonder if *Ange* was all right.

"I guess she does seem a little . . . scatty," Ange said vaguely. "But having a baby that doesn't sleep can make you a little crazy."

She was right about that. Fran hadn't slept properly herself in days. She'd been too busy thinking about what Dr. Price had told her. She *could* get a paternity test without Nigel's permission, if she used DNA from Rosie, but he neither recommended this nor would perform this service. He thought it would be a much better idea to tell Nigel the truth with support. She nearly laughed. Support? Where would she find that?

Besides, things had been great with Nigel lately. He'd been the perfect husband. A devoted father to Ava and Rosie. A loving husband. That was why her constant back-and-forth was so ridiculous. Why would she go and get a paternity test when things were so great between them?

She wouldn't, she decided. Of course she wouldn't.

Keys jangled in the door and then Essie's mum appeared in the front room. At the same time Essie came out of the bedroom, carrying Polly.

"Oh, thank God," Essie said, nearly collapsing with relief at the sight of her mother. "I'm going insane. Polly's barely had a wink of sleep all day. I'm losing my mind."

Essie thrust the baby at her mother. Fran ached with jealousy. Why didn't she have a mother like Barbara? Someone who would swoop in and take over when things got too tough. Her own mother wasn't the kind who helped out, and she was certainly not the type you confided in. She imagined her mother's response if she were to confess her infidelity.

"What a mess you've gotten yourself into," she would say in a hushed voice. "You need to forget this paternity business and just put this whole thing behind you." Then she'd probably add: "I don't think we should tell your father about this," and the matter would be laid to rest.

Her mum had other strengths, of course. Intelligence, a good moral compass, a passion for travel. But handling a situation like this was outside her many capabilities. Which meant Fran didn't have a person in the world to confide in.

Barbara put her purse down and adjusted Polly on her hip. "She looks exhausted. Did you try rubbing her back?"

There was a short silence while Essie, presumably, gave her mother the unhinged look of a woman whose baby hadn't slept.

"Why don't I try?" Barbara said quickly, and she disappeared from the room with Polly. She was the mother every woman with small children wanted.

The mother than Fran needed.

Essie fell into her armchair. "Ah. Silence. I have no idea how she does it. I swear to God, if that baby cries again I'm going to lose my . . . Fran, are you all right?"

"I'm fine," she said, realising in horror that she was crying. Ange and Essie sat forward in their chairs. This was new territory for them. Fran didn't know who was more uncomfortable.

"What's going on?" Essie asked.

"I don't even know where to start."

"The beginning is always a good place," Ange suggested gently. She edged her chair a little closer to Fran's and laid a hand on her arm and that was all the encouragement Fran needed.

"I had an affair," she blurted out. The relief of confessing was instantaneous. "I mean, it wasn't really an affair. More of a friendship and a handful of one-night stands. It was a year ago, a guy from work."

Ange withdrew her hand, and rose to her feet.

"Ange? What is it?" Essie blinked wildly, trying to get a handle on what was going on.

Ange glared at Fran. "What is it? I'm shocked and upset, that's what it is. Infidelity is a lot more damaging than 'a handful of one-night stands.' It can break up families, destroy lives! Anyway, I think I should leave before I say something I regret." She snatched up her purse. Her face was contorted as though she was fighting back tears. Her hands, Fran noticed, were shaking.

Fran felt a little shaky herself.

Ange wrenched open the door.

"Oh no no no!" Essie flew to her feet. "Ange, please don't slam the . . ."

She closed her eyes at the same time as, in the next room, Polly began to wail.

24

ANGE

Ange gave Essie's door a terrific slam on her way out. It felt surprisingly good to be angry. So much of her life was spent controlling anger—when speaking to clients who had messed up, with her children whose life's purpose seemed to be testing her limits, and even with her parents. At some point, clearly, she had internalized the belief that anger was meant to be tempered. What a ridiculous idea. Feeling it, as it turned out, was pretty fantastic.

She charged her way down Essie's path, but annoyingly she had nowhere to go. It was Sunday afternoon. Lucas had gone to the supermarket, and then was headed to the gym—and the boys were with friends. Ange wondered if she should go kick-boxing or running—something to get all this adrenaline out of her.

She noticed Isabelle coming out of her house.

"Isabelle," she called.

"Hi, Ange."

"I've been meaning to catch up with you." Ange said, heading up her path. Annoyingly, she already felt herself reining in her anger, her polite voice going on. The euphoria of her rage faded as though it had never existed.

"I had a call from my assistant about your employment checks. She has been in touch with your nominated workplace and they haven't been able to confirm your employment."

"Oh." Isabelle seemed to flush. "Yes, well, they wouldn't. Actually I don't work there anymore. That was my job in Sydney, but now I'm here I'm looking for something else."

Ange blinked. "You're . . . not employed?"

"Not currently. But I have enough money to cover the rent, don't worry."

Isabelle smiled. Ange felt a flicker of uncertainty. Hadn't she said she was moving to Melbourne for work? Ange was *sure* she had.

"We really require our tenants to be employed when they rent a house. If I'd have known—"

"Is that Lucas?" Isabelle said, pointing over Ange's shoulder.

Ange turned. Lucas's car was turning out of the cul-de-sac. "Yes, I think so." He'd probably dropped off the groceries and now was headed for the gym. But as she watched him turn out of the street, a funny feeling came over her.

She turned back to Isabelle. It took her a moment to recall what they were talking about. "So . . . er, you'll give me the details of your new employer once you find a job?"

Isabelle smiled again. Her smile, Ange noticed, wasn't entirely warm. "Of course. You'll be the first to know."

"Well . . . good. Thanks."

Ange turned and scurried down the path. When she reached the bottom she pulled up short, realizing what had caused her funny feeling.

Lucas had turned right. The gym was left.

25

BARBARA

"Barbie?"

Barbara suppressed the urge to snap at Ben for calling her that since he had, after all, answered the phone. She knew a lot of sons-in-law who would have let it go to voice mail, and she knew she should consider herself lucky.

"Yes, it's me," she said. "I need to talk to you."

"All right," he said, but he sounded distracted. She could hear someone talking to him in the background whispering something about a Zumba class.

"Ben," Barbara said, "I really need you to listen."

There was a bit more whispering and then Ben said, "All right, Barbie. You have my full attention."

"Thank you. Look, I was just over at your place and Polly hadn't slept."

Ben was quiet a moment. "Okay?"

"She doesn't seem herself, Ben. I'm worried about her."

"Polly?"

Barbara dug her nails into her palm. She wondered if Ben was intentionally trying to infuriate her. She wouldn't have put it past him. "*Essie*."

"Essie doesn't seem herself?" Now she had his full attention. "In what way?"

"She's exhausted. She's irritated with Mia and she's struggling with Polly. And I wonder if she's become a little too consumed with Isabelle?"

"Isabelle?" From Ben's tone, he clearly didn't share her concern. "What has *she* got to do with this?"

Barbara tried to figure out how to explain it in a way that Ben would understand. The fact was that ever since Essie was a little girl, she had gotten into these intense friendships. She'd become friendly with a girl from school that Barbara had never heard of, and all of a sudden, the girl would be coming for sleepovers every weekend. Essie would be constantly on the phone with the girl and mentioning her name in every other sentence. Often she'd even start *dressing* like the other girl. And she'd lose all sense of who she was. It made her a good target for people who needed something. All they had to do was offer their friendship and Essie would offer everything she had in exchange.

"I just think she should be focusing on her family right now," Barbara said. "After last time, I don't think she can afford to be investing all this time in a new friend."

"I don't know, Barb. She seems to like Isabelle a lot. She's been happier since they became friends. And it's nice for her to have someone around . . . other than you and me, I mean. For company."

Barbara pursed her lips. Like Essie, Barbara had been an only child so she knew about loneliness. But there were upsides to having your parents as your closest confidants. As a child, Barbara had never been relegated to the kids' table or sent off to play in the garden—she'd always had her parents' undivided attention. From an early age she'd gone to galleries and bookstores and plays with them. Every evening she'd regaled her parents with tales about her day, which they either found enthralling or at least did an excellent job of pretending they did. She never felt like the child, more like the three of them were part of a team. It made it all the more shocking when, just shy of twenty, Barbara lost them both in quick succession, to cancer, then a heart attack. So yes, she understood what it was like to want a friend. She also understood that the wrong company was worse than being alone.

"Look, you were the one who said you were worried about her the other day and I said I'd keep an eye on her. Now that I'm telling you that something doesn't seem right, don't you think you should do me the courtesy of listening?"

Ben was quiet for several seconds. "You're right. All right. I'll talk to Essie."

"Thank you," she said.

"Hey," Ben said, in a softer voice. "It's okay. We'll take care of her. You and me. Essie will be fine, Barb."

Barbara wasn't so sure. But he didn't call her Barbie, at least, and that was something.

26

ANGE

Could you stalk your own husband? Ange wondered, as she sat in her car in the parking lot near Lucas's studio. She'd been sitting there for nearly half an hour. In the first ten minutes Ange had just about convinced herself she was being ridiculous. After all, Lucas going to the studio on a weekend wasn't proof of anything, was it? Maybe he had some pictures to develop, or some maintenance to do? And it *would* be just like him to get it done over the weekend. But then Ange had seen her.

Erin.

She'd pulled into the parking lot, and parked a few spaces down from Lucas's car. Then she walked directly to his studio, clutching the hand of her little girl. That was how she knew for sure it was Erin—the child. Charlie's face was burned into Ange's mind.

Well, so what? Ange thought. It didn't necessarily mean any-thing. Perhaps when Erin had seen Lucas at the hospital it had reminded her to call up and book another photo shoot and Lucas had opened up a weekend appointment to squeeze her in. The last photo was probably when Charlie was born, and now she must be—how old?—two or three maybe? Time for an up-date. That was what Ange herself would say when she ran into one of Lucas's clients. She'd eyeball the children and say, "Time for an update."

So that was all it was. An update.

Ange was losing it, obviously.

She thought of her behavior earlier at Essie's. Storming out of there and slamming the door. Why had she done that? She'd call over later with flowers, she decided. There was no excuse for be-ing so rude. There was no excuse for what Fran had done either, but that wasn't for her to judge.

She didn't have enough to do, clearly. Ange thought of her clients who fussed over every little detail of the properties she showed them. ("I couldn't possibly keep these bathroom cabinet handles," they'd say. "They are a different silver from the ones in the kitchen!") They didn't have enough to do, those people.

Tomorrow she'd spend the day cold-calling for new listings. She'd run herself ragged. A busy brain was a happy brain. Who had said that? Someone. Perhaps she'd call another neighbor-hood watch meeting too? Essie and her mum hadn't attended the first one, and it would be good to see how the surveillance cameras were working out.

She pulled her diary out of her purse—*her trusty old-fashioned paper diary that she wouldn't replace even if Apple came up with a version that floated in front of your eyes and made entries using data directly from your brain*—and scribbled on today's date. *Set up neighborhood watch meeting.* There. She snapped it shut again, feeling better already. On the cover of her diary was a picture of Will and Ollie aged three and four months, respectively. Will was kneeling on a blanket holding Ollie around his belly—Will beaming, Ollie screaming. Ange couldn't help but smile. Ollie had spent the best part of the first six months of his life screaming, something Ange blamed on the fact that he was always hungry. It was because he was born so small, Lucas was fond of saying. He had to catch up to his brother's birth weight. But the truth was, he wasn't that small. Not if you took into account that he was born three weeks early.

Ange thought about that night that she'd told Lucas she was pregnant. He'd been about to tell her he wanted a divorce, she knew it.

"I'm pregnant, Lucas," she said, before he could say it.

"What?" he'd exclaimed.

"You heard me."

He blinked slowly, as if the idea of his wife being pregnant— his wife—was the absurd part of this conversation, instead of the fact he wanted a divorce. He rose to his feet and started to pace, trying to make sense of it all.

"But we haven't really . . . done it . . . much lately."

It was true. Clearly he'd been too busy being with Josie to have sex with his wife. "It only takes once," she said.

Lucas looked so miserable Ange almost felt sorry for him. But she knew he wouldn't leave his pregnant wife. He'd work through it, for her sake and for Will's, and for the sake of the unborn child. By the time the baby was born, Ange would have built up their marriage sufficiently that he'd never need to look elsewhere again. This would blow over, she told herself.

But life, of course, had laughed at her.

Lucas had done the right thing, as Ange knew he would. Josie had disappeared from their lives with an unlikely ease. Lucas had been surprised by Ange's libido during the month that followed. She remembered him saying as much, when she woke him early one morning, right on the heels of a late evening of lovemaking.

"Intimacy is important," she told him, "to get our relationship back on track."

Of course he didn't protest too much. But with a ticking clock at her heels, Ange couldn't afford to be blasé. She'd remembered hearing women saying things like "I ovulate early" or "I have a long cycle"—things that sounded important to know when you needed to get pregnant in a hurry. But Ange had no idea about her cycle. When she'd been trying to get pregnant the first time around, she'd simply gone off the pill and a couple of months later, *voilà!* But this time she needed to be smarter about it. She visited the pharmacy and picked up some of those ovulation predictor kits. Every morning she stared at the test window, waiting for an indication that today was a fertile day. On the day a smiley face appeared in the test window, she showed up at Lucas's studio to surprise him. She remembered trying not to think about the last woman he'd had in there.

It was that time that had done the trick.

After an emergency C-section with Will, her obstetrician recommended scheduling an early C-section anyway. And Lucas didn't pay attention to things like dates, especially the second time around. So, at thirty-seven weeks, when Ange sent Lucas off on a golf trip in Tasmania, he went along happily.

By the time he got back, they had another son.

Lucas was disappointed to have missed the birth, of course, but nothing made up for disappointment like a new baby boy.

Ange had thought everything would go back to normal after that. And admittedly, in the years that followed, there were long periods where she didn't think at all about what she'd done. But then she'd be sitting at her desk one day, or driving the boys to school, and she'd be hit by a pang of guilt so strong she'd double over. Karma, as it turned out, really was a bitch.

The studio door opened and Ange sat up on alert. The little girl appeared first running, with Erin running behind her. Lucas held the door, watching them. Ange scrutinized him. He appeared to be fully dressed and he wasn't showing any outward affection to Erin. Ange's gaze turned to little Charlie, who was lying on the grass now, her T-shirt riding up as Erin tickled her. Her legs kicked. *Get your camera, Lucas,* Ange thought. *This is the money shot.* But Lucas's camera was nowhere to be seen. He just watched them thoughtfully from the doorway. There was a softness to his expression that was a knife in Ange's stomach. She became aware of her heartbeat; a quiet, urgent hammering. This wasn't nothing, she realized. This was definitely *something.*

Charlie stood now, weary from laughter, but Erin wasn't finished. She came at her again, fingers outstretched, tickling the air. Charlie shrunk away from her mother, back behind her forearm. There was something familiar about it, Ange realized. It reminded her . . . of Will.

Of *Lucas.*

Ange's gaze snapped back to Lucas. His expression was unmistakable now. Soft and fond and bursting with pride. It was the way he looked at Will and Ollie. Ange had always thought it was a look reserved for his . . .

She slapped a hand over her mouth.

No. Vomit rose in her throat, but she forced herself to keep looking, to scour the scene for any evidence that she was right. Because if she *was*, things weren't going to blow over this time.

Things were going to blow *up*.

27

FRAN

Fran was sprinting so fast she couldn't hear her thoughts. It was bliss; it was agony. Her throat tasted of something—blood? bile? guilt?—but her legs just kept on pumping. The park was deserted but for a few dog walkers. It was midday and most kids were at home having lunch or taking their afternoon nap, she supposed. Rosie was at home with Nigel and Ava was asleep in her jogger pram, flying up and over the hills. It should have been creepy, being alone with her baby in a deserted park, but Fran found herself wanting to stay here. It was less confusing than being at home.

She came to a stop at the bottom of a hill and drained the last of her water from the bottle. She had a great affection for this park with its wide expanse of lawn, its huge wooden play-fort for the kids, and its wildly expensive pony rides on Sundays. Most weekends, children's birthday parties were held by the barbecues.

It was the park Rosie referred to as the "wood park" and the one she requested to go to most often. It was also the park where Lucas's studio was located, and where, three years ago, he'd taken that fabulous photograph of them.

Three years ago. When things had been good.

How had she let this happen to them? Nigel had made mistakes too, but his mistakes were out on the table. It was *her* that was hiding things. The irony was that if she had less of a conscience, everything would have been fine. She would have put it in the past and moved on. Instead, it ate away at her.

She wandered over to the water fountain to fill her bottle. There was the undeniable fact to consider, of course—they had at least one child together. And Rosie was happy. Fran tried to imagine telling Rosie that Mummy and Daddy weren't going to be married anymore. Rosie would want to live with Nigel. As the mother, Fran might still get primary physical custody of her, but at what cost? She'd be breaking up Rosie's life, and her own, to clear her guilty conscience. What kind of mother would that make her?

But what about in fifteen or twenty years, when Ava found out that the only father she'd ever known wasn't her father? When she found out her mother had kept the secret all this time?

What kind of mother would *that* make her?

Fran grabbed her stroller and was heading out of the park when the door to Lucas's studio burst open and a sweet little girl came out, running. Her mother ran after her and tickled the girl until she squealed. Lucas watched them from the doorway smiling—he must have just done a shoot with them. Fran continued walking but pulled up short when she noticed Ange's car just a few meters away. Ange, it seemed, was also watching the little girl and her mother. There was something about the way she was staring at them that made Fran pause. Her eyes didn't look right.

Fran looked back at the woman and the child. At Lucas, smiling over at them. And suddenly, she understood Ange's outburst earlier.

Suddenly, she understood it all.

"Is it a boy or a girl?" I asked.

The doctor and nurse exchanged a glance.

"Your baby was a girl," the doctor said finally.

I smiled. A girl. I knew it.

The doctor cleared his throat. "But, as I said, I'm afraid your baby didn't survive. It was stillborn."

Stillborn. I turned the word over in my head. Still. Born.

I pictured her little face. She'd be wrapped up in a blanket now, probably wearing a little knitted hat. What did she look like? They said all babies' eyes were blue at first. But would they eventually be brown like mine?

"Can I see her?" I asked.

Silence. Then the doctor looked at the nurse. "Have you managed to contact her husband?"

The nurse shook her head.

I felt like I might explode. Under my hospital gown, my breasts were tingling. I'd already waited this long. Why were they making me wait longer? "I want to feed her as soon as possible. That's good for the baby, right?"

The doctor's expression baffled me. Did most mothers not want to see their babies? Perhaps they were too exhausted. I found that reassuring. I was a special kind of mother. I wanted my baby more. I loved her more.

He stood. *That's right,* I told him silently. *Go get my baby. Finally!*

He walked to the door. The admission paperwork was still on the bedside table, untouched. I couldn't have cared less about paperwork—I wanted my baby. The anticipation was unbearable. From my bed I could see the doctor in the corridor, talking to the nurse. Another person in a white coat had joined them. I felt like I was in a dream. It must be the drugs. Oh well. If they weren't going to get my baby, I would.

I lowered myself gingerly off the bed. I felt the coldness of the floor under my feet, which meant I had some feeling back in my legs. Good. Clutching the metal railing on the side of the bed I hauled myself to standing. There was a hospital-issue robe on a hook on the back of the door. I took a step toward it but all at once the floor came up to greet me, hitting me with a smack. Suddenly the little crowd that had gathered outside my door rushed into the room. I started to shake.

"Bring me my baby!" I began to scream. "BRING ME MY BABY!"

I continued shaking and screaming until a needle went into my arm and everything went black.

28

ESSIE

"Mum, it's me again. Can you call when you have a chance? Thanks so much."

Essie hung up. Polly, bleary-eyed, let out a sob of exhaustion.

"Go to sleep if you're so tired," Essie begged.

She might have been imagining it, but it looked like Polly was steeling her jaw, saying, *Oh yeah, try me.*

Essie's baby book said Polly should have been having three naps per day, each an hour to two hours long. *Two hours!* It was like the book was just trying to taunt new mothers, make them suffer. For the last week, Polly hadn't slept more than twenty minutes at a time during the day, and today, she hadn't slept a wink. To add insult to injury, Mia had decided to decline her afternoon nap as well and had just had a huge meltdown because Essie had given her pasta for lunch and she "hated pasta." (She did not hate pasta. Two days ago she'd declared that she wanted spaghetti for breakfast because it was just *sooooo* good.) Now Mia was watching cartoons and Polly was attached to her hip, a pathetic, sobbing mess. Meanwhile, all Essie wanted was to eat a bowl of pasta and go to sleep.

Essie walked to the front window and looked out. Her mum's car wasn't in her driveway. Where on earth *was* she? For the past week, she had been around constantly, staying all day and only leaving when Ben arrived home at night. But today, she was nowhere to be found. Rationally, Essie knew it wasn't reasonable to expect her mum to be available every time she needed her, but Essie wasn't feeling logical right now. All Essie wanted was for her mum to arrive on her doorstep and put both girls (and Essie) to bed. Then, in an hour or two, she wanted to wake up to find the laundry done and dinner on the stove.

Was that so much to ask?

It was just that her mum was such a natural mother and grandmother. Once upon a time, Essie had thought *she* would be a natural mother. The first time had clearly been a disaster, but this time, she'd had higher hopes for herself.

So much for that.

Essie had already left a couple of messages for Ben, even though she knew he had a busy day at work today. She was looking for a sympathetic ear, but all she got was his answering machine. She sat on the couch and tried to breast-feed Polly to sleep (again). Through the window she could see her mum's driveway, so she'd know the moment her mum got home.

"Mummy!" Mia whined, pointing to the TV. "It's finished."

"Something else will come on in a minute," Essie said tiredly.

"What will come on?"

Essie tried to remember what day it was. On Monday and Tuesdays *Peppa Pig* was up next, on Wednesday, Thursday, and Friday it was *Sesame Street*. Essie was shamefully aware of which kid shows were on which day, just not so great at remembering what day it actually was. She thought hard.

It was . . . Thursday.

Shit. Her mum went to the movies with Lois on Thursdays. So *that's* where she was. Essie felt a shameful wave of jealousy. Sometimes, when she had a moment to herself, Essie would fantasize about being retired. The endless, empty calendar filled with whatever she wanted. Sleep, evenings out, movies. She could take up a hobby, go on vacation somewhere that wasn't kid-friendly. Go to the theater. Stay up all night reading, and then sleep it off the next day. Her mum was constantly doing that. She'd come over to Essie's midmorning and hand her a thick novel that she'd stayed up all night to finish. "You must read it," she'd exclaim. Essie would stare at it as if it was a foreign body. *Read?* An actual book (and not about parenting)? When was she supposed to do that?

"*Sesame Street* is on," Essie told Mia, and she promptly started to wail again. Essie felt like wailing herself.

There was a knock at the door.

Essie shimmied from her chair, with Polly still attached to her breast (but utterly and irretrievably awake). As she wandered over to the door, Essie wondered if giving her a shot of whisky, like they did in the old days, really was such a bad idea.

"Hi," Isabelle said, when Essie threw open the door. Then her face fell. "Are you all right?"

"I'm . . . yes, well, I'm . . . it's just that . . ."

Essie found herself unable to finish the sentence. The words she needed had momentarily (or perhaps permanently) left her, and all the alternative words seemed to be mushed and jumbled and running together. In the meantime, Polly had unlatched and was smiling gummily at Isabelle while milk leaked through Essie's shirt. Mia was throwing a fit to the *Sesame Street* theme song.

"Give her to me," Isabelle said, taking Polly and shutting the door behind her. Mia, seeing they had company, quieted down and stared at Isabelle.

"Don't like *Sesame Street*?" Isabelle asked Mia.

"The bird," Mia said. "He's too big."

"Big Bird?" Isabelle said. "I know what you mean. No bird is that big in real life. Quite frankly, it's ridiculous."

Mia nodded seriously.

'Tell you what, why don't we put a movie on instead?'

Essie went and changed her shirt. By the time she got back Isabelle and Mia were on the floor and Mia was telling her that Big Bird was even taller than her daddy who was really tall and wasn't that silly? Also yellow wasn't her favorite color, it was her *third* favorite after pink and purple and sometimes green. Amazingly, Isabelle managed to follow the conversation as well as provide meaningful commentary, put on the movie (*The Little Mermaid*) and stop the meltdown all while holding Polly in her lap. Polly, newly animated by the surprise guest, had lost any trace of drowsiness brought on by the breast-feeding, but watching them, Essie found it hard to be upset.

"Shouldn't you be at work?" Essie asked.

Isabelle was dressed in skinny black jeans and a racer-back white tank that didn't look very workish. Her bra was black, and a single lacy strap crept up her spine and split into two at her nape.

"I took the day off," Isabelle told her. "And lucky I did. You look like you could use some help."

Essie fell onto the couch. "I do. Not that you can tell now. Clearly you have a gift with my children." She gestured to Mia who sat so close to Isabelle she was practically on her lap.

Isabelle smiled. "Your mum isn't around today?"

"She's at the movies! Can you *believe her*?"

"The gall!"

"I know, right?"

Essie giggled, then sighed. "The wheels have just fallen off today. It's Polly, mostly. She used to be my dream baby and now . . . well, she's decided to develop a backbone like her sister. I don't know where they get it from. Neither Ben nor I have backbones." She giggled again. She was delirious, clearly.

"So Mia wasn't a dream baby?"

Essie shrugged. "It was me, really. The fact is, Mia could have been the most wonderful baby in the world and I wouldn't have appreciated it."

Isabelle laid a hand over Essie's, giving it a short squeeze. Essie felt an unexpected, deep sense of peace.

"How are you coping this time?" Isabelle asked.

"Okay, I guess. I mean, when I look at the girls I feel love. Mostly love. Love, mixed with exhaustion and a little irritation."

"A little" may have been understating it. In fact, an hour ago, when Polly remained awake despite forty minutes of patting, Essie had just about cried. *Go to fucking sleep!* she'd shrieked in her mind. At the same time she'd had a lot of uncharitable thoughts about her mother. *Shut up about back patting. It doesn't work! Unless I missed the step when you slip her a mild sedative before patting.*

She must have left her mum a dozen voice messages today. She'd called Ben several times as well, demanding to know the exact time he would be home. When he'd made a joke about being thirty seconds late, she didn't laugh.

"It's hard work being a mum," Isabelle said. "Everyone struggles from time to time."

Essie yawned. "I guess so."

"Look, why don't you have a sleep? I'm happy to stay here with the girls. I don't have any plans this afternoon."

Essie reached out and grabbed both of Isabelle's hands. The idea of having a nap was impossibly appealing, but doing it while Isabelle remained in the house was, for some reason, nicer still.

"Don't say that if you don't mean it. It's very dangerous playing games with a desperate, overtired mother." Essie hoped she sounded funny and charming rather than psychotic.

Isabelle withdrew her hand and laid it over her heart. "I mean it. I'm happy to hang out here for a few hours. You look like you need the rest."

"This is the part when I'm supposed to refuse, right? Tell you I have everything under control and offer you a cup of tea? Well, I'm not going to. Do you understand that?"

"I do," Isabelle said solemnly. She looked like she was about to crack a smile but before she had the chance Essie lunged forward, gathering her into a hug. "I think I may actually love you," Essie said, then she raced off to her bedroom and slammed the door.

When Essie opened her eyes, Ben was leaning over her.

"Oh, hello," she said sleepily. She rubbed her eyes. Ben looked . . . strange. His mouth was pulled tight and his eyeballs were flying back and forth.

"Essie, where are the girls?" he demanded.

She blinked a couple of times, then sat up quickly. Where *were* the girls? She tried to think. Her brain wasn't awake yet.

"Oh," she said, remembering, "they're with Isabelle." She lay back against the pillows. "What are you doing home?"

"I got your messages about Polly not sleeping. I thought I'd duck home to see if I could settle her for you."

Essie smiled. "How sweet."

Ben didn't smile back. Lines bracketed his mouth and he kept rubbing his left temple and wincing as though it was causing him pain. *That* was why he looked strange, she realized. He was worried. Ben was never worried.

"Why are the girls at Isabelle's?" he asked.

"They're not. Isabelle is watching them for me *here*."

"There's no one here, Essie."

She faltered for a second. "Are you sure?"

"I checked every room. I didn't think you were here either, until I came in here."

"Well . . ." Essie's brain was still fudgy from her sleep. "Maybe

Isabelle *did* take them to her house? Maybe they were being noisy and she didn't want them to wake me?"

In three huge paces Ben was gone, presumably to check Isabelle's place. Essie decided to double-check the house. Ben wasn't the most observant person in the world—it was entirely possible that they were playing hide-and-seek in the lounge and he hadn't noticed. Still, it was hard not to absorb some of his panic.

Walking from room to room, Essie listened and looked, on alert for a giggle or a whisper, or a little foot poking out from behind a curtain. But after doing a quick lap of the house, she found that the house was indeed empty. She had to admit, it was odd.

The door crashed open and Essie looked at Ben's giant form in the doorway.

"There's no one at Isabelle's." Ben's jaw was tight.

Essie shoved her panic aside in an attempt to think logically. This wasn't a worrying situation, she reminded herself. She hadn't *misplaced* the children, she'd left them with a perfectly capable adult. "There'll be a good explanation, Ben. Maybe they've gone to the park? Was there a note anywhere?"

"Not on the kitchen counter. Not on the hall table. And the pram is still on the porch."

"Well, I'm . . . sure they'll turn up."

"Jesus, Essie! What were you thinking, leaving them with a stranger? If you weren't coping, you tell me. Or Barb."

"I tried to get in touch with both of you but you weren't available. Besides, Isabelle isn't a stranger. She's a neighbor and friend. And it's not like I had a heap of other people offering to help me. You weren't answering your phone, and Mum was at the *movies*!"

But Essie could see Ben wasn't listening to her. "I'm calling the police," he said.

"The police? For goodness' sake!"

"Essie," he said slowly and carefully: a teacher to a child who just wasn't getting it, "our children are missing and so is the person who is supposed to be taking care of them. We don't know anything about her and we have no idea how long they've been gone."

Essie felt the first quiver of uneasiness. "Is Isabelle's car in the driveway?"

"I'll check."

Ben headed for the front door, but before he got there, the back door flew open. Mia bounced inside first, followed by Isabelle who was holding Polly. Both girls had pink, flushed faces.

"Daddy!" Mia ran headlong into Ben's legs. He fell to his knees, taking her little face in his hands.

"Oh . . . Oh, wow. There you are."

"Is everything all right?" Isabelle frowned, casting her gaze from Essie to Ben and back again.

"No, everything is not all right." Ben sat back on his haunches. "We were about to call the cops!"

"Why were you about to call the cops?" Isabelle asked, perplexed.

"Because I got home to find Essie asleep and the girls missing!"

"We were playing outside," Isabelle said. "Mia needed to run around and I thought the fresh air might help Polly sleep."

Right on cue, Polly let out a giant yawn and then rested her head on Isabelle's shoulder. Ben stood and snatched Polly from her. His eyes closed as she snuggled into him. Essie wasn't sure she'd ever seen Ben so rattled. "I thought they'd been . . ."

Isabelle's face paled. "Kidnapped? Oh God, no . . . I'm *so* sorry."

"*Don't* apologize," Essie said quickly. "It's our fault. We should have checked outside." Essie shot an irritated look at Ben. "Isabelle was helping me out because I was exhausted and needed a break. She was a lifesaver."

"Well, Ben's home now, so I'll leave you guys to it. I'll talk to you soon, Essie. And again . . . sorry."

Stay, Essie thought, as Isabelle gathered up her bag. *Stay!*

It was a strange thought, given what had just happened. She should have wanted alone time with her husband so they could talk through what had happened. She should have wanted to hold her children close and thank the gods that they were, in fact, safe. There were a million things she should have wanted to do.

But all Essie wanted was Isabelle.

"What's going on?" Ben asked Essie that night after the girls were in bed. Essie had just poured herself a glass of white wine and had put her feet up on the coffee table.

"What do you mean?"

"I mean . . . talk to me. You promised you'd tell me if you ever felt yourself getting out of your depth again."

"I'm *not* feeling out of my depth. I had a bad day and a friend helped me out. Why are you making such a big deal of this?"

Ben sat beside her. "It's not just me. Your mum is worried too. She rang me at work the other day."

Essie felt a shot of betrayal. "Well . . . Mum worries."

"Yes, and I'm starting to think she has reason to. She said you're giving Polly to her at every possible opportunity. And there were four hysterical messages on my machine today when I returned from my meeting."

"They weren't hyst—"

"And this new friendship with Isabelle! You've never even left them with a babysitter besides your mother, and now you let Isabelle watch them straight off, before you even know her properly. Why?"

"I may not have known Isabelle for long but I feel like I've known her forever." Essie knew she sounded a little petulant, but she couldn't help it. "Anyway, why are you so upset about it? She didn't kidnap our children, in case you hadn't noticed. Or are you still worried she might?"

"Why not? You hear about it all the time. Single women approaching forty who take a shine to a neighbor's children and suddenly they disappear."

Essie rolled her eyes and took a sip of her wine.

"That's another thing—you've been drinking a lot lately," Ben said.

"Just because *you* don't drink doesn't mean no one else can."

"Essie, how can I trust you with the girls if—"

"How can you trust the girls *with me*?"

Ben's cheeks flushed red. "Listen, I'm sorry to bring this up, but you did, in fact, desert one of our children in a park once. How can I be sure that you won't do something like that again? Or something worse?"

They stared at each other for several beats. Then Ben sighed, and the tension went out of him like the air from a balloon. "Listen I'm sorry, I shouldn't have said that. It's just . . ."

Essie's phone buzzed on the table beside her and she glanced at the screen. Ben paused, perhaps waiting for her to silence it.

Essie picked it up.

"You're not going to answer it?" Ben looked at her incredulously. "Essie, we need to talk."

She accepted the call. "Hi, Isabelle."

"Sorry, is this a bad time to talk?" she said.

Ben stood before her, so shocked and dismayed. So worried.

"Not a bad time at all," Essie said, curling up. "What's up?"

29

ISABELLE

"Melbourne's great," Isabelle said into the phone.

Jules clicked his tongue. She could sense his skepticism, even over the phone.

"Really," she insisted. "You should come down here sometime."

She pictured him, stretched out in the window seat of his Sydney apartment, staring out over the waves. One of the few things his 1960s brown brick building had going for it was its killer view of Bondi Beach. It had always struck her as ironic, as he must have been the only guy in Bondi who didn't surf, preferring leather over wet suits and motorbikes over surfboards. Isabelle was the same, really—she loved the gorgeous Sydney beaches, but she wasn't one to lie around on the beach, sunbathing or swimming. In fact, it was fair to say that Isabelle and Jules resembled Melbourne people rather than Sydney people, with their love for the music scene, art galleries, and coffee. (Melbourne took its coffee seriously. The other day, Isabelle had noticed a "deconstructed coffee" on the menu at a local café, and deduced that it was a coffee served on a paddle in three separate cups—one with espresso, one with milk, and one with water. It was, perhaps, a little ridiculous, but she suspected Jules might actually like it.) She opened her mouth again, to try and convince him of this, but he got in first.

"I could come on the motorbike," he said.

Isabelle smiled. "That would be nice."

"So are you causing quite a stir down there in Melbourne?"

"Of course not," she said, though Isabelle suspected that was exactly what she was doing. Her being there was obviously causing trouble between Ben and Essie, and Ange had discovered she wasn't working for the Abigail Ferris Foundation. The truth was she'd *never* worked for the Abigail Ferris Foundation even though she'd had a lot to do with it. After Sophie was taken, they'd provided her with support as well as a few leads that didn't pan out—the most interesting one about a young woman who had given birth to a stillborn the day Sophie was taken, but who had never filled out any paperwork as labor had come on too fast. Then, she'd disappeared from the hospital again and no one had any record of her. Isabelle had searched far and wide. She'd scrolled through birth announcements and tried to find the details of people in the area who'd had baby girls around that time. All roads had lead to nowhere. Until now.

"Listen, babe, I have to go, I'm actually in the middle of something. Can we talk more later?"

She hung up the phone and looked at the table in front of her, cautioning herself against excitement. She'd gotten to this point before, after all, only for it all to turn out to be a false alarm. That had been crueler, in a way, than losing Sophie in the first place. But this time would be different, she knew it. This time, instead of going in half-cocked, she was going to be thorough.

She took a deep breath. *Go on*, she told herself. *Get on with it.*

Her hands shook as she reached for a piece of white paper. She lay six or seven reddish-brown hairs across it. She'd managed to pluck them from Mia's hair elastic while playing in the garden today. Hair wasn't the most accurate DNA to test, but short of holding the child down and swabbing her cheek with a cotton tip, it was the best she could do. About four of the hairs contained the root, and Isabelle prayed it would be enough. In her drawer she had two envelopes, both of which had been provided by the DNA testing company. One should contain Mia's DNA and the other, hers. She got out the instructions for her cheek swab and began to read. She wouldn't make any mistakes. She couldn't.

Once she'd mailed off the test, it would take seven days to get results. Seven days was so fast. Seven days was a lifetime.

In seven days, Isabelle would have her answer.

In seven days, she'd be taking back what she'd lost.

30

ANGE

Ange was making dinner, like she always did. An hour ago Will and Ollie had gotten home from their friends' house and Ange relented when they begged for a milk shake, like she always did. Then she yelled at them for leaving their stuff all over the floor and told them she'd be telling their father when he got home. Like she always did. There had been no tears, or anger, or bargaining. She was doing everything as she always did, even though everything was different.

Lucas had another family.

The words had pinballed around in her head all afternoon, yet she still couldn't make sense of them. It was as though someone had told her she lived on Mars rather than Earth—it was curious, mind-blowing even, but the ramifications remained unclear.

For now, she was merely hunkering down, waiting for more information.

Lucas had another family.

Ange turned on the oven and caught at her reflection in the glass. Her mother's reflection stared back at her. Bitter, detached, and a little crazy. Ange had a sudden, sharp yearning for her. Her mother had been dead almost twenty years, and for the ten years before that she'd been virtually dead, just sitting on the couch watching *Oprah* and ranting at Ange that she must never let a man have control over her happiness. Now, she heard her mother's voice in her head: *They're all the same.* Ange longed to fall into the recliner beside her mother and say, "I should have listened to you, you bitter old goat. As it turns out, you were quite right."

Keys jangled in the door.

"Hey," Lucas called. He rounded the corner, winking at her. Winking had always been their thing. Over the years she'd never seen a greeting she liked as much. Some husbands planted a perfunctory kiss on their wife's cheek, others merely grunted as they walked in. But Lucas's wink always seemed so genuine, so full of affection. It was like a little secret they shared.

One of many secrets they shared.

"Something smells good," he said. "What's for dinner?"

It was such an ordinary question. It was absurd given the magnitude of their situation but also, surprisingly comforting. Ange glanced back at the kitchen, taking in the onion, ground beef, eggs, and bread crumbs that were out on the kitchen counter.

"Burgers?"

Lucas laughed. "Is that a question?"

It was. The truth was, Ange had no recollection of what she'd made, no idea at all beyond the ingredients she could see on the counter. Maybe she was in shock? The idea wasn't unappealing. If she were in shock, someone would wrap her in a warm blanket and give her some sweet tea, and watch over her until they were sure she was "out of the woods." She'd seen paramedics do that on TV, after people had been involved in car accidents and such. Surely there was a service like that for women who'd found out their husbands were philanderers. And if there was . . . where the HECK was her blanket and sweet tea?

"Ah, meatballs," Lucas said, peering into a pot on the stove.

"Yes," she said. "Meatballs."

Of course, she thought. *Meatballs*. Most women, Ange imagined, screamed and threw things when they found out their husbands had alternate families.

Ange made her husband's favorite dinner.

Lucas wandered over to the boys who were playing Xbox and, miraculously, they grunted a hello to their father.

They'd become a family, Ange realized. Her boys, Lucas, Erin, and their little half-sister, Charlie. One day, at their weddings, they'd thank "Dad and Erin for all they'd done over the years." Then they'd smile over at the table, where Ange was sitting, date-less, trying to look happy so she didn't ruin the special day.

Ange went to the fridge and got out a half-full bottle of wine and two glasses. She very nearly laughed. *Two* glasses! In ten years, when Lucas was married to Erin, would she still get out two glasses when she opened a bottle of wine? Would she still make minestrone without celery because Lucas hated celery? Would she still tell the boys to "just wait until their father got home"?

"I'm *starv*ing," Ollie called out dramatically.

Ange was about to tell him dinner would be ready soon, but Lucas intervened. "You're not starving. Children in Africa are starving. You're simply hungry."

Oh, fuck off, Ange thought.

Usually, when Lucas said something like that, Ange felt proud. What a good husband she had. What a lovely role model for her sons. Often she took it one step further, into self-flagellation. Why didn't *she* think to say something like that? Thank goodness they had Lucas, she'd think, to give them a moral compass.

Now it felt laughable. Lucas's moral compass!

Ange filled one glass and walked over to the lounge. Lucas was perched on one arm of Ollie's chair. Ange slid onto the other. He glanced at her wineglass, perhaps wondering why she hadn't offered him one, but not mentioning it. Guilt, maybe? *Well, I do have a girlfriend and an illegitimate child, so I'd better not give my wife a hard time about not offering me a glass of wine.*

Maybe he did have a moral compass after all?

"You're not in your gym clothes," Ange said casually.

He hesitated only for the slightest second. "No," he said. "I went into the studio for a few hours."

"On a Sunday?"

"Yeah," Lucas said. "It came up at the last minute."

"Oh yeah?" She took a large gulp of wine. "Who did you shoot?"

The thought had occurred to her that she had no proof of anything. Not a shred. She imagined standing up in front of a judge and saying: *Yeah, well, the little girl moved her arm in ex-*actly *the same way my older son does. Uh huh. And also, my intuition.*

A woman's intuition is never wrong. Sentence him to death, Judge! Or at least, some hard labor.

The judge would laugh in her face. Maybe that was why she was pushing him now. She wanted her theory disproven.

"Is there any more of that wine?" he said.

"In the kitchen," she told him, then she stood and followed him. "Who was the client?" she asked him again.

"A repeat client with her three-year-old," he said, filling his glass to the top.

Ange took another large swig of her drink. "A three-year-old," she said, after forcing herself to swallow. "That must have been fun."

"I'm *starving*!" Ollie cried again, from the other room.

"Tough," Ange yelled at the same time Lucas said: "You're *not* starving!"

Lucas looked at her. "Honey, you seem stressed. How about I run you a bath?"

"But dinner is—"

"I'll finish it. Go on. I'll bring you another glass of wine. And I'll keep a plate warm for you to eat when you get out."

She wanted to slap him around the head. She wanted to know how he could do this to her and, more important, how he could do it to their sons. She wanted to know how he could stand there and pretend to be the perfect husband after spending the afternoon with Erin and Charlie. She wanted to hear him tell her the truth. Instead, she heard herself say: "A bath would be lovely," and she headed out of the room.

31

FRAN

Fran had been for a blissfully intense run. She'd run so fast and for so long that she wasn't conscious of a single, solitary thought. People often said they went for a run to "clear their head," but those people wanted their thoughts to *become clearer*. Fran wanted the opposite. She wanted her head entirely empty, devoid of thoughts, and a run always did just that for her. Unfortunately, it didn't last. Which meant Fran was going to have to try something else. The truth.

She let herself inside. Nigel and Rosie sat at the dining room table, with LEGOs sprawled out in front of them. Fran felt a jolt of surprise at seeing Rosie. In the middle of her thoughts about life-changing confessions, she'd forgotten her children existed.

"Mummy!" Rosie said. "I've built you a house. You won't be

able to live in it, because it's tiny and it's pretend and it's made of LEGOs."

Fran felt touched. Rosie never made her anything. Everything was always for Nigel. She was also surprised to see them playing with LEGOs. It was rare to see Nigel engage in noneducational toys.

"It's great," Fran said, pulling up a seat next to Nigel. "I like red."

"There's also some green and a bit of yellow," Rosie added.

Indeed there was. Fran felt a wave of affection for Rosie's spectrum-like accuracy. She looked at Nigel. He'd sorted the entire box of LEGOs into colors, which he had divided into clear ziplock bags, with another bag for all the instructions. She should have known he'd have come up with a better use of his time than actually creating something.

A sudden, aching pang of love nearly knocked her over. *Why did I cheat on this man?* she thought. *Why couldn't I have supported him through the rough times like a good wife would have done?*

"I'll just go check on Ava," she said, starting to stand. She was halfway out of her seat when Nigel reached for her.

"Ava's fine," he said. "Just . . . sit for a little while. We want Mummy here with us, don't we, Rosie?"

Rosie nodded enthusiastically. "We love Mummy."

They beamed at her, identical smiles that very nearly made Fran feel happy. But it was too out of character. Nigel must have spoken to Rosie, said something like: *Mummy's not doing very well right now so we need to be nice to her.* They were both looking at her a little too often. Their eyes were a little too soft.

"I love you too—"

"I need a wee," Rosie said, jumping up. She scampered off. Fran felt relieved to have one less pair of eyes on her.

Nigel scooted his seat a little closer. "I feel like I've been neglecting you," he said. "And I'm sorry. Rosie and I have decided to make it up to you."

Stop, Fran thought. *Please stop.*

"I know you're struggling, and I'm going to step up. Maybe we should have a date night? I know you don't want to leave Ava, but we could ask Isabelle to babysit, or maybe Essie's mum. Barbara *loves* babies."

Fran picked up Rosie's pretend LEGO house. It had a tiny purple flower on one of the red bricks that Rosie had failed to mention when reciting its colors.

"Why don't I speak to Barbara and I'll book La Svolta for dinner," he said. "One night next week, maybe. We could—"

"I had an affair last year, Nigel. And Ava might not be yours."

Her voice was even and clear, soft and serious. There was no room for misunderstanding. She put down the LEGO house.

Rosie ran back into the room. "I want to make a car. But you won't be able to drive it because it's too small and it will be made of LEGOs."

Rosie clambered onto the chair opposite them and took the house that Fran had been holding. She reached for the blue LEGOs and began assembling her car while Nigel and Fran stared at each other over the top of her head.

32

ESSIE

"Are we just doing a trim today?"

Essie stared into the shockingly well-lit mirror in the front window of her hairdresser. She wore no makeup, of course, and she looked awful. *Old*. Her eyes were circled with purple and her skin had a faint sheen to it, like she was getting ill. And there was something else too. She looked thin. Almost . . . gaunt. When had she gotten thin?

The hairdresser—a new girl named Kym who was in her early twenties with ironic gray hair and huge pale blue eyes—clearly misinterpreted her lengthy pause.

"Or do we want a restyle?"

Kym was pulling and tousling Essie's hair and peering into it as if she was searching for treasure in amongst the strands. It looked like a reddish-brown sea of tangles, long and shapeless, hanging halfway down her back. No wonder Essie's mum had taken it upon herself to book her an appointment. "Uh . . . a restyle?"

Kym lit up. "Cut *and* color?"

"Well . . ." Essie had never colored her hair before, largely because she knew color took a long time. Upward of three hours. Who had time for that? But today the idea of three hours away from her children filled her with joy.

"Sure. Cut and color."

"Perfect," Kym said, and disappeared to get her "color board." She left Essie with an iPad to google styles she liked. While Kym was gone another girl came to ask if she'd like a tea or coffee. Essie ordered a peppermint tea, but the moment the girl disappeared to make it Essie thought: *Did I just order peppermint tea?*

Something isn't right with you, Essie.

And she wasn't the only one who thought so.

"Right," her mum had said when she arrived this morning. "I'm looking after the girls at my place today. I've made you a hair appointment first thing, and afterward you can go out for lunch, get your nails done, or just come home and sleep. Up to you."

Essie knew she should feel grateful, but she couldn't bring herself to feel anything at all. Ben had still been at home when her mum arrived, which meant they were clearly in cahoots.

Don't leave her alone with the children was the implication. *She can't be trusted.*

Maybe they were right. In the past few days she'd drifted past exhaustion into some sort of deadened state. Instead of constantly lusting after sleep, she'd accepted she would never sleep properly again. When Polly cried, she lurched to her feet like someone had flicked a switch, robotically feeding, bouncing, and replacing the pacifier in the child's mouth. She did everything that was expected of her, but she didn't feel a thing. The only time she'd felt vaguely alive was when she was with Isabelle.

The nicest thing about Isabelle was that she found Essie so interesting. It was unfamiliar. Usually when Essie spoke to other adults she played the role of interviewer—asking questions, listening, nodding. But with Isabelle she became the focus of every conversation. Isabelle wanted to know every detail about Essie— how she'd met Ben; had she always wanted children; had it been difficult to conceive? How about Essie's childhood—was it happy, was Barbara a good mother? She asked about her father, and Essie explained that he had run off with another woman while her mum was pregnant. She didn't usually tell people that. Her mum had never spoken much about her dad and Essie had deduced from this that it was an insult to her mother to talk about him. But there was something special happening between her and Isabelle. It felt like that time after you'd started dating someone special when you wanted to share every detail about each other.

Isabelle shared details about her life too. Her mother died when she was twenty, but her parents had gone their separate ways years before that. She had a brother called Freddy and two half-sisters. Her dad had married a much younger woman who was nice enough, but Isabelle kept her distance, as she'd never felt part of that family. There was genuine sadness in her voice when she talked about that. It made Essie want to wrap her arms around her and hold her. She didn't remember wanting to do that to another woman before.

By the time Kym returned with the color board, Essie had a couple of pictures ready to show her.

"Oooh," she said. "A big change!"

Was it? Essie wondered.

"I love it!" Kym squealed before she could change her mind. "It will really suit your face shape."

Well, good, Essie thought, sipping her peppermint tea, and then spitting it out and putting the cup on the bench in front of her. Kym gave her a strange look, but Essie didn't care. When you were a sleep-deprived mother of two in your thirties, you could spit out your tea if you didn't like it.

As Kym pasted color onto her hair with what looked like a pastry brush, Essie found herself feeling overwhelmingly tired. She let her eyes close. Maybe she'd catch forty winks while she was here? When you were a sleep-deprived mother in your thirties, you were allowed to do that too.

33

ANGE

"Ange! Is that you, dear?"

Ange had been about to head out to her Pilates class when the phone had rung. Now, she cursed herself for answering. Her mother-in-law always called the landline, probably because Ange always screened the calls to her cell. In the early days of her relationship with Lucas, Ange would make him call her back. (*Your family, your problem*, she'd say). But at some point she'd stopped saying things like that to him. At some point his family became her problem. *Everything* became her problem.

"Hello, Leonie," Ange said, standing by the counter with her rolled-up yoga mat by her feet. She never sat when her mother-in-law called. It was better to remain on guard.

"It's nice to hear your voice, Ange. My word. How long has it been?"

Not long enough.

"I've been meaning to get in touch forever," she continued without a pause. Leonie had an irritating tic of filling even the slightest pause with meaningless chatter. After a conversation with Leonie, she always felt like she'd been the victim of a minor assault.

"How are my grandsons? Growing like weeds? I really must plan a visit."

"Will and Ollie are fine, and you're welcome anytime, Leonie," Ange said, safe in the knowledge that Leonie only ever left Perth to come to Melbourne at Christmas, when she stayed for a week at an Airbnb in the city. She refused to stay in the spare room because "she didn't want to intrude," which would have been wonderful, had she not gone on about it so very much. Apparently her own mother-in-law used to descend when her children were little and demand to be waited on hand and foot. Clearly, she'd set the intention to not be that grandmother, and more important, to make sure everyone *knew* she wasn't. In spite of this, Leonie was a wonderful grandmother. Whenever she did visit, Leonie could always be found engaging with the kids. She read books and did role-plays and played the dullest of games for hours. Because of this, the boys adored her and because of this, Ange found she couldn't quite bring herself to hate her.

"And how's my boy?" she asked, talking about Lucas, of course.

"He's great," Ange said on autopilot.

Ange could practically see her beam. "Well, I suppose he's busy. What with work and the boys and running the household."

Once, when Leonie was visiting, Ange had sat on a barstool with a glass of wine while Lucas stacked the dishwasher. Leonie had never fully recovered. ("Let me do it," she'd insisted to Lucas, shooting a glance at Ange. "Honestly, you've been on your feet all day, you shouldn't have to do this too." It didn't seem to matter to her that Ange worked and earned the lion's share of the money. In Leonie's opinion it was a woman's job to take care of her man in the home.)

"We're all tired but happy," Ange murmured, all the while wondering: *Why am I playing this game with my mother-in-law? What sense of shame or pride is so deeply ingrained in me that I cannot be real?*

She imagined what an honest conversation with Leonie would sound like:

"How's Lucas?" Leonie would ask.

"Well, he's had at least one affair that I know about . . ."

"Oh, dear."

"Also he has a secret phone and I'm almost positive he has an illegitimate child."

"My word."

"And I'm thinking about leaving him, but despite what he's done I can't really bear the idea of it, and frankly, I'm not sure why I have to be the one to make the decision when he was the one who has had the affairs!"

But you couldn't have conversations like that with your mother-in-law. You couldn't have conversations like that with anyone.

"So, how is work?" Leonie asked her.

This was a departure. Leonie's usual repertoire was to ask about the kids, then ask about Lucas in a way that made Ange feel inferior, then finally get to the point of the call (which was usually to ask for some real estate advice for a friend of hers). The only time she asked Ange about work was to make a point of the fact that she worked too much.

"Not bad," Ange started. "Though I'm finding—"

"It's good that you work," she interrupted. "The brain doesn't like to be idle. It can make you start to overthink things."

Ange paused. That felt like a loaded statement. "What kind of things?"

"Oh, you know. Things. I remember when my kids were little and Lucas's dad was off at work, I used to send myself crazy with thoughts. About my friends, my children . . . my marriage. But you can wonder too much about things, can't you?"

This time, Leonie didn't fill the silence with chatter or noise. Ange lowered herself into the seat beside the phone. Had Lucas spoken to her? It was unlikely, but not impossible. Suddenly Ange wondered about Leonie's marriage. Had it also involved infidelity? Had she made it her philosophy to turn a blind eye? The thing about people who lived by a philosophy was that they liked others to follow their philosophy too. Otherwise there was the risk of their philosophy being wrong.

"Life is all about attitude, Ange," Leonie continued. "If you tell yourself enough that life is perfect . . . somehow, it is."

Maybe, Ange thought. *Or maybe you end up living a perfect-looking lie.*

34

BARBARA

Barbara was standing at the window when she saw Essie's car pull into her driveway. She hesitated, wondering whether to go out. On the one hand, she wanted to see if she was feeling better after her hairdresser visit this morning. On the other, she wanted Essie to enjoy her day off without any interference from her. As she watched her emerge from the car, Barbara felt herself descend into the kind of internal dispute that her friend Lois often had about her daughter.

"Does she want me to visit or stay the heck away?" Lois often lamented.

Barbara never had any sage advice to offer Lois. Essie always told her what she wanted. If Barbara rang Essie and she was in the middle of something she'd say, "Mum, can't talk, Fran's here," and Barbara would hang up the phone without the slightest hint of offense. But now Barbara had no idea what Essie wanted or needed.

Barbara watched her through the window. Essie had her head in the backseat, getting out some groceries perhaps. Maybe she could go there under the guise of helping her bring them inside? Both girls had gone down for a nap; it wouldn't hurt to pop outside for a moment. Barbara had a feeling that if she just *saw* Essie—up close—she'd get a good idea of her mental state. But when Essie emerged from the car, Barbara did a double take. Her hair was dark brown, and short. Chin-length. With bangs.

Barbara walked out the front door and headed toward her.

"Essie!" Barbara called, when she was a few yards away. Essie turned around and Barbara caught her breath.

"Oh," Essie said, self-consciously. "Yeah. I went for a restyle. What do you think?"

She touched her hair, with pride or perhaps embarrassment. She reminded Barbara of those women on TV who had complete makeovers and then had to perform a catwalk to show off their "new look." Barbara liked those shows. But Essie didn't seem to have any understanding that she didn't have a *new* look. She had a look that belonged to Isabelle.

"Gran?" Mia's voice came from Barbara's front door. "I'm awake!"

Mia scurried across the driveways in her T-shirt and undies and bare feet, her skinny pale legs a perfect pair of matchsticks. Her hair was sweaty and mussed from sleep. A few paces away from them, she stopped and frowned. "Mummy?"

"Hello, sweetie."

"Your hair is different." Mia blinked up at her mother, scratching her bottom absently. "You look like Ithabel."

Okay, Barbara thought. *I am not being paranoid.*

"It is similar, I guess," Essie admitted. "But I like it. Anyway, Isabelle doesn't have the copyright on bangs, does she?"

Essie tried for a laugh but it fell flat. It was the strangest thing. Barbara's daughter was standing in front of her, but it wasn't her daughter. She didn't even *look* like her daughter. She needed to call Ben.

"Can we go home, Mummy?" Mia said.

"Oh, no, Mia," Barbara said quickly. "Mummy's having a rest day. You can stay at Gran's for a bit longer."

"No! I want to stay with Mummy." She wrapped her arms around Essie's leg.

"It's fine, Mum," Essie said, but Barbara reached for Mia's shoulder and yanked her away from her mother. She didn't want Mia going anywhere with Essie.

"Gran!" Mia shrieked. "That hurts!"

"Mum, let go of her."

But Barbara didn't let go. It may have been Mia's reaction, or perhaps the strange look in Essie's eyes, but Barbara felt *herself* becoming a little hysterical. "Really, I think it's best if I—"

"Mum!" Essie slapped Barbara's hand clear of Mia's shoulder. "For heaven's sake, what is the matter with you?" She picked Mia up and held her on her hip.

Barbara stepped back, breathless. "Funny. I was about to ask the same of you."

Essie shook her head, perplexed, then turned and walked back to the house with Mia. Barbara would have followed but Polly was still asleep at her house. Instead she stood on the street between the houses, a strange feeling of déjà vu creeping over her.

It was happening, she realized. Her daughter's demons were coming out again.

35

ISABELLE

"Hello?"

It was just starting to go dark when Isabelle's phone rang. She snatched it up without glancing at the screen.

"Hi," Essie said. "Is this a bad time?"

"Of course not." Isabelle sat up straighter. "What's up?"

"Actually I was wondering if you could come over. I have something to show you."

"You do?" Isabelle said. Essie sounded different; she was talking too loud or something. Isabelle heard Mia babbling in the background.

"Yes, well. I hope it doesn't freak you out . . ."

"Okay, now I'm intrigued."

Essie giggled. Isabelle felt a whisper of worry—a tremor underfoot. Essie had been struggling last time she'd seen her.

Exhausted and verging on delirious. And something in Essie's voice told Isabelle that things may have worsened.

"Right, just give me a few minutes then. I'm just finishing something up and I'll come to you . . ."

"Don't be too long," Essie said.

Isabelle had no intention of being long. She hung up the phone and pushed back her chair, eager to investigate sooner rather than later. Perhaps Essie'd had another night of hardly any sleep? That could certainly make a person sound odd. She was only just on her feet when there was a knock at the door.

"I said I'd be right there!" she called jokingly. She threw open the door and stopped short.

He was dressed in jeans, a gray T-shirt, and a denim jacket, his shaggy black hair pushed back over one ear. His dusky-blue eyes shone with something like mischief.

Jules.

"What . . . what are you—"

"I said I'd come down on my bike."

"You did but . . . I . . . I wasn't expecting . . ."

Jules guided her backward into the house. He stripped off her dress, letting it fall to the floor. In a matter of moments they were both naked.

"I'm meant to be going to see Essie," she protested against his mouth.

But by the time he lowered them both into the armchair, Isabelle had forgotten all about Essie.

36

FRAN

Fran sat on the floor in the dark room with her head in her hands. She and Nigel had spent the day pretending everything was fine. They'd spoken in odd, jovial voices about trivial day-to-day topics like meals and baths and who would read bedtime stories—a peculiar little show they'd put on for Rosie's sake. Was it doing her any favors, Fran wondered, not being real in front of her? Obviously there were some topics too mature for a three-year-old, but did they have to talk with faux smiles and cheer? Fran didn't know. She didn't know anything anymore.

Rosie had been fussy and clingy at bedtime, so maybe they hadn't done such a great job of keeping things from her. Kids were intuitive, wasn't that what everyone said? She'd kept asking for one more story, one more cuddle, one more drink of water. Fran and Nigel had both indulged her, perhaps wanting to put off what was coming. But eventually there was nothing else left to do but turn off her light and go and talk.

Once the questions started, they came like a train. Nigel wanted to know everything. How it had happened, how many times, what feelings were behind it. Did she ever plan to tell him? Did she ever plan to tell Mark? (She didn't. In an odd way, the whole thing felt like it had nothing to do with Mark.) Nigel's mood rolled from calm to angry to shocked to upset. There were periods of silence. Then more questions. It felt like the questions would never end. They started broad and vague, and then became grotesquely specific. *Did they perform oral sex? Him to her? Her to him? What was the position? How long did it last? Did she orgasm?* Fran wondered if it was helpful for him to know, but she was relieved she didn't have to be the one to decide for him anymore.

"Enough," she said eventually. "I think we've covered it all. Maybe we should talk about what to do now."

Nigel stood up and walked to the window. Fran wanted to go to him, to put a hand on his shoulder, but could she do that? Was she *allowed*? He looked like a statue at the window, so still she couldn't even see him breathing. Fran wasn't sure she was breathing herself.

When Ava began to cry, Nigel moved quickly—out of the room before Fran could even get to her feet. When he was gone, she gazed out the window. Lights were starting to come on in the street and Fran pictured the neighbors in their homes watching Netflix, brushing teeth, filling out paperwork for school excursions, paying bills. She wondered if any of the neighbors were looking back at her house, wondering what she was up to.

He'd been gone several minutes when Fran realized. Nigel was with *Ava*. The child she'd just told him might not be his.

She bolted.

Nigel was in the rocking chair in the darkness, with Ava splayed across his chest, exactly as she'd found him a few weeks ago, both of them blinking into the darkness.

Fran pressed a hand to her heart.

"You thought I might have hurt her," he said with a sneer.

Fran didn't respond. Obviously it was what she'd thought. But suddenly she saw how ridiculous that was. She slid down onto the carpet and rested her back against the wall.

Nigel met Fran's gaze, dead-on. "Do you think she's mine?"

"I don't know."

"I know you don't know. I'm asking what you *think*." He watched her steadily. He'd stopped rocking the chair now. Ava's eyes had closed and her breathing was loud in the silent room.

"I can't answer that," she said. "What does it matter what I think?"

"It matters to me."

And clearly it did. The reason she could hear Ava breathing, she realized, was because Nigel wasn't.

Fran took a moment to think. "Some days I do. Other days—"

"For fuck's sake!" Nigel's calm snapped like worn elastic. It occurred to Fran that during their marriage, she had only seen him angry a handful of times. Even when he was depressed, it was rare. She hadn't looked for a husband with a gentle temperament. She'd looked for several things, but that part had been sheer good luck.

"Fine! I *do* think she's yours. If I were forced to guess, I'd say she was yours. But—"

"But you don't know."

"Exactly."

Silence. Oblivious to what was happening around her, Ava let out a contented sigh.

"We'll get a paternity test," Fran said. "Now that you know . . . we can do that. And then we'll know."

"We'll know what?"

Fran understood what he meant. They could find out the paternity of Ava. But there would still be so much they wouldn't know. Like how they would move forward after this if she wasn't his child. How they'd move forward, if she *was*.

"Do you know what the worst part is?" Nigel said. "Worse than you having an affair or a potentially illegitimate baby? Worse than becoming a part-time dad to Rosie and possibly losing Ava altogether? It's that because of all this I might lose my relationship with you. And you are the one thing I don't think I can live without."

It was the loveliest knife she'd ever been stabbed with in her life. Fran closed her eyes and rested her forehead against her knees.

37

ESSIE

It was dark outside now and Isabelle still wasn't here. Essie stood by the window, catching her own reflection. Her hairdresser was right, her hair *did* suit her face shape and coloring. She'd changed when she'd gotten home, into a tank top and long skirt so she could feel the breeze around her ankles, but she still felt hot and bothered. Where *on earth* was Isabelle?

Essie stepped from foot to foot, unable to stand still. She felt vaguely breathless and her heart hammered in her chest. Was it was normal to feel like this at the prospect of a visit from a friend? She hadn't had a lot of good friends in her life, so she wasn't sure. She also wasn't sure about some of her . . . other thoughts. Women admired each other's bodies, of course. ("You skinny bitch," or "I'd do anything for your boobs.") But was it normal to think about reaching out and stroking the line of your friend's jaw? Was it normal to wonder what it would be like to kiss the pink cupid's bow of her lips?

Lights flashed into the street and Essie watched as a motorbike drove up Isabelle's driveway.

"What are you looking at?" Mia asked, appearing beside her. She'd abandoned her ham and cheese sandwich at her little table.

"Nothing, honey. Eat your sandwich."

Essie craned her neck to see the person standing at the front door.

"Mummy! Can I see?" Mia ripped open the curtain.

"Mia!" Essie whipped the curtain back into place. It was a small street, and it didn't take much commotion to catch people's attention. Essie peered around the curtain again just in time to see Isabelle's front door close. Who *was* that?

Essie charged toward her door, powerless to do anything else. It was the same feeling she'd had a few months back when she'd been away from Polly for a few hours, and her body literally *ached* until she could get back to her. Now she was aching for Isabelle. She couldn't wait.

"I'll be right back," she said to Mia.

Outside, Essie stepped over the plants dividing their houses and started up Isabelle's driveway. Barefooted, she found herself running. At the door, she raised her hand to knock then she stopped herself, peering through the thin strip of glass alongside the door instead. Isabelle's shoes and underwear were lying there, trailing toward the lounge room.

Essie lowered her hand without knocking.

She made her way down the side of the house, her heart hammering. She squeezed past a shrub and stepped into a garden bed next to a window. It had a clear view of the living room. Essie moved closer. Isabelle lay across the armchair, one bare leg kicked over the arm. Her body was on an angle, long and lean and pale. She moved suddenly, and that's when Essie noticed the man kneeling before her.

She jumped back. She felt the sting as hard as if she'd been slapped.

And then, in an instant, it was clear. She loved Isabelle. She *loved her*. It wasn't the same way she loved Ben. She loved Isabelle in a pure, perfect way.

She loved Isabelle more.

"Essie."

Essie jerked around. The security light cast a blinding glow, but from his size, Essie could see right away that it was Ben. She blinked at him, waiting for her eyes to adjust.

"What are you *doing*?"

Essie looked back at the window and his gaze must have followed because a moment later, he clapped a hand over his mouth.

The sensor light flicked off.

"Essie," he whispered urgently. "We need to leave."

She shook her head. She wasn't trying to be difficult. She simply *couldn't* leave. She was certain that if her feet were pulled off this soil, she would actually cease to exist.

Why did she feel like that?

"Essie. Let's go." Ben sounded, not angry exactly, but agitated. He gripped her arm just below her shoulder and started to lead her back toward the street. Essie dug in her heels.

"No."

"Essie," he said, softer now. "Let's go home. We can talk there, okay? Essie, I'm going to help you . . ."

There was a flash of movement at the front door and then the light flicked on. Leaves rustled. And then someone else was there.

"Essie? Is that you?"

It took Essie a moment for her eyes to adjust. It was Isabelle. Her shirt and skirt were all askew.

I love you, Essie thought. I love you, Isabelle.

"What's going on?" Isabelle said. She sounded wary. "Ben?"

"I'm not sure," Ben said.

It was utterly silent and still. Essie felt their eyes on her. She wished Ben would go away. Emotions were coming at her so fast. A splash of anger, a flurry of nerves, a burst of panic. It made her bold. She shoved past Ben and looked Isabelle dead in the eye. *Just look*, she told herself. *Look in Isabelle's eyes. You'll know. You'll know if she feels it too.*

Isabelle glanced toward the doorway where a disheveled man stood, half-dressed. The man on the motorbike. The one from inside. Essie watched the silent language that passed between them. And after a few seconds, she realized she had her answer.

Essie let out a whimper.

This time when Ben tried to guide her away, Essie let him. He led her past Isabelle and the disheveled man, back toward their home. Essie wasn't sure if she was imagining it, but when she walked past Isabelle she was sure she heard her whisper, "I'm sorry."

38

ANGE

Ange sat in her favorite armchair with a glass of pinot grigio while the TV played some kind of house-flipping show. The boys were in their bedrooms doing whatever they did in there, and Lucas sat opposite Ange in his trendy jeans and V-neck T-shirt—one bare, tanned foot resting on the coffee table. The *V* in Lucas's shirt seemed to have gotten deeper lately, exposing a taut hairless chest that usually filled her with longing. Today, it filled her with rage. *Put a proper shirt on,* she wanted to yell. *A button-down and a pair of chinos. And while you're at it, be a different kind of man! The kind who loves his wife and can keep it in his pants.*

There was a knock on the door and they looked at each other, then raised their eyebrows in unison.

"I'll get it," Ange said, when Lucas remained seated. Had he always been so useless? she wondered. Had she been blind to it because of his deep V-neck T-shirts, or was she simply happy to put up with it so long as he wasn't a philanderer with another family?

It was Barbara at the door. She stood there with Polly in her arms and Mia by her side. Polly was smearing a segment of orange into her white blouse and Barbara seemed neither bothered nor aware. "I'm sorry to bother you, Angela," she said, "but is there any chance you could look after the girls for an hour or so. Essie is . . . well, she's ill, so Ben and I are taking her to the hospital."

"To the *hospital*? Is everything all right?"

"She's physically fine . . ." Barbara drifted off, glancing at Mia.

Ange read between the lines. Physically Essie was fine. Mentally was another story.

Ange felt a twist of guilt. She'd noticed Essie didn't seem herself these past few weeks. She and Fran had even *discussed* it, at Essie's place. Why hadn't she reached out to her? Why hadn't she offered to help out with the girls, bring her a few meals, pop by for a chat? Ange knew what Essie had done last time, with Mia. Now she was unwell again and no one had helped her. She couldn't help feeling that she, like *all* the neighbors, should shoulder some responsibility for that.

"Of course I'll look after them," Ange said, taking Polly from Barbara. "Why don't you give me Essie's keys and I'll take them home and give them dinner and put them into their own beds? Then you can come back whenever you're ready."

"That would be wonderful."

Barbara found the keys and handed them over and then kissed

the girls good-bye. By the time Ange had brought the girls into the foyer, Lucas was there.

"What's going on?" he said.

"Essie isn't well and is going to the hospital. I said I'd take the girls back home and look after them for a few hours."

Lucas nodded. Ange didn't have to tell him not to ask any more. He squatted next to Mia. "So I suppose we're going to have to get you home somehow. Hmmm. I don't suppose you like piggybacks?"

Mia glanced at Ange, then back at Lucas. She nodded shyly.

"You don't?" Lucas cried. "Who doesn't like piggybacks?"

She smiled. "*I do.*"

"You don't?"

Now, she was flat-out giggling. Even Polly was smiling. "I said . . . I DOOO!"

Ange watched Lucas. The Lucas who had affairs and illegitimate children. The Lucas who also understood when to ask questions . . . and when to give piggyback rides.

"Hold on tight," he said to Mia as he hoisted her onto his back.

Ange told the boys where they were going (she often left them home alone while she popped over to the neighbors) and then she and Lucas walked across the road to Essie's. The house was in a surprising state. Breakfast dishes were stacked in the sink, toys were strewn all over the place, a half-eaten sandwich sat on the coffee table. Usually, when Ange went over to Essie's it was clean and welcoming, with everything in its place.

"I'll get the dinner started," Lucas said, as Ange did a sweep of the room, gathering up the dirty dishes and taking them to the kitchen. When the boys were little, they had a similar routine— one of them tidying while the other made dinner. Later, one would read stories while the other did the dishes. No matter how stressful her day had been, when Lucas showed up, things made sense again. For years, Ange had listened to women talk about how their husbands were terrible with the kids, how they always did the wrong thing, or forgot to check the temperature of the bath, or did up the diaper too tight . . . or something. Ange had always nodded and smiled while being secretly smug. How lucky she was! Lucas wasn't one of those husbands. He checked water temperature, and made lunch boxes and sang songs and put children to bed. He was a dream husband!

A dream husband to two women.

Ange unstacked and stacked the dishwasher, gathered the toys into their wicker baskets, and folded the laundry and put it away. Meanwhile Lucas had found a jar of pumpkin and zucchini mash for Polly, and had got some pasta and veggies started for Mia. When it was ready, he pretended the pasta was worms, which had Mia laughing hysterically. *How is it possible?* Ange thought. *How can you be such a good guy and such a bad guy? How can I love you so much . . . and hate you so much.*

After dinner, they bathed the girls. Then Ange sat on the couch feeding Polly a bottle while Lucas played trains on the floor with Mia.

"Thanks for helping," she said to him.

He smiled at her. "It reminds me of when the boys were little."

"Me too."

Mia rammed a train into Lucas's foot. "Oww," he said, theatrically, rolling around while Mia chortled. "A train ran over my foot!"

"I don't suppose you get to do this with Charlie very often," Ange said.

Lucas glanced over, still holding his foot and pretending to wince. He raised his eyebrows. "Sorry?"

"Erin's little girl?" Ange continued. "Your daughter?"

Mia rammed Lucas's foot again, but this time he didn't react. Frustrated, she tried again. And again. Ange scanned Lucas's face for confusion or bewilderment, but it wasn't there. All that was there was understanding.

"How did you know?" he said.

Finally the tears she'd been waiting for welled up in her eyes. "I know," she said, "because you just told me."

39

ISABELLE

When Isabelle opened her eyes the next morning, Jules was beside her, fast asleep. Until that very moment, Isabelle hadn't been aware of how much she'd missed the weight of his body beside her, his slightly woodsy, minty scent. She basked it in for a moment until everything came flooding back.

She jerked upright and reached for her phone. She'd texted Essie twice last night. Even though she hadn't been optimistic for a response, she was disappointed to find no messages. If she'd had Ben's number, she would have called him but she didn't. And since she had no intention of talking to Barbara, it left her out of options.

Jules opened his eyes all at once, without a single stir or yawn. He always woke like this, and it was always unnerving. He frowned. "You okay?"

"No, I'm not," she said, jumping out of bed.

"Where are you going?"

"I need to see Essie," she replied, and headed for the shower.

40

ESSIE

Essie had been in Summit Oaks for two nights and there hadn't been any mention of a release date. It was fine by her. She was nuts, after all. A married, mother of two, becoming obsessed with a female neighbor? Spying on her from the side of her house like a stalker? It was like a *Jerry Springer* episode. Everyone agreed she'd had "another postpartum episode," and the humiliation of this was all encompassing. Another one? Was it not enough that she had dumped her first baby in the park, but now she'd had a complete mental breakdown after her second?

The medication helped keep thoughts at bay. Thoughts of . . . what would it be like when she had to face Isabelle? It was hard enough to face Ben. She'd thought he would be angry with her, horrified and embarrassed, but he wasn't. He'd been at her bed-side every moment he wasn't with the kids. As far as she knew he hadn't been to work in days. If her mum hadn't begged him to go home and be with the girls, she suspected he'd have spent the nights on the floor of her hospital room as well.

Ange had phoned and so had Fran. Essie was touched, even though she couldn't bring herself to speak to them. She knew she'd have to face everyone eventually, but for now, she was happy to remain in a foggy, drugged-out world where reality didn't exist. Essie's mum was the only one she'd speak to, besides Ben. She sat in Essie's room now, flipping through a magazine. For the last two days, she and Ben had tag-teamed, either at the hospital or looking after the girls. In her typical style, her mum didn't ask anything of Essie. She brought magazines or snacks, and then sat by the window, refolding Essie's clothes and throwing out wrappers from candy bars she'd eaten. Making things right again. Essie knew she had lucked out in the mother department, but what about Mia and Polly? Who would make things right for them?

Essie began to get tired—a combination of the medication and the depression. Even as she started to drift off, she sensed her mother's movements. She was grabbing her purse from the table, rummaging for her keys, checking for her sunglasses on her head, looking around to see if there was anything else she could do before she left—anything else she could *give*. Her lips brushed Essie's forehead and then the door gently closed.

A few minutes later Essie heard a nurse come in. She waited for the scrape of the chart lifting from the end of the bed, the filling of the water jug, the scrawl of a pen against paper—but she didn't hear them. Even the soles of her shoes on the floor sounded wrong, more of a clack than a squeak.

Essie opened her eyes.

"Did I wake you?"

Isabelle stood at the end of the bed, looking down at her with a tentative smile. Her hands were clasped together in front and she looked nervous, which Essie found odd. What did *she* have to be nervous about? She wasn't the one who'd humiliated herself. Unless . . . maybe she was worried that Essie might do something crazy again?

"I'm sorry to show up like this," Isabelle said, "I just . . . needed to see you. After the other night, I was worried."

Essie struggled to her elbows, then sat up. Despite the circumstances, Essie couldn't deny she was happy to see Isabelle, if very sheepish. "You were *worried*? About your crazy neighbor?"

"You're not crazy, Essie."

"With all due respect, you haven't been inside my mind for the last few weeks. You haven't heard my thoughts."

Isabelle pulled up a chair and sat. "That's true. And actually, I was hoping you would share those thoughts with me. If you'd humor me, I'd really like to know."

"Trust me, you don't."

"Trust me, I do."

They locked eyes. It seemed, despite all odds, that she *did* want to know. Essie didn't understand why, but she also didn't have much to lose. She'd already spied on Isabelle through the window of her house. How much worse could it get?

"Fine. When I wake up, I'm thinking about you. When I go to sleep, I'm thinking about you. I think about kissing you and touching you. I *love* you. I feel like if I lost you, I'd be like a sieve, full of holes, and everything that is good would leach away. I . . . I'm obsessed with you, Isabelle."

She snuck a look at Isabelle, and was surprised to find her nodding. She slid her chair a little closer to Essie. "What if I told you that everything you just described made absolute sense?"

Essie laughed once, a "pah" of ridiculousness. "I'd say *you* were crazy."

"And I'd say I'm not crazy," Isabelle said. "I'm your sister."

I left the hospital that afternoon. I wasn't in any position to argue. I'd feel much better once I was at home, I told myself, though I'd miss the medication. The ward was busy so I packed my own bag, ready for discharge. I waited in my room for a while, but when no one came to see me I just left. And then I was going down in the elevator and headed for the taxi stand. Going home.

Except something was wrong.

What was it? It felt like I was missing something, but I had it all—bag, purse, keys. I must have laughed when I realized.

My baby! I'd forgotten my baby.

I turned around and walked back into the hospital. A nurse glanced up when I came back inside. She was on the phone, busy, so I pointed at my room and kept walking. I found you right there in the hallway, still in your wheely-crib. A pang of fear went through me. They'd found you. Could I get reported for this? Would children's services come beating down my door? I could already read the headline: NEW MOTHER FORGETS HER BABY.

I wasn't thinking rationally, of course. It was the medication. Surely they wouldn't report me? Mothers were often disoriented after having their babies, it probably happened all the time. Still, I didn't see the need to draw any more attention to my mistake. So I just gently lifted you from your crib and took you downstairs to the waiting cab.

41

ISABELLE

"What do you mean you're my sister?" Essie said.

Isabelle was shaking. She'd been waiting for this moment since she was eight years old, but now it was here, she felt the enormity of it like a boulder on her shoulders. She moved to Essie's bedside, twisting the bedcovers in her nervous fingers. "I know it sounds crazy, but you were nineteen days old when you were abducted from the Royal Sydney Hospital. Your name is Sophie. Sophie Heatherington."

"I don't understand," Essie said. "Why do you think *I* am Sophie?"

Essie sat up straight, pulling her knees up in front of her. Her eyes were wide and interested—she was obviously curious, but a long way from believing *she* had a role in it.

"I saw you on the news when there was the fire in Pleasant Court and I nearly fainted," Isabelle said. "You look exactly like my mum. *Exactly.* I may have only had nineteen days with you, but I was eight and you were my baby sister. I remember everything about you. The shape of your nose, the color of your skin. Your eyes—one brown and one blue."

Mention of her eyes caused the slightest flicker of uncertainty in Essie. "But . . . I'm not the only person with a birthmark in my eye."

"That's true. And I've had a false alarm before—a girl from Adelaide with a birthmark in her eye. But this time, it was more than just the birthmark. After Sophie was taken, Mum and I trawled the newspaper announcements for weeks. We tried to get the police to follow up on all the people who announced the births of baby girls in Sydney in the week after Sophie was taken. When I saw your name on the news after the fire I knew there was something familiar about it. I double-checked and sure enough there was a birth notice for Esther Walker in the newspaper three days after Sophie was taken. It wasn't proof, but I was convinced enough to try and find out more. So I took a leave of absence from my job and moved to Melbourne. The goal was to try and get some DNA, but I didn't know how to get it from you so I took some of Mia's hair. I did a DNA test. Our kinship index is greater than one point zero, which means Mia and I share DNA."

Isabelle held out the document to Essie.

"You took Mia's hair?"

"Read the document, Essie," Isabelle said, more determined now. Now she'd started this, there was no going back. She needed to make Essie understand this, or she'd lose her all over again.

Essie glanced at the document briefly, then waved it away. "I don't understand this . . . what does it mean?"

"It means Mia is my niece."

"No. No, that can't be right. I don't believe you."

"You don't have to believe me," Isabelle said. She stabbed a finger at the papers between them on the bed. "This is proof."

Essie glanced down at the document again, keeping her distance as though it could infect her with something.

"What's your birthdate, Essie?" Isabelle asked gently.

"June tenth."

"Is that what it says on your birth certificate?" Essie handed the document back.

"I don't have a birth certificate. But if I did, that's what it would say."

"Why don't you have a birth certificate?"

"I don't need one. I'm a homebody. I hardly want to leave the house, let alone the country."

Isabelle watched her steadily. Essie rolled her eyes.

"Okay," she said. "Then for the sake of argument, how did this happen? How did I end up with my mum instead of yours?"

"You weren't well," Isabelle started. Her mind drifted back to the day she came home from school and found Sophie screaming. It was a shock after the quiet, content baby she'd been for the previous few weeks.

"I'm taking her to the hospital," Isabelle's mum had said. "She has a fever."

Isabelle had wanted to go to the hospital too, but instead she and Freddy were sent to a neighbor's house. A few hours later when their dad collected them, her mum and Sophie still weren't home. They were staying the night at the hospital, her dad told them.

The next day, Isabelle's dad picked her up from school. The

phone was ringing when they arrived home and Isabelle and Freddy ran to answer it. Isabelle got there first.

"Hello?"

"Izzy, it's Mum. Can I speak to Dad?"

"Mom! How's Sophie?"

"Just put Dad on the phone," she said.

Her mum sounded different. Sophie must have gotten worse, Isabelle thought. As she handed the phone to her dad, she got a funny feeling in her belly.

"Hi, Linda," her dad said. A split second later, his brow became furrowed. "What? What do you mean?"

He began blinking rapidly. He was still holding Isabelle's schoolbag with one hand and gripping the phone with the other. His knuckles became white. "Where was Sophie while you were sleeping in the nurses station? Well, check again. Find the nurse. I'm not yelling, I'm just . . ."

Isabelle got scared then. Her dad was calm, jolly. He wasn't one to yell or get flustered. "I don't care if she's off-shift. Why are you asking *me*? Okay, I'm coming now."

Her dad walked straight to the door. He was still holding Isabelle's schoolbag. Isabelle and Freddy hurried after him. They didn't speak a word on the way to the hospital. There was already a policeman there when they arrived and that's when Isabelle realized how serious it was.

"You were in the hospital and someone took you from your crib while our mum was sleeping," Isabelle said to Essie. "We never saw you again."

It was such a simple ending to the story, though not an entirely accurate one. Because it wasn't the end of the story. After Sophie's disappearance life became a whirlwind for the Heatheringtons—doing press conferences, putting up posters, endless meetings with the police and people who worked for missing children foundations. People shuttled Isabelle and her brother to school and activities to help them maintain "a sense of normalcy"—as if that were possible. After a few months the counseling started—family counseling—which was basically putting them all in a room together to watch her mother cry while her father, dry-eyed, patted her back. The counseling had been horrible. But when things had started going back to normal—that was worse.

After six months, Isabelle's mum packed up Sophie's bassinet. Isabelle tried to stop her, but she explained, "Sophie won't need it anymore. She's too big. She needs a crib." That had made sense to Isabelle. Her father had begged her mother, "No, don't put up the crib." They'd had a fight. But her mother put it up anyway, while Isabelle sat on the floor and handed her tools. (Her mum wasn't handy. It took them all night to put up that crib.)

They put her toddler bed together when she would have been three. Isabelle's dad had left by then. Isabelle and her mum celebrated every birthday. Freddy went along with it, but like her dad, he seemed to have moved on in a way Isabelle and her mother couldn't. When they went on vacation, they brought something back for Sophie, so she'd have a memento of what she'd missed. The family photos they took somehow held a space where Sophie should have been. They talked about her as if she would come back one day. For years, Isabelle believed she would.

Isabelle lost her mum to cancer when she was twenty. After that, Isabelle was the only one still looking for Sophie. Everyone else had moved on.

Essie was staring at her.

"You're not crazy, Essie," Isabelle told her.

"Really?" Essie said. "If what you're saying is true, it's worse. It means I've fallen in love with my own sister!" Essie laughed loudly, but Isabelle heard a note of uncertainty in it.

Isabelle took a breath. She hadn't wanted to get into this part so soon. "Actually, that part even makes sense. Have you heard of genetic sexual attraction?"

Essie blinked, her smile sliding off her face. "Have I heard of *what*?"

"Genetic sexual attraction is an attraction that can happen between relatives who meet as adults. It is most common between a birth mother and an adult child who was adopted out as a baby. It also can happen between siblings who were conceived by the same sperm donor or separated at birth."

"Sorry . . . *what*?"

"The other night, when you looked at me like you were in love with me? That is classic behavior of someone experiencing genetic sexual attraction. You were feeling something toward me that you couldn't put your finger on, so you read it as attraction. Essie, I know this is a huge shock, but does this make even the slightest bit of sense to you?"

Essie glanced down at the DNA results again. "How did you do this?" she asked softly.

"The DNA test? Well, it was one of those—"

"—one of those online tests that are advertised on TV? Seven ninety-nine for peace of mind? Guaranteed test results in fourteen days?" She looked up. Her eyes were wild and disbelieving. "Why are you doing this to me?"

Isabelle had known she'd get pushback from Essie. She was prepared for it. She was unprepared for the situation to be turned around on her.

"I didn't do it to you. *Barbara* did. Barbara kidnapped you, Essie."

Essie laughed. "Have you *met* my mother? Does she seem like a kidnapper?"

"Actually, yes. She fits the profile of a baby snatcher exactly."

Essie paused. Clearly, she hadn't expected that. "In what way does she fit the profile of a baby snatcher?" Essie's chin was held high, disbelieving, but she was listening. It was, Isabelle figured, the best she could hope for.

"For one thing, she looks nothing like you. For another, she moved you both away from Sydney when you were a newborn and you have no contact with her friends or family. You have no father in the picture. Often women take babies to hold on to a man but it rarely works. They usually end up alone in a codependent relationship with the child, exactly like you and Barbara are."

Isabelle didn't know if any of this was registering with Essie. Her jaw was set—which may mean she was refusing to listen, or possibly, that something had struck a chord.

"Essie," she said as the door opened. It was Barbara.

"Oh! Hello, Isabelle. Sorry, am I interrupting?"

Barbara held a pile of magazines and an overnight bag, and she smiled warmly at them. After a moment, her smile faded. "Is everything all right?"

"Fine," Essie said, "though I am a bit tired. You probably should go, Isabelle. And I think it's best if you don't come back while I'm in here. I need to focus on getting better."

There was a moment's silence. Barbara glanced at Isabelle, a question in her eyes.

"I'd really like to come back in a few days," Isabelle said. "You might be feeling a bit better and we can talk further."

"No," Essie said, avoiding her gaze. "Mum, can you tell the nurses, please? No more visitors. I need to rest."

"All right," Barbara said, disconcerted. She sent Isabelle an apologetic look. Isabelle slid her gaze to the floor.

"Thanks for coming, Isabelle," Essie said.

"I'll call you," Isabelle replied, but Essie's expression made it clear that she wouldn't be answering.

42

FRAN

Fran was in purgatory. Or limbo. Or perhaps it was hell? It was certainly hot enough. After a few days of slightly cooler temperatures, the heat had surged again and today the winds were set to pick up, so the fire authority was on high alert for bushfires.

Fran was on high alert too, for a verdict on the future of her marriage.

She and Nigel sat on the floor of the lounge room while Rosie crouched inside the little puppet theater that Santa had brought last Christmas. Ava sat in Fran's lap, gurgling happily. Fran had been pleased when Rosie suggested putting on a show, partly because it was far more common for her to conduct a science experiment or read an atlas, and partly because it would be a few minutes where she and Nigel wouldn't have to find other things to do to avoid speaking to each other.

For the past few days she and Nigel had gone about their lives as if nothing had happened, save for a few small changes. Now Nigel shut the bathroom door when he showered, and he dressed in pajama pants and a T-shirt for bed, rather than just boxer shorts. In the morning, when Fran woke, he was already out of bed and making breakfast, and as they ate, they both talked only to Rosie. He needed time to think, he'd said. It was so typical of Nigel. He was methodical and fair, even when it came to matters of the heart.

Fran wished she had someone to talk to, but everyone seemed to be caught in their own personal drama. Essie, it seemed, was in the hospital. Ben hadn't given details, but Fran gathered it was more postpartum issues. She couldn't help feeling guilty about that. She'd noticed Essie wasn't doing well. She was just across the road. But she'd been too wound up in her own life to do anything. What kind of a person did that make her?

Rosie's hands were stuffed into a pair of frog puppets, which were wrestling or dancing or doing something that was illegal in public on the stage of Rosie's little theater. Fran flicked a smile at Nigel. His gaze, she noticed, was on Ava.

He'd been looking at her a lot, these past few days. Checking her out from different angles, in different lights. She didn't blame him, of course, she'd been doing the same thing if the situation were reversed. Problem was, it wouldn't tell him much. Ava changed constantly. She was starting to lose that newborn look now. Her face was filling out and her little hands had gained a nice layer of fat, making them look like they were screwed onto her arms. She looked entirely different from Rosie as a baby. But that didn't necessarily mean anything.

"We should get a paternity test done," she said.

Nigel stiffened, but he kept his gaze right ahead at the puppet show. Rosie was singing a song about a frog on a log. "If you like."

"I mean . . . isn't that what you want?"

He turned to her, slack-jawed. "No. I do not want to get a paternity test on a child that I thought was mine. That is definitely not what I *want*."

Fran looked back at the show.

"Daddy! You're not listening."

"I am," he said, not missing a beat. "Frogs don't make that noise."

The frogs disappeared from the stage, and Rosie's head appeared. "What noise do they make?"

"It depends on the species. But it often sounds like a chirp, like this." Nigel made a noise that Fran had never heard before, but she didn't doubt that he was right. Neither did Rosie. Nigel was the encyclopedia Rosie went to whenever she needed facts. Nigel was the one she went to for *everything*. He was, for that matter, the one *Fran* went to for everything. Nigel was the heart and soul of their family. It was why, when he was struggling, the whole family struggled with him.

Rosie imitated the frog's call perfectly, then disappeared again. The show resumed.

"I'm sorry," Fran whispered. "It's just . . . you've had a few days to think about things. What *do* you want?"

He didn't say anything for a while. Rosie kept making that frog noise, that irritating but accurate frog noise.

"I want to believe we'll find our way through this, Fran."

Her body went limp in relief. "Oh. Nigel. Thank goodness, so do—"

"—I *want* to believe it," he repeated over the top of her, "but I'm not sure I do."

43

ANGE

This is what it will be like, Ange thought as she watched the boys play Xbox. *This is what single parenthood will be like.* It was early afternoon and the boys were just home from school. She'd made them a snack—nachos, which they'd demolished like a pair of wild dogs, leaving scatterings of cheese and corn chips all over the coffee table—and then she'd sat on the arm of Ollie's chair begging for snippets about their day. The other arm of Ollie's chair was empty. Because Lucas was gone.

Ange didn't know if he'd left forever, or just for a few days. He'd taken only an overnight bag, so presumably he'd be back sometime. The shameful truth was that she was desperate to call him up and ask when that would be. She could pretend it was for the kids' sake, even though they'd barely batted an eyelid when she told them he'd gone away for work. But she had just enough pride to stop herself, instead choosing to suffer in silence, hanging on to the few shreds of dignity she had left.

The most shameful thing was that she hadn't even asked him to leave. She hadn't had to.

"I should probably leave," he'd said the night before.

"Moving in with Erin?" she'd said offhandedly, as if talking about it casually made the idea less unspeakably awful.

"No." He'd frowned. "No. Erin and I aren't together anymore. We haven't been for a long time."

That had been a surprise. Ange had thought Erin was Josie no. 2—that it was *true love*. Fleetingly she wondered what would have happened had she not stepped in with her bogus pregnancy and allowed Lucas to have his moment in the sun with Josie all those years ago. Maybe he would have come back after realizing his mistake, and been a different man from then on.

Maybe not.

"We stay in touch for Charlie's sake," he said. "But that's it."

"How did this happen, Lucas?" She'd leaned forward as if she really wanted to know. In fact, what she wanted to do was turn back the clocks to when this whole thing had been merely a suspicion. The whole conversation felt so odd it was as though she was watching it on TV, rather than taking part in it.

"Remember a few years back—Ollie's first year of school?"

Of course she remembered. Ollie's first year of school had been a great year. With the boys both at school, she'd finally gotten her life back. She'd decided to branch out on her own, starting her own real estate office. She'd expected it to take years to turn a profit, but by the end of that first year, she'd been making good money. Ollie, of course, had adjusted to school life instantly and Will was settled in the second grade. Lucas worked flexible hours and spent more time with the boys. Surely that couldn't have been the year that Lucas strayed? The year she'd been so happy?

"You were working so hard and I'd taken over the lion's share of the parenting, doing school drop-offs and pickups. It was a real transition time . . ."

Ange's spine straightened. Was that a trace of martyrdom in his voice? It was true, he had taken over as lead parent that year and it had been a relief for Ange. Unlike her, Lucas relished those mind-numbing aspects of parenthood—the idle conversations with other parents, the school notices, the Book-Week costumes. But she had taken over most of the financial responsibilities! With her new business, she was earning enough that he could work flexible hours doing his photography and be available to the boys. It catered to both of their strengths. She remembered Lucas saying so at the time.

Now it was a real *transition time*?

"You worked late a lot—"

"No, I didn't," she snapped. "I was always home by seven P.M. Eight P.M. at the latest. And Saturday mornings. No more than you'd expect any dad to work!" Strangely, making this a gender issue was easier than making it about her failings as a wife. She understood gender issues—as a businesswoman, she dealt with them every day. She made it her business to mentor younger women in the office on claiming their place at the boardroom table. As she squared off against Lucas, she almost heard Beyoncé singing in the background. "I worked hard to support my family.

To allow you to work part-time doing what you loved and staying home with our children. It was the arrangement *you* wanted! If I were a man, I'd be applauded. Because I'm a woman, I'm a neglectful wife and mother!"

"I never said that. And I never would." Lucas's eyes fell away from hers. "It's just that . . . I found myself alone a lot."

And that's when Ange realized. It didn't matter that she was justified working the hours she did, that she was doing her best for her family. It didn't matter if she was right and he was wrong. Nothing they talked about or fought over made the blindest bit of difference. Charlie existed. The damage had been done.

"Erin used to jog in the park next to my studio. We became friends."

"I don't need to know details." Ange pressed her fingers into her temples. "God, at least spare me that."

"Okay. Well . . . our relationship only lasted about six months. We'd already ended things when she found out she was pregnant. All she wanted was for me to be a part of the child's life. And I agreed, as long as it didn't affect my relationship with you."

In a grotesque way, Ange was impressed. All these women prepared to hide Lucas's secrets, just to keep some part of him. All these women protecting him from facing the truth.

"Were you at Charlie's birth?"

"No," he said.

"Regular visitation?"

"We work it out on an informal basis."

"Do you pay her money for . . . child support?"

All at once, the logistics seemed vitally important. There must have been illicit visitation, hushed phone calls, birthday presents purchased and squirreled away. *Years* of deception on a daily basis.

"I pay her out of my own money from the studio. I have never used a cent of your money to support Charlie."

The martyrdom was back. It incensed Ange. "You understand that your money is *our* money, don't you? That everything you didn't bring home to me and the boys was coming out of our pockets? Unless you think that the money I earned was mine and mine alone?"

"I guess. I just . . . I felt better that way."

"Well. As long as you felt better." A thought suddenly occurred to her. "Does she call you Daddy?"

"She calls me Lucas. She thinks I'm a friend of the family."

"Do Erin's friends and family know you're her dad?"

"Her mum and her sister do. No one else."

"What was the plan for when she got older? When Charlie asked who her dad was? When she wanted her dad to come to ballet concerts and graduation ceremonies?"

Lucas sat on the coffee table, his face pressed to his palms. With each question, he sank a little lower. He was ashamed, obviously. Or maybe he was just annoyed? Annoyed that he was found out and that he had to have this conversation. "Erin said she'd make something up."

"How very accommodating of Erin," Ange said cattily, aware that she'd been just as accommodating when, for all these years, she'd closed her eyes and ears and focused on what she had instead of what she didn't.

When she was younger, Ange had always been so clear about what she would and wouldn't put up with in a relationship. At the top of the list was the Holy Grail—if he cheats, kick him to the curb. Back then everything had been so clear, so simple. Now, despite everything Lucas had done, nothing was clear.

He was a good father, that was the problem. Women were prepared to overlook just about anything for a man who was a good father. The opposite was equally true. There was no amount of love in the world that would have made her stay with Lucas if he wasn't good to her kids. Erin obviously felt the same. The irony was, she and Erin had a lot in common.

"Right," she said now, standing up decisively. "We're going on an adventure."

Both Will and Ollie looked up at her skeptically.

"Where's Dad?" Ollie said.

"Not here. This is an adventure for just the three of us. A Mum adventure."

They looked back at the Xbox.

"Come on, boys," she said. "It'll be great."

Will at least had the decency not to turn away. "What were you thinking?"

She had no idea. A meal in town, probably. Not the most *adventurous* adventure in the world, but it was all in the attitude. Wasn't that what Lucas always said?

"It's a surprise."

"Is Dad meeting us there?"

It was Will who asked, but Ollie turned around at this. They hadn't mentioned Lucas's absence last night but now Ange wondered if it had been on their minds. She looked at their gorgeous expectant faces. They were nearly young men. And they were babies.

"No," she admitted.

They both turned back to the Xbox.

"But we can have an adventure without him! It will be even better than one of Dad's adventures. And, there will most likely be pizza."

Ollie's body stilled, and Ange found herself holding her breath. He was thinking it over. Pizza was a big draw card. Even Lucas didn't often let them have pizza—he was too busy being sanctimonious, saying things like "Our bodies are our temples." Often, they'd all come home from an adventure sucking down green smoothies. *Cop that, Lucas,* she thought. *Mum's playing the pizza card. Just try and compete with that!*

"Can we order in?" Ollie said after a moment. "Then we can keep playing Xbox."

Will glanced over his shoulder, gauging Ange's reaction. He liked Ollie's idea, no doubt, but if she dug her heels in, Will would go along with her adventure. He might even pretend to have a good time. Sweet boy.

"Maybe when Dad gets back, we can go on the pizza adventure?" Will suggested, ever the diplomat. "That will be *even more* fun, don't you think?"

He smiled at Ange and she realized he was trying to spare her feelings. Was this how it would be when he came home from a weekend with his father? ("It was okay, but not that great," he'd say, while Ollie would unapologetically proclaim it "the BEST weekend EVER!!!!") She had a sudden urge to hug Will, cry, then hug him some more.

"What the heck," she said. "Let's order in. And let's get ice cream too."

The boys whooped, and Ange chose not to take it personally. They wanted their father, she understood that. *Of course* she understood.

She wanted him too.

44

ESSIE

Essie watched her mum in the corner of her hospital room, thumbing through a magazine. A cup of tea sat on the table beside her, her third in an hour. Only Essie's mother could drink tea in this heat. She'd arrived a little while ago with an armful of books, a lemon tart from Essie's favorite café, and a photo of Mia in a frame. (Essie hadn't printed or framed any photos of Polly yet. More proof she was a terrible mother and she *had* had another postpartum episode.)

Essie glanced at the photo of Mia on her bedside table. It was a preschool picture, and she was doing that peculiar wince she always did when she knew she was having her picture taken. (Ben did the exact same wince in photos—her mum had said it had all but ruined their wedding pictures, but Essie thought it was adorable—on Ben *and* Mia.) Mia's nose was wrinkled (she had

Essie's nose—small and ever-so-slightly turned up at the end) and her large forehead (lots of brains, everyone always said) was furrowed. Essie looked at her mother, who carried on reading, oblivious. Her mum had a strong, straight Roman nose. She had a smallish forehead and unremarkable chin. There wasn't much of a resemblance, Essie noticed, perhaps for the first time. No resemblance at all, actually.

Her mum must have felt her gaze, because at that moment, she looked up from her magazine. "Are you all right, honey? Do you need anything? A cup of tea?"

"Actually I wondered if you could tell me about my birth."

Her mum blinked, then flicked her magazine closed. "Well," she said. "This is out of the blue."

Essie rolled onto her side, propping her chin in her hand. She was, for reasons that weren't quite clear to her, trying to act nonchalant. "There's not much else to do around here, is there?"

"Yes, I suppose that's true." Barbara uncrossed and recrossed her legs. "Okay, let's see. I think I've told you it all. It was long. And painful." She smiled. "But all worth it, in the end."

"And . . . the moment they handed me to you?" Essie concentrated on speaking in a slow, offhand manner. "What was that moment like?"

"I guess . . . honestly, honey, I don't really remember. I was so tired at that point. I'm sure I was delighted."

"Surely you remember?" Essie pressed. "That first moment with your child?"

Her mum's eyes focused in the middle distance, searching for the memory. But how could she not know? Essie had been exhausted after giving birth to Mia and Polly. She had felt like she might *die* from the exhaustion. But she still remembered Mia's cross little face—so disturbed from being ejected from her comfortable resting place. And Polly—she was so calm and alert it was almost as if she'd rested up for the big day and it was exactly as she'd expected. Essie could have described every fold in each of their faces during their first moments together. Then again, their births weren't thirty years ago.

Barbara's gaze darted back and forth like she was scanning the insides of her brain. "I . . . you were . . . quiet, as I recall. A serious baby. You had . . . very long fingers. Piano-playing fingers. I said that to someone, I think. 'She'll have a career as a concert pianist.'"

Essie smiled. A concert pianist. She felt a wave of relief. Of course her mum remembered her birth. Because she *was* her mum. Isabelle's theory was nothing more than just that . . . a theory.

Her mum smiled and reopened her magazine. Essie glanced down at her fingers, admiringly and that's when she noticed they weren't particularly long at all.

An hour or so after her mum had left, Essie reached for her iPad. She had several messages waiting for her—from Ange, from Fran. *Several* from Isabelle. She ignored them all. Instead she opened up Google. She hesitated a second, then typed in GENETIC SEXUAL ATTRACTION.

Genetic sexual attraction (GSA) is sexual attraction between close relatives, such as siblings or half-siblings, a parent and offspring, or first and second cousins, who first meet as adults.

Essie shuddered. The idea was just so . . . sickening. Before she knew it, she was clicking on another link.

The phenomenon of genetic sexual attraction is sexual attraction between two close relatives. It's believed to be triggered when two family members are estranged early in life. Failing to form the family bonds which create a natural taboo around sexual bonding, they risk interpreting intense familiarity as sexual attraction.

Barbara Gonyo coined the term in 1980. She reported feeling overwhelmingly attracted to her own estranged son upon meeting him later in life. However, her son's unresponsiveness towards her attraction meant she never acted on it. Known as GSA, genetic sexual attraction is reported in a full 50 percent of reunion cases between related adults separated in their early years.

Essie closed down the browser quickly and put down the iPad. It was interesting enough, in a really creepy way, but it was of no relevance to her. She wasn't actually entertaining the idea that Isabelle could be her sister. She refused to believe that her mother would have snatched her. Her mother was the most honest, upstanding citizen she knew. She wouldn't so much as park in a No-Standing Zone, let alone steal a baby! No. It was ridiculous.

Although . . . what if something else was going on? A

terrible misunderstanding? Essie had heard stories of children who had been switched at birth . . . what if that had happened? What if her mum had given birth to another baby—a lovely, long-fingered baby—and somehow had ended up with Essie instead? It would explain everything. The reason why, at age thirty-two, Essie was suddenly attracted to a woman. The reason why just the thought of Isabelle brought about strong, physical urges she'd never had for any man.

Yes, it was possible. But it was a stretch. A long stretch. She thought of what Isabelle had said. *Our kinship index is greater than one point zero, which means we share DNA.* What did that even mean? After all, didn't everyone share DNA? Wasn't everyone related in the grand scheme of things?

It was a mistake. This whole thing was a mistake.

Essie lay down on the bed. She had about an hour before Ben arrived. She should get some rest. The doctors said rest was important. She could just buzz the nurse right now and ask for a sleeping tablet and they'd give it to her. Perhaps that's what she'd do.

She sat up again. But instead of reaching for the buzzer, she reached again for the iPad. She opened up a new browser and typed in: DNA TESTING. HOW ACCURATE IS IT?

45

BARBARA

Barbara was driving home from the hospital when she felt a sudden jolt—like her heart had missed a beat. Her skin started tingling, her breath became shallow and her thoughts began to race: fast and furious. *Am I having a heart attack? A stroke? A panic attack?* But the loudest, most prominent thought was . . .

Why do I not remember the doctor handing me Essie?

She pulled to the side of the road. She still appeared to have full use of both arms, which was good. She glanced in the mirror—neither side of her face had slackened. But she'd felt strangely off-kilter since leaving the hospital. Perhaps she was coming down with something? Lois had been ill with a nasty virus these last few days, maybe she'd caught it. She *did* have a slight ringing in her ears.

Suddenly she realized that ringing was her phone.

She scrambled for it in her purse on the passenger seat of the car. It was Lois.

"I was just thinking about you," Barb told her.

"I know," Lois said. "My ears were burning."

"That only happens when someone *talks* about you, Lo."

"I doubt it happens at all," Lois said, pausing to sneeze. She sounded dreadful—all stuffed up. If Barbara wasn't going through her own personal catastrophe she'd have gone straight over there with chicken soup and lemons.

"I fear I haven't been a very good friend these last few days," Barbara told her. "I should have dropped by with soup or something."

"Don't be ridiculous. You've had enough on your plate with Essie. Besides, you need to stay away. This thing's awful. It started as the stomach flu, now it's morphed into a dreadful cold. I'd feel terrible if you caught it."

"It might be too late," Barbara said. "I feel like I might be coming down with something already."

"Are you sick to your stomach?" Lois asked. "Headache? Sniffles?"

"No, not exactly."

"It might be this god-awful heat."

"Maybe," Barbara said. Her legs were stuck to the seat beneath her and the back of her hair was damp. But it felt like something more.

A comfortable silence drifted between them as Barbara tried to analyze what was going on with her. She had no symptoms. And yet, she felt terrible.

"Ah," Lois said, finally.

"What?" Barbara said. "What does *ah* mean?"

"You have a dreadful case of WMS."

"WMS?"

"Worried mother syndrome."

Barbara let her head fall back against the headrest. *Of course!* She was worried about Essie. What mother didn't become shaky and erratic when something was wrong with her child? That was all it was.

"I know you need to be there for Essie, Barb, but you need to look after yourself too. You're not as young as you used to be."

"Thanks a lot."

"It's the truth. I'm ordering you to go home and take a nap. Let Ben take care of the girls today."

"Ben *is* taking care of the girls today. You're probably right, I do need a nap. I haven't slept properly since this whole thing went down with Essie."

"Of course you haven't. You're a good mother. But it's time to look after you."

Barbara suddenly felt much better. She should have known a chat with her old friend would fix everything. "All right," she said. "I will."

"Right. I'll call you tomorrow to check in."

"Thanks. Oh, and Lo?"

Lois blew her nose again. "Mmm?"

"Do you remember the moment the doctor handed you Teresa after she was born?"

There was a pause. "Vaguely. She was covered in white gunky

stuff. I remember asking the doctor whether that was normal. I don't remember much else. Why?"

Once again, Lois had proven to be the best friend Barbara could've asked for. "No reason," she said. "No reason at all."

46

ISABELLE

"Are you just going to sit there looking out the window for the rest of your life?" Jules asked.

"Probably," Isabelle said, because maybe she *would* stay in this window forever. She couldn't focus on anything except Essie. She'd called and texted her a dozen times and, as expected, Essie hadn't responded. The whole thing had left her feeling flat and empty. After all these years she'd finally found Sophie—and she couldn't see her. And while she understood that Essie needed time to catch up, it still hurt.

Jules came and sat behind her in the armchair and began massaging her shoulders. "I don't know if I could do this without you, you know," she told him.

"You definitely couldn't."

She smiled, getting a glimmer of understanding of what it

must be like to be in a real relationship—a relationship where you shared things, talked things through, sorted things out. It was . . . nice. She was about to say so when, through the window, she noticed Barbara letting herself out of Essie's place, holding Mia's hand. Before she knew what she was doing, Isabelle was out of her seat and out the front door.

"Barbara!"

Barbara stopped and looked around.

"Oh, hello, Isabelle." She looked so nice, so normal. The quintessential woman next door who stole her sister. "I'm glad I ran into you. I'm sorry about yesterday. I don't know why Essie has decided not to see visitors. But it's probably for the best."

"Best for who?"

Isabelle hadn't meant to confront Barbara—she wanted to give Essie a chance to catch up first, but all at once, she couldn't help herself.

"I'm sorry?" Barbara said, her smile slipping.

"Who is it best for? You? Is it best for you that Essie doesn't see visitors? After all, you like to keep her separate from people, don't you? Isn't that what you've done all her life?"

Barbara blinked. "I . . . I'm sorry, I'm not sure what you mean."

"I think you do."

She laughed, a little disconcertedly. "I can assure you, I don't."

"I know Essie is not your daughter."

To her credit, Barbara did a good job of acting surprised. Amused even. She glanced around, as though she suspected Isabelle was playing some sort of joke on her. *"What?"*

"On June tenth, 1985, my sister Sophie Heatherington was

snatched from the Royal Sydney hospital. The same day Essie was born at the same hospital."

Barbara's head drew back into her neck, like a turtle into its shell. "Your sister was stolen from the Royal Sydney hospital?"

"And never found."

Barbara was at a loss for words. "I'm sorry, Isabelle. I can't imagine what that must have been like for your family."

"No, you *can't* imagine. If you could, you never would have stolen her."

Barbara scratched her head, perplexed. "Isabelle, why do you think your sister is Essie?"

"I have proof, Barbara. DNA evidence."

Barbara's frown deepened. "Well . . . I also have proof. I gave birth to her. I brought her home from the hospital as a newborn."

"A large newborn?" Isabelle said. "A nineteen-day-old newborn? And then, swiftly moved to Melbourne?"

Barbara hesitated. Then she shook her head. "Look, this is all very strange. But I can assure you I would never, ever, steal a baby. The idea is absolutely abhorrent. As a mother, I can understand the pain it would cause—"

"But you're *not* a mother! What did you do, fake a pregnancy? Was it to hold on to a man? Or did you lose a baby? Did you just have an insatiable need to be loved?"

"Gran," Mia said. "Why is Isabelle yelling at you?"

Barbara's hand found Mia's face and stroked it. But her gaze remained on Isabelle. Something had changed. She was hearing what Isabelle was saying. Still, there was no guilt on her face, only shock. She was either a wonderful actress, or something else was at play here.

"You say you have proof?" Barbara said, after a moment.

"Yes," Isabelle said. "DNA."

"And that DNA says I'm not her mother?"

"It says that I am Mia's aunt. Which means Essie is my sister."

"That's impossible," Barbara whispered. She muttered something softly, something Isabelle couldn't make out.

"Gran!" Mia said.

"Yes, darling?"

"I thought we were going to see Mummy."

"We are," she said. "Yes. We are."

She took Mia's hand and headed away from Isabelle without another word. The car was parked at the end of the drive and in stiff, robotic movements Barbara loaded Mia into her booster seat and then walked around to the driver side. From there, she held Isabelle's gaze above the car. It occurred to Isabelle then that it might not be a good idea to let Barbara drive away with Mia, but before she had a chance to do anything about it Barbara had got into the driver's seat and was driving away.

47

ESSIE

Essie got out of her bed and sat in the chair in the corner. In the last few hours it had occurred to her that it was strange for her to be in bed all day. After all, she wasn't sick, was she? She didn't *feel* sick. Stressed, maybe. Confused, certainly. But not sick.

You're not crazy, Essie. Was that what Isabelle had said to her? Essie had to admit, the idea that she wasn't crazy *was* appealing, if she didn't think too much about what it meant. That her mother *wasn't* her mother.

Her mum and Mia were due here any moment. Essie imagined having this conversation with her: *Okay, Mum, this is going to sound weird, but I'm not sure you are actually my mum. Would it be okay if you got a DNA test to confirm that we are related?*

Essie knew exactly how her mum would react. She would blink a few times, and then her head would retreat a few inches, giving her a frightening number of chins. Finally, she'd agree. She'd be baffled, of course, but she wasn't the obtuse type. If Essie wanted a DNA test, her mum would take one. It was possible she wouldn't even ask why.

She'd been coming around to the idea of having a sister. She didn't believe Isabelle's assertion that her mother had kidnapped her, of course, not for one minute. If she did happen to be Isabelle's sister, there would have to be another explanation. After all, Essie was thirty-two years old. In the old days hospital systems weren't like they were now. It would have been easy to mix two babies up. Didn't it happen all the time? But while the idea of being related to Isabelle appealed, Essie wasn't sure she could handle the idea of not being related to her mum.

She sighed and sat back in her chair. She glanced at the clock on the wall. It was later than she thought. Her mum should have been here with Mia over an hour ago.

Where *were* they?

48

ISABELLE

As Isabelle walked inside, she was still thinking about Barbara. She'd reacted so strangely. Not like she'd been caught in the act. More like she'd just found out something she didn't know. But how was that possible? Isabelle had pictured confronting the person who'd taken her sister a million times over the years, and never once had it involved a startled, confused-looking middle-aged woman shooing her granddaughter into the car.

Isabelle got down a glass from the cupboard, turning the whole thing over in her mind. She shouldn't have let Barbara take Mia while she was in that state. For all she knew, Barbara wasn't fit to drive. Isabelle thought about calling Essie, but she doubted she'd answer. She'd just decided to call Ben when she saw him through the window, walking down her path.

Isabelle made it to her front door at the same time as Ben.

"Ben," she said, throwing open the door. He looked spent. He was in his shorts and tank top and was sweaty, like everyone else. He looked like he'd been through the mill. Polly was in his arms. "Hello."

"Have you seen Barbara?" he said. "Or Mia?"

"Yes. I saw them this morning in your driveway. They were going to see Essie at the hospital." The first flutters of panic started in Isabelle's chest. "Why?"

"How long ago was that?"

"Uh, I guess . . . two hours? Three? Haven't they—"

"Shit." Ben turned and started walking back down the driveway without another word. Isabelle ran after him. The concrete was hot under her bare feet. "What's happened?"

"I can't find her and she's not answering her phone. Essie's worried she's had a car accident but I've traced the way to the hospital and there's no sign of any accidents. I'll have to start calling hospitals." Ben was walking purposefully down the path and Isabelle was on his heels. But hearing this, she fell back.

"This is all my fault."

Ben stopped short. "What do you mean, all your fault?" He half turned, both curious and impatient. He clutched Polly around her waist so that she dangled rather than rested on his hip. She gave an irritated squeak.

"I . . . may have upset Barbara when I saw her earlier," Isabelle said.

"Upset her how?" Isabelle could see from Ben's expression that Essie hadn't told him anything.

"I need to see Essie," she said.

"Isabelle, if you know something, can you please just spit it out? Barbara never does anything like this and I am worried."

"I just . . ."

Ben stared at her. He was usually so patient, so easygoing, but he looked like he was about to throttle her. *"What?"*

"I'm sorry to tell you this, Ben, but . . . I think Barbara may have kidnapped Mia."

49

ANGE

Lucas would be here any minute. Ange sat in the front room, trying to psyche herself up for it. He'd called an hour ago, saying he'd like to come to see the boys. The *boys*, he'd said; not her. After fourteen years of marriage, this was what they had been reduced to. This was what happened, she realized, when secrets came out. This was the reason she hadn't wanted to tell, hadn't wanted to know.

Lucas had been somber on the phone—almost reverent, as if he'd been calling to give his condolences after someone had died. The conversation had been stiff and awkward and had lasted a total of forty-seven seconds. Ange had wanted to make a joke, or tell him to stop and pick up some milk on his way over—do something that made them feel like *them* again. But then, they weren't them anymore, were they?

Over the past few days she'd formulated a loose sort of plan. She would stay in the house; Lucas would find somewhere else to live. Heck, she might even help him find a place! Part of her liked the idea that she would be the bigger person for the sake of her sons, another part of her longed to stand on an upper floor and hurl Lucas's belongings out of the window while screaming like a fishwife. She looked at the armchair opposite her, where Lucas normally sat. They'd bought these armchairs as a pair when they were newly married—the first items they'd actually *purchased* rather than inherited from their individual homes or from their parents. Ange remembered sitting in them in the store, side by side, talking about how one day they would sit in these chairs with a pair of toddlers in their laps—first their own kids, then their grandchildren. That was their future, she'd been so certain of it.

She was still sitting in her chair a few minutes later when she heard the knock at the door. That was a surprise. Lucas still had his key, why wouldn't he just let himself in? Perhaps he was setting a boundary. *I don't live here anymore. From now on, I knock.*

She opened the door. Lucas's cheeks were pink and it wasn't just the heat. He looked like he'd been crying. Another surprise. "Lucas," she said. "For goodness' sake. Come inside." She led him back into the front room. The boys were in the lounge room out back, engrossed in their game. Without being directed to do so, Lucas fell into *his* armchair and dropped his head into his hands.

"Come, now," she said. "You don't want the boys to see you like this."

"I'm sorry, Ange," he sobbed. "I'm so sorry."

Ange reluctantly put an arm around him. There were many

bizarre things about finding out your husband had an illegiti-mate child, she realized, not least of which was patting his back while he sobbed in your front room. "I never wanted this to hap-pen," he said. "I want to keep our family together."

"Shh," she said watching for the boys. She hadn't expected this level of upset. He hadn't been this upset after Josie. As much as she didn't want to buy into it, Ange found it giving her hope.

"This wasn't the first time, Lucas," she said, to herself as much as to him.

"I know," he said, looking up. His face was anguished. Infuri-atingly, it made him look even more handsome. "I can't explain it. I don't know what's wrong with me."

I don't know what's wrong with me. The words were surprisingly healing. It occurred to Ange that for years, she'd felt like Lucas's infidelity meant something was wrong with *her.*

"You never did anything to deserve a husband like me. You were so . . . so—"

"I wasn't pregnant."

Lucas stilled. Even his tears appeared to halt halfway down his cheeks. "What?"

"With Ollie. I told you I was pregnant because I knew you were going to leave me for Josie."

Lucas scoffed, dismissing her admission out of hand. "But you *were* pregnant. We *had* Ollie."

"Remember how much sex we had after our reunion, Lucas? I got pregnant pretty quickly. Within a few weeks."

Lucas stared at her. She could tell from his face that he still didn't get it. Of all his wonderful qualities, Lucas had never been quick.

"So you weren't pregnant," he said slowly. "But you said you were so I wouldn't leave you."

Congratulations, darling, she thought. *You finally got there.*

"Yes."

It was surprisingly therapeutic, airing all these truths. Ange exhaled back into her chair, feeling the weight of the secret leave her. Lucas stood up and walked to the mantel.

"Okay," he said turning to face her. "I forgive you. And I have to ask . . . would you consider . . . forgiving me?"

Lucas didn't look quite so desperate anymore, Ange noticed. Her admission had been therapeutic for him too. After all, they were equals again now, weren't they? He'd lied; she'd lied. Now they could bury the hatchet. Even-stevens. She knew that was what he was thinking, because she knew everything about Lucas. Ange thought back to the day in the store. The two plaid chairs side by side. The imaginary children and grandchildren in their laps. She thought about forgiveness. How much was too much in a marriage? How much was not enough?

Ange heard the thunder of feet in the hallway.

"Dad!" Ollie cried, tearing into the room. "Will! Dad's here!"

A mass of head rubs and sweaty hugs followed while Ange looked on. If the boys noticed their father's face was tearstained, they didn't show it—they were too busy telling him the level they'd made it to on the Xbox. Little narcissists.

"Can we have pizza for dinner?" Ollie asked him. "Mum let us have pizza yesterday."

He met Ange's eyes over the tops of their heads. She might have been imagining it, but it looked like he was giving her an admonishing look. "Two nights in a row?" he said. "That sounds a bit—"

"Great idea," Ange said. "Hawaiian for me."

Ollie and Will gave each other the side-eye. "Hawaiian? But—you and Dad always get Greek salad or fish. You never eat pizza."

They weren't wrong. Ange tried to remember the last time she'd eaten pizza. Probably back in college. Definitely sometime before she'd met Lucas. Before she started drinking the Kool-Aid about her body being her temple. Before she started trying to maintain a body that would stop her husband from straying. Fat lot of good it had done her.

"Well, guess what?" she said. "I eat pizza now."

50

BARBARA

The road in front of Barbara was hazy from the heat. The wind had picked up. Barbara could feel it all around them, pushing and pressing the car as though trying to sweep them off the road. Barbara glanced at Mia in the rearview mirror, staring boredly at her lap, fiddling with the hem of her skirt. Her features—her reddish hair, her clear blue eyes, her delicate build—were so at odds with Barbara's own. It was so obvious and yet, Barbara hadn't paid much attention to it before.

As she drove, Barbara cast her mind back to the day she found out she was pregnant with Essie. She'd had two pregnancies before, both of which had ended in miscarriage during the first trimester, but this one, she was certain, was going to stick. She'd been married for three years by then. The first year had been average, the second worse. The third year had been unbearable.

She'd met John at a casino at 1 A.M., a few weeks after her father's death. John had just won a game of cards and he'd insisted on buying her a drink. Their wedding, six months later, was a knee-jerk reaction to losing her parents', she knew that now. She wasn't used to being alone, and the desire to create a new family to replace the old was stronger than she imagined.

They lost the car first, on a horse that "just couldn't lose." Next was the house they'd bought with her inheritance. They ended up renting a one-bedroom apartment. She questioned the logic of a one-bedroom when they were about to have a baby but John said they'd make do. The yearning for her parents was unrelenting. Her mother would have brought her home and cared for her during her pregnancy, and her father would have given John a stern word, then taught him how to better manage money. They may have even loaned them money to buy another modest house, in exchange for letting them oversee the finances. It would have been a learning experience and they would have done better in the future.

But Barbara's parents weren't there.

John wasn't there a lot either. He'd been emotionally absent for most of their marriage, but as her pregnancy progressed he was physically absent a lot too. *Everyone* seemed to be absent. Barbara had had friends earlier in her life, but one by one, she stopped visiting them, instead spending all of her time holed up in the apartment, worrying. She worried about what would happen if they were evicted from the apartment for not paying the bills. She worried she'd have nowhere to bring home her baby. It started to get inside her mind, the worry. The only thing that got her through the worry was the knowledge that a baby was coming.

She found a crib for the baby at the charity shop, a few items of clothing, and a teddy bear. She set it all up in a corner of the bedroom. Some days she'd just sit in the bedroom and look at the things she'd set up. It comforted her, somehow.

John had disappeared by the time Barbara went into labor. She'd been getting ready to go to bed when she felt the first contraction— so strong it took her breath away. By the time her taxi arrived to take her to the hospital, she couldn't talk.

"It's early," she remembered telling the nurse. "Thirty-five weeks."

The nurse nodded. There hadn't been time to fill out the paperwork, to talk . . . to do anything but push. It didn't take long. Barbara tried once again to remember the way Essie looked when she was placed in her arms, but she couldn't. She remembered other things. The averted eyes of the hospital staff. The coldness of the room. She remembered the feeling of the baby in her arms, the barely-there weight against her hospital gown.

Why couldn't she remember her face?

And just like that, the face started to come. Perfect closed eyes. Bright red, blistered skin and deep purple lips. She was tiny. Too tiny.

"Why . . . why does she look like this?" she'd asked.

"Maceration," the doctor said. "The epidermis has started to separate from the dermis. Judging by the color of her skin, she probably died four to six hours ago in utero, around the time you went into labor. I'm sorry but your baby was stillborn."

Stillborn.

Barbara swerved off the road and onto a side street, pulling up sharp.

Your baby was stillborn.

No. That wasn't right. Barbara glanced in the rearview mirror. She was there in the backseat. Essie was right there. She wasn't stillborn. She was healthy and perfect, a toddler now.

"Where are we?" she asked. She looked hot and bothered and on the verge of sleep.

"Sorry, honey. Mummy just had a horrible daydream."

Essie looked puzzled. "Did she?"

"We're going home now, baby," Barbara told her. But when she looked around, nothing looked familiar. How far had she drifted while daydreaming? Was she even in Sydney anymore?

She got out her road map and tried to get her bearings.

When I got home from the hospital, everything was exactly as I'd left it. A half-drunk glass of water sat on the end table; my pajamas lay on the floor of the hallway where they'd been discarded. I came inside and set your basket on the sofa. Your eyelids flickered in sleep and I felt a sense of peace. I wasn't alone anymore.

John had been gone for three months. The other woman's name was Laurel. She was his hairdresser, of all things, and I knew her. Whenever John went in to get his hair cut, I always poked my head in and said "not too short," and Laurel laughed. Then, as I headed off to the greengrocers, Laurel always waved at me through the window, her shaving blade still in her hand. I should have known that was ominous.

Laurel wasn't especially attractive. She had brassy-blond hair and she always seemed to be wearing a floral dress covered by a black PVC apron. I had never looked closely enough to notice whether Laurel had an ample bosom or nice hips under than apron. John obviously had.

"But I'm pregnant," I'd told John, when he'd made the confession. He knew that, of course, since I reminded him every day. Not to mention the fact that for the first time I actually had a bump. I called John the day you were born and told him he had a daughter. He'd seemed pleased and said he'd put an announcement in the paper. But there was no request to visit. No offer of financial assistance.

If it weren't for Esther, my generous aunt in Melbourne, giving me rent money, I wouldn't have survived as long as I had. It seemed as good a reason as any to name you after her.

That day as I sat in my apartment, I lifted you out of your basket and placed you to my breast. When you were finished, I realized you'd need a fresh diaper, which meant a trip to the store. I hadn't expected you for a few more weeks so I was unprepared. But the idea of a trip to the store filled me with anxiety. The only time I'd been out of the house in the past few months was to go to the hospital and to go to the grocery store. It was at the grocery store a month ago that I'd run into Laurel. She'd smiled at me for a quick moment before recognition had come to her face. I'd abandoned my shopping cart immediately and run back to the car.

I needed to call Esther. She'd offered to come to Sydney to help out for a few weeks after the baby was born. Without any other help, I had no choice but to accept her offer. Or did I? After I finished feeding, I could pick up the phone and call Esther . . . or, I could get on a bus to Melbourne. In Melbourne

I wouldn't have to worry about who I'd bump into in the street. I wouldn't have to worry about what people thought. I could make new friends. Start over somewhere a long way from here where no one would know us.

51

ESSIE

Essie looked up when she saw movement in her doorway. But it wasn't her mum and Mia standing there, it was Ben and Isabelle. Somewhere in the back of Essie's mind, it struck her that they were an odd pair to arrive at her door together, but she was too worried about her mum and Mia to address it.

"No word from Mum?" she said.

Ben shook his head.

"Well . . . where's Polly?" she asked.

"I left her with Ange."

Essie felt her panic rise a notch. If Ben had left Polly with Ange then obviously he was worried too. "Well, I think we should call the—"

"I've called two hospitals," Ben said. His facial muscles were tight, she noticed, making him look older. "And I'll keep calling.

But the road is clear between home and the hospital. And your mum would have had ID on her, someone would have called us."

"What about Lois?" Essie suggested. "Have you tried her?"

"I don't have her number."

"I have it." Essie retrieved the phone number and gave it to Ben and he walked into the hallway to make the call.

"Are you all right?" Isabelle asked Essie when he was gone.

Essie wrung her hands. "It's so unlike Mum to disappear like this."

"Is it?"

Essie looked at Isabelle for a long moment. "Isabelle, I know you think that Mum kidnapped me, but it's just not possible. I accept that it's possible that we are sisters, and I want to take my own DNA test to confirm this. But if we are, it's not because Mum kidnapped me. If anything it's—"

"I confronted her."

Essie blinked. "You confronted *my mum*?"

"I was going to wait until you had a chance to digest the news, but then I saw her outside my house and I couldn't hold back. I just—"

"And?" Despite Essie's confidence that her mum was an innocent party, she had to admit she was curious. "What did she say?"

"She denied it," Isabelle admitted. "But she seemed . . . confused. When I told her I had proof she seemed very rattled."

"Rattled?" Essie said. Her mum was never rattled. She might have laughed (politely, of course). She'd have been puzzled as to why Isabelle thought she'd kidnapped a baby—who wouldn't be? Essie imagined her inviting Isabelle in (for tea!) so they could sort the whole misunderstanding out. But she wouldn't have been *rattled*. "How do you mean?"

"She sort of glazed over," Isabelle continued. "Then she put Mia in the car and left. That was a few hours ago."

"Lois hasn't heard from her today," Ben said, reentering the room. He tossed the phone down onto the bed with more force than necessary.

"Mom seemed rattled?" Essie repeated. "And then she put Mia in the car and we haven't seen her since?"

Isabelle looked like she might cry. Ben pressed a hand against his forehead. A nurse peeked her head around the door, assessed the situation, then ducked away again.

"You're telling me my mother is a child abductor," Essie said slowly. She was looking at Ben and Isabelle, but she was talking to herself. "And now she's missing and she has my daughter?"

Ben looked from Essie to Isabelle and back again. Finally he reached for the phone again.

"All right," he said. "I'm calling the police."

52

FRAN

No good will come out of this, Fran told herself, as the phone rang in her ear. *No good at all.* And yet, she continued to wait on the line.

Nigel was gone. He'd left a few days ago, ostensibly on business. It was good timing, he said. They both needed time and space, and this trip—to a conference in Brisbane, would give them that. Fran didn't know when he was coming back, or *if* he was coming back. All she knew was that she was bereft without him. So was Rosie. Even Ava seemed down in the dumps.

Ange hadn't returned her calls. If Essie hadn't been in the hospital, she might have tried her. She couldn't speak to any of her former work colleagues, for obvious reasons. But there was one person she *hoped* she could count on. If only she'd pick up the phone.

"Hello?"

Fran cleared her throat. "Mum? It's me."

"Francesca?" There was a pause. Fran pictured her, making eyes with her father, showing her surprise. "What is it? Is everything all right?"

In her defense, it wasn't a ridiculous question. Fran and her mother didn't call each other to chat. They didn't bother with casual niceties or "catching up." They spoke on the phone to make arrangements or report facts. "Just a reminder that it's Rosie's birthday on Monday." "Did Dad get the results of his blood work?" "I passed my final exams." Fran had always told herself it was because they were all busy people; too busy to make idle chitchat. But the fact was, these last few months, Fran had plenty of time to talk. She just didn't have a lot of people to talk *to*.

"Actually everything isn't all right."

Her mother sucked in a breath. *Good girl, Fran,* she thought. *Spit it out.* This was, after all, the reason for her call. She was sick of keeping things hidden. It might have preserved her dignity and her façade, but it stopped people from being able to support her. And now she needed support.

"Oh no. Is it one of the kids?"

Yes, Fran thought. *It's Ava. She might not be Nigel's.*

"Do you have a moment to chat, Mum?"

"Of course. I mean . . . I'm going out in a few minutes. I have a do at your father's golf club. But if there's something wrong—"

"I cheated on Nigel. And Ava might not be his."

Fran held her breath. She had never said anything like this to her mother before. They'd never talked about anything shameful or negative. Never shared a laugh about the indignity of slipping down the stairs at work, or failing a math test, or missing out on a job that she really wanted. They saved their conversations for things that had gone well. The tests she had *passed*. The jobs she had *gotten*.

"Is this . . . true?" she said finally.

"Yes. I'm sorry to dump it on you. I know it must be a shock."

"It . . . certainly *is*."

Her mum had been caught off guard, clearly. High achievers didn't have problems like this. Or if they did, they didn't talk about them. Fran imagined her mother sinking into the blue-and-white gingham chair in the hallway off the kitchen, slipping her feet out of her kitten heels, and taking out her pearl earring on the phone side.

But when she finally spoke again, she sounded like she'd recovered slightly. "Okay. You'll need a paternity test. I don't think they're hard to organize. If Ava is Nigel's, he'll be far more inclined to forgive you. You'll be able to move on and pretend this never happened."

Something about her tone got Fran's back up. "And if she's not Nigel's? What then?"

"Well, I don't know, Francesca," she snapped. "Let's just hope that she is. You're a silly, silly girl, you know that? Why would you go and have an affair?"

But she wasn't asking, not really. It was a shame because Fran wanted to tell her. *He was depressed, Mum. It was horrible. Did Dad ever get depressed? How did you handle it? If you had shared your difficulties with me, instead of just your successes, I might have been in a better position to navigate them myself.*

"I'm not going to tell your father about this," her mum said.

"And you should keep it to yourself too. You don't want people knowing your business or gossiping about you."

"Mummy?" Rosie said. "Ava's hot."

Who isn't? Fran thought. She'd left the air-conditioning off and instead had the fan going, as a nod to Nigel, even in his absence. But enough was enough. She grabbed the remote and switched on the unit.

"I don't care who knows my business," Fran said. "Nigel knows, it's not like it's a secret."

"You need to protect yourself, Fran. Not to mention Nigel and the children. People talk."

"Support," she said. "That's what I need, Mum. That's why I called. Clearly it was a waste of a phone call."

"How *dare you*? How dare you call me up and start acting like a teenager after you've gotten yourself into this mess? I expected better from you, Francesca. You're a smart, capable young woman."

"Smart, capable women make mistakes."

"Not these kinds of mistakes."

But the biggest mistake she'd made was expecting her mum to be any different. She wouldn't make that mistake again.

"She's still hot, Mummy."

Fran glanced over at Ava, lying on a blanket. She didn't look right. Fran walked closer.

"I don't know what you want me to say," her mum was saying "You're not a little girl anymore. I can't swoop in and fix this . . ."

Rosie was kneeling beside Ava, blowing on her face. Trying to cool her down. Fran dropped to her knees. Ava's eyes were not closed and not open, just cracked open slightly. Fran picked her up. She *was* hot. Too hot.

Something crawled over her heart.

"Marriage is hard work," her mother was saying, "but the harder it gets the harder you . . ."

Fran hung up the phone and called the ambulance.

53

BARBARA

Barbara stopped at a fuel station a few hours later. When she and Essie got out of the car, the heat hit them like a warm, wet cloth.

"Gran," Essie said. "I'm tired. I want to go home."

She chuckled. "What did you call me?"

"Gran."

"Gran?" Barbara repeated, incredulous. "I'm not that old, am I?"

Essie's face crumpled up, confused. She opened her mouth to say something else, but Barbara beat her to it.

"We'll be home soon," Barbara told her. "Let's go pee and then I'll get you a candy bar."

This got her moving, of course. In the restroom, there was another mum with twin boys who were peeing into the second toilet, attempting a "sword fight." The mother smiled at Barbara, a little embarrassed.

"Boys!" she said, rolling her eyes.

"I'd love a boy," Barbara told her. "I've only got Essie so far. Maybe next time. It would be nice to have a pigeon pair."

The woman frowned at the same time as Essie shouted: "Finished, Gran."

Barbara opened the door and started plucking stiff sheets from the paper dispenser. "So it's still Gran, is it?"

"What?" Essie slid off the toilet, her underwear still around her ankles.

Barbara glanced at the other mother and shrugged. "Could be worse, I guess. She could be calling me Grandpa." She started wiping her. "My name isn't Gran, Essie. It's Mummy."

Essie looked perplexed. "I'm not *Essie*. I'm Mia!"

Barbara pulled up Essie's underwear. The little boys from the next cubicle were washing their hands and getting pink soapsuds everywhere.

"All right, all right," Barbara said, defeated. "I'm Gran. And you're Mia."

Essie washed her hands and Barbara shot the other mum a look that she hoped said "we're in this motherhood thing together." But the other mother looked as puzzled as Essie.

Barbara sighed—*I give up!*—and left the restroom with Essie to pay for the fuel.

"Would you like to choose a candy bar, Ess?"

Barbara was surprised when Essie narrowed her eyes, instead of squealing in delight. "STOP CALLING ME THAT!" she cried. "I. Am. Not. Essie. And you are GRAN!" She stamped her feet, quite worked up now. She must have been exhausted from the long drive. But Barbara was exhausted too. And she'd had enough of these games.

"Fine. If you're going to be silly, no candy bar."

Barbara paid for the fuel as Essie went boneless on the floor, wailing that she wanted a candy bar.

"Where are you headed?" the cashier asked.

Barbara watched Essie rolling about on the floor. "Sydney."

"Not today you're not," he said. "The Hume Highway's closed. Bushfires."

Barbara groaned. Essie continued to cry that she wanted to go home, she wanted her mummy. It was too hot and Barbara was at the end of her tether.

"Well," she said. "I guess we're going back to Melbourne for tonight."

She picked up Essie—an almost impossible act with a flailing toddler—and struggled to the car. She expected a sympathetic look from the mother of the two boys, but she didn't get it. *All very well for her to be judgmental now that her boys had covered the bathroom in pink detergent!*

Barbara had made it halfway to the car when she lost her grip and Essie wriggled from her arms. She ran back toward the shop, probably to claim her candy bar, and Barbara reached for her, catching the back of her T-shirt and pulling tight. She'd had enough of this. Essie let out a high-pitched wail.

The woman with the two boys and a man who looked like a truck driver came toward them.

"Are you all right, sweetheart?" the woman asked Essie.

Barbara couldn't believe it. Another mother taking the side of a tantrumming toddler? Where was the solidarity? The woman squatted down in front of Essie and asked. "Do you know this lady?"

Before Barbara could respond that *of course she knows me, I am her mother,* the truck driver said to Barbara: "Please let the little girl go, ma'am. You're hurting her."

Barbara was absolutely indignant. She was being shamed for trying to teach her daughter some manners. She was about to let go of the T-shirt, because what else could she do, but in the face of these strangers, Essie had backed toward Barbara anyway. Clearly the mother who deprived her of candy was the lesser of the evils when compared to strangers.

"Do you know her?" the woman asked Essie again.

Now Essie nodded. "She's my Gran."

Barbara sighed.

"She's your grandma?" the man repeated, at the same time as the woman said to Barbara: "Are you feeling all right, ma'am? You seem a little confused."

Barbara was done. She grabbed Essie and shoved her into the backseat of the car, holding her down with one hand and buckling her in with the other.

"Ma'am," the man said again. The woman, Barbara noticed now, was pointing her phone at them. Barbara ignored them both and put the car into gear, heading back to Melbourne.

54

ISABELLE

Talking to the police proved to be a difficult affair. Apparently they weren't inclined to issue a red or amber alert for a child who had gone missing for just a few hours and was under the care of her loving grandmother. Isabelle scoffed at that. Explaining that Mia's grandmother was a baby snatcher wasn't straightforward, given that Isabelle's proof wasn't legally binding, and even if it was, Barbara hadn't been convicted of anything. If Isabelle's story was true, they said (with heavy inference that it wasn't), it was far more likely to have been a case of the switched-at-birth type of situation.

They were speaking with Ben and Essie now, but in the meantime, they said, they'd be keeping an eye out for Barbara's car, and checking for car accidents.

"In most cases like this," a jolly, slightly overweight copper with a handlebar moustache told them, "we find the people involved, unharmed, having taken a spontaneous outing and then had their cell phone run out of batteries."

Essie and Ben hung on that. "Yes," Ben said. "Of course that's what's happened. Mia probably begged Barbara to take her to the zoo, and we all know Barbara is powerless against Mia. They probably headed out on the excursion and lost track of time. And Barb isn't one to keep her phone fully charged, is she?"

"Never," Essie agreed. "They may have even run out of fuel somewhere. We'll hear from them soon."

Isabelle understood why they needed to believe this, but she didn't share their confidence. They hadn't seen Barbara's face cloud over when she'd confronted her about Essie, as though she'd suddenly awoken from a dream.

Then again, perhaps they were right. No one would be happier than Isabelle if Barbara walked in that door right now with Mia. After all, Isabelle had come to Melbourne to try and get her sister back—not to start this nightmare all over again for another family. She'd never forgive herself if something happened to Mia. Worse, Essie would never forgive her.

"Isabelle."

Jules appeared in the doorway. She'd called him half an hour earlier to tell him what had happened, and his response had simply been: "What is the address?" Now he was here. She walked into his arms.

"What can I do?" he said at the same time as Essie gasped.

The policeman with the handlebar moustache was holding out his phone and Essie was looking at it. Isabelle went to her side. It was a low-quality video at what looked to be a gas station.

Barbara held Mia by the neck of her T-shirt. There was something about her face—a blankness. Her jaw was hard and tight. She muttered something irritably to whoever was holding the camera then grabbed Mia uncharacteristically roughly, then shoved her into her car seat, buckling her in without care or concern.

"This is your mother and daughter?" the policeman asked Essie. It was Ben, finally, who confirmed that it was. Essie was too stunned to say anything at all.

"Where are they?" Isabelle asked him.

"The video was taken at a fuel station near Albury, headed for Sydney."

"Albury?" Ben cried.

Essie slumped back against the bed. Ben reached for her but she pushed him away. She glanced around the room and finally her eyes landed on Isabelle. Isabelle opened her arms, and, without hesitation, Essie fell into them.

55

FRAN

The emergency room was full, but Ava was seen straight away. Fran couldn't decide if that was a good thing or not. She wanted Ava to be seen quickly, of course. But if it was just a minor temperature, surely she wouldn't have been rushed through like this? Wasn't she always hearing stories about people waiting hours in emergency to be seen by a doctor?

Fran stood in a hospital room with Rosie by her side, while a bunch of people in hospital scrubs stripped Ava naked and examined her. Fran presumed they were doctors, but who knew? The doctors, nurses, and other hospital staff all seemed to dress the same. *Be doctors*, she willed them. *Be the best doctors around*.

She remembered the feeling of Ava's skin when she'd picked her up. So so hot. Burning hot. She'd had to follow the ambulance in her car because she couldn't find anyone to watch Rosie, and they weren't both allowed to travel in the back of the ambulance. It was a five-minute drive to the nearest hospital, and as she drove, questions swirled in her mind. How had she not noticed Ava was so ill? Hadn't she been fine an hour earlier? She'd been a little irritable maybe, but who wasn't in this heat?

It was her fault. She'd missed something, clearly. She was the mother, it was her job to stay on top of things. As she stood in the corner of the hospital room, she peppered hospital staff with questions.

"What's wrong with her?"

"Will she be all right?"

"What can I do?"

"Is this my fault?"

Rosie had her own stream of questions.

"What are they doing to Ava?"

"Will they give her medicine?"

"What kind of medicine does she need?"

Nigel had bought Rosie a book a few months back, *The Human Body*. She'd been obsessed with it, before she'd started her puzzle phase, and had taken to reciting little facts from it, like "The human body has two hundred and six bones." She probably understood the human body better than any other three-year-old. Perhaps she understood it too well. Clearly the hospital staff thought so, because after a minute or so, one of the people in scrubs came over and squatted down in front of her. "Do you like secrets?"

Fran looked down at her. It occurred to her that she didn't really know whether Rosie liked secrets. She may have thought they were silly. That information was for sharing. Which, when Fran thought about it, was a good philosophy.

But Rosie nodded.

"I can only tell you if you promise not to tell anyone else."

Rosie promised.

"Okay. There's a secret stash of Popsicles in the freezer in the maternity section. Some of the women like to have one while they're in labor. Would you like me to find someone to take you there?"

Rosie broke into a grin. Fran felt appreciative and at the same time suspicious. Why was this person getting rid of them? Were they annoying the staff with all their questions? Or was it that they were going to do something terrible to Ava, and didn't want them to see? Ava looked so tiny, lying there on the hospital bed. The last thing Fran wanted was to leave her in this room all alone. But what could she do? Fran supposed she couldn't send Rosie to the maternity section alone.

This was why you needed two parents, she realized.

"Okay," she said. "Let's go."

A few minutes later they were following a hospital administrator to the maternity section. "You can use your cell phone if you have any family or friends to call," she said to Fran as they walked. Fran tried not to read too deeply into that, but how could she not? If everything was fine, would they be sending her for Popsicles and suggesting she make phone calls?

As they walked, Fran fiddled with her phone. Who could she call? The list of potential people in was worryingly short. She quickly ruled out her mother. She'd probably be at her golf function now, cracks forming in her wide smile as she insisted that everything in her life was perfect. She might have tried to call Essie, but obviously she wasn't going to be able to help her today. She could call Ange, she supposed. But there was only one person she wanted to call, and it was the one person she wasn't sure she should call. Still, before she knew it, she was dialing the number.

Nigel answered on the second ring.

"Hey," he said. "I'm just heading into a—"

"I'm in the hospital," she said. "It's Ava."

Her stomach clenched. If it were Rosie, she knew, he'd already be on his way. With Ava, she wasn't so sure.

"What happened?" he said urgently.

She filled him in on the details, which were sparse. She was hot. Listless. Her lips were dry. Nigel took it all in with comforting urgency. She felt more reassured than when she was with the doctors. He asked which hospital they were in. He asked if she was all right, if Rosie was. And then he said the words she'd been longing to hear.

"Sit tight. I'll be there as soon as I can."

56

ANGE

Ange was driving to Summit Oaks. Polly Walker was strapped into the backseat in Ollie's old infant car seat. She'd spent the morning looking after Polly. It had been quite lovely, having girl time. It seemed ridiculous now that she'd spent so much time feeling resentful about not having a daughter when there were four little girls right across the street from her. She could have girl time any time she wanted, all she had to do was ask. In fact, if she had asked, perhaps everyone would have been better off.

She *would* ask from now on, she decided.

Ben had asked her to bring Polly in to see Essie and Ange had been grateful for the task. Lucas was back in the house for now, and while Ange was being civil, every now and again she'd think about Erin and have a bitchy outburst. A classic case of Betrayal Tourette's. ("Yes, just grab some milk, bread, and an illegitimate child from the supermarket, thanks so much.") She knew it was juvenile, but for now it made her feel better and that was all she cared about.

When she arrived at the hospital, a nurse pointed Ange in the direction of Essie's room. She found Ben in the doorway. His face was ashen and his hair was all mussed as if he'd been running his fingers through it. When he caught a glimpse of Polly he grabbed her, cradling her as if she were a much smaller baby.

"Is everything all right?" Ange asked.

For a moment, Ben didn't answer, just rested his forehead against Polly's. After what felt like an eternity, he glanced back toward the room. Essie was propped upright, her head on Isabelle's shoulder. A policeman stood beside them.

"I'm not sure."

Ange was curious, but she forced herself not to ask. She had enough going on in her own life without prying into other people's. "Is there anything I can do?" she asked instead.

"I wish there was," he said, looking into the room. Ange was quiet for a moment. Ben's eyes remained on Essie. "I just thought it would give her a boost to see Polly. Thanks for bringing her in."

He gave Ange a nod of thanks, and took Polly to Essie's side. He was right: the moment Essie laid eyes on her she visibly lifted. She cradled Polly next to her heart, the exact way Ben had. Ben slid in beside them and put his arms around them both.

Ange knew Ben wasn't perfect. Essie had told her about how he left his sweaty gym clothes on the bathroom floor, how he often worked late, how he rarely did the grunt work of the parenting. Ange remembered feeling quietly smug. After all, Lucas was faultlessly tidy, he was always around, and you'd be hard-pressed to find a more hands-on dad. But Ben had something going for him, Ange realized now, something that obliterated everything else.

He only had eyes for Essie.

57

BARBARA

Barbara snaked through the streets of St. Kilda, wondering what to do. She'd been forced to head all the way back to Melbourne because of the bushfires, but what had she been doing here in the first place? And why didn't she remember coming here?

Maybe she had Alzheimer's? As horrible as that would be, at least it might be some kind of explanation for what was going on. She didn't want to admit it, but the longer she drove in this heat, the more frightened she became. She pulled the car to the side of the road and tried to decide where to go. A hotel? A bed-and-breakfast?

"Can we go on a twam ride, Gran?" Essie asked. She pointed a chubby finger at the tram that wove down the street they were on. "Please?"

Her eyes were two shining beacons.

"Not right now, honey. I have to figure out where we need to go first."

Barbara looked around. Nothing looked familiar, but then again, she hadn't spent a lot of time in Melbourne before. Her aunt Esther lived in Melbourne, but it had been a while since Barbara had visited her. Barbara glanced over her shoulder. There was a tourist information booth a few meters up, on the opposite side of the road. She'd go there, she decided. They'd know what to do. They might even have information on the bushfires and tell her when she could get back on the road to Sydney.

"Please, Gran?" Essie said. "Please can we go on the twam?"

"No, sweetie," she said. "Just stay here for a moment. I'm going to talk to the people at that booth."

And she got out of the car.

Two minutes later she got back into the car with the name of a hostel and a bushfire update.

"Is your seat belt on?" she asked, turning around. But Essie wasn't there.

"Essie?" Barbara twisted to look in both foot wells. They were empty. "Essie!"

Panic rose in Barbara's throat. She jumped out of the car and scanned the sidewalk but there was no sign of a child in either direction. Suddenly a car's brakes screeched. Barbara gasped. Essie was on the road; a car hurtled toward her. It happened in an instant. Barbara stepped off the pavement and bolted, narrowly missing a car coming in the opposite direction. She caught Essie around the waist and heaved them both off the road and onto the tram tracks. This was the superhuman strength mothers talked about having when they saw their child in danger. This was it.

We're okay, she thought. *We're okay.*

On the tram tracks, they stood, catching their breath—their hearts pounding as one.

"Gran," Essie said, sobbing.

"Shh. It's all right," Barbara said. The sun beat down on them. She needed to get them both to a hotel and give Essie a nice cool bath. Some clean clothes. And a nice long sleep.

She lifted Essie safely onto the island platform and that's when she heard the commotion start up again. More brakes screeching. *What now?* Barbara thought. "Ma'am!" came a voice. Barbara glanced around.

And then the tram came.

58

ESSIE

As she rested her head against the wall of her hospital room, Essie had an overwhelming feeling that this was penance. She'd left her daughter once before—in a park of all places—and as punishment, she'd been taken from her. It was karma, pure and simple. Ben was pacing the hall with Polly and Isabelle stood by the window. The police had left, or maybe they were out in the hallway, Essie didn't know. She found it hard to concentrate on what everyone else was doing when her little girl was missing.

Missing. Essie had no idea how to react to that word. It wasn't as though Mia had been snatched by a stranger. She was with her grandmother, for heaven's sake! Then again, Essie didn't know if that was true. Was Barbara her grandmother? Was she Essie's mother?

Would she ever see Mia again?

The police seemed to think she would. They reassured her with all sorts of stories—*misunderstandings!*—involving children who were returned home by the end of the day. They were confident this was one of those cases. But Essie was anything but confident. She wanted nothing more than to find her mother, to sort this whole situation out. At the same time, a thought hovered at the edges of her consciousness—if her mother *was* capable of taking Essie, and never returning her—*if*—what did that mean for Mia?

Essie let out an involuntary sob. She felt Isabelle stand and move to her side at the same time as there was a tap at the door, and a policeman walked in.

Essie sat up. "Is there news?"

"Yes, ma'am."

Essie scanned his face. It wasn't the relieved, delighted face of an officer coming to tell a mother everything was all right. She wasn't sure what kind of face it was. "Have you found Mia?" she asked tremulously.

"We have."

Essie felt a flicker of hope. "Is she all right?"

"She's absolutely fine. Not a scratch on her."

Ben melted at the news. He fell to his knees, with Polly still in his arms. But Essie kept looking at the police officer.

"And my . . . mum?" she asked in a small voice. It felt wrong to ask, as if asking was a betrayal to Isabelle. To Mia. At the same time she had to ask.

"Well," he said, "that's a little more complicated. You see . . ."

Essie sucked in a breath.

59

ANGE

"We need to talk," Ange said.

Lucas looked surprised. That, in itself, was irritating. He was back in the house, so he obviously figured that was the end of it. Erin—and Charlie—had simply been another aberration, like Josie, and now they were going to move on with their lives.

At least that's what he thought.

Ange thought of the way Ben had looked at Essie at the hospital. It wasn't a look of infatuation or even affection—it was true, deep concern. He cared about her more than anything else. He put her before everything—and everyone—else.

"What is it?" he said.

They were in their bedroom. With the boys around, it was difficult to find a place to have a private conversation and the boys seemed to be *always* around—it was almost as though they sensed something was up and were staying close. But having them close did have its upsides. Twice Ange had seen Ollie watching something he shouldn't on the iPad, and half an hour ago, when she glanced over Will's shoulder while he was texting, she found out that he had a *girlfriend*—Candace! Why hadn't she always kept them close, she wondered. Will and Ollie . . . and Lucas too. Maybe if she'd kept him close, she might have glanced over Lucas's shoulder and realized *he* had a girlfriend too.

Ange sat on the bed. "I can't be married to you anymore."

Even as she said the words, a voice inside her head screamed: *SHUT UP! SHUT UP! SHUT UP! Every marriage has problems. Isn't it better to have some of him than none at all? You'll never find someone else—even someone old and haggard—at your age. For God's sake SHUT UP!*

But she kept talking.

"We will be in a relationship forever, because we have two children. But you also have a child with another woman which means you will always have a relationship with her too. And knowing the kind of man you are, you'll always have a relationship with Charlie—as you should." She took a deep breath and forced herself to continue. "But that's too many relationships for me, I'm afraid. Too much to sweep under the rug."

"But it's over with Erin," Lucas started.

"It's not just Erin," Ange said. "It's the other women. The ones I don't know about."

Even as she verbalized the thought, she knew it was true. After all, what were the chances she'd just happened to have discovered the only two women Lucas had been unfaithful with?

Lucas didn't deny it. When Ange turned to face him again,

his head was down and his hands were laced around the back of his neck.

"You say the right things, Lucas, and you even do the right things. At least, you do a lot of things right. But being faithful isn't an optional extra in a marriage. At least it isn't for me."

He looked at her pleadingly. "Please, could you give me one more chance? The last one. If I do this again, I will leave without being asked."

Ange thought back to the day in the store. The two plaid chairs side by side. The imaginary grandchildren in their laps. Then she thought about the man she wanted to sit next to in those chairs.

"You're not a bad person, Lucas," she told him. "But you're a terrible husband."

"Ange—" he started.

"The answer's no," she said and walked out of the room before she could change her mind.

60

ESSIE

"But will she . . . be all right?"

The policeman told Essie that Mia had darted into traffic and Barbara had whisked her out of the path of an oncoming car, only to be hit by a tram herself. Apparently Mia was totally unscathed but Barbara had been rushed to the hospital in critical condition.

"I'm sorry, Mrs. Walker. We don't have a lot of answers yet."

Mia was being brought to Summit Oaks by a female police officer and Ben had already left to meet them. Isabelle sat beside Essie with Polly on her lap. Essie had so many questions, but she couldn't seem to project any. Every word had caught in her throat, tangling with other words.

"What did Mia see?" Essie asked finally.

"We don't know," the police officer said. "But she's aware her grandmother was hit by the tram."

"And they were back in Melbourne? What were they doing in *Albury*?"

The policeman's shrug was clearly well-practiced. "Unfortunately we see this kind of thing regularly. "Often it's drug related but not always. It can be mental illness—a psychotic break. With some older folks, it's dementia. Or perhaps just a temporary confusion."

Essie tried to reconcile what he was saying with her mother. But . . . Barbara was the most levelheaded person Essie knew. She didn't have temporary confusions, she certainly wasn't into drugs. She was *her mother*.

Except maybe she wasn't.

Another policeman appeared at the doorway and the policeman in the room stood. "Your daughter will be here any minute," he said. "And I'll be right outside."

Essie felt the room start to sway. Isabelle was looking at her; she could feel her eyes.

"I want my mum," she said quietly.

"I know," Isabelle said.

"She was a good mother, you know. A great mother. I know you don't want to hear that—"

"Actually I do want to hear that. I know Mum's worst fear was that someone was mistreating you. She always said that if you couldn't come back to us, she prayed you were with someone who desperately wanted you and cherished you."

Tiny, precise footsteps echoed in the hallway. Essie and Isabelle stood in unison as Mia charged into the room. Essie swept her daughter up in her arms. "Mia!"

Mia let herself be hugged for just a moment before she pulled back. "Gran had to go to the hospital."

"I know, sweetie."

"And I went in a police car."

"I heard." Essie hugged Mia again. She caught eye contact with Ben who stood behind her. "Any news about Mum?"

"She's in surgery," Ben said. "The next twenty-four hours will be crucial. She had a significant head trauma."

"Can I play on your bed, Mummy?" Mia said.

"Of course," Essie said, and Mia leapt onto the bed, immediately reaching for the control to make it go up and down. Isabelle went over and helped her operate it.

"I spoke to the doctor in the hallway, and he's coming in to see you," Ben said. "He's going to start working on your release papers. Then we can all go home."

Essie nodded at him. It should have been a reassuring thought. She wasn't crazy. Her daughter was fine. She was able to go home with her family. But as she packed up her things, getting ready for release, all she could think was: *We're not* all *going home. Mum's not going anywhere.*

61

FRAN

Nigel had got the first plane out of Brisbane. He got a cab right from the airport and arrived in the hospital, as the sky was just getting dark. When he got to Ava's room, Rosie asleep on Fran's lap and Ava was in a hospital crib.

Nigel walked directly over to Ava. "How is she?"

"She has heatstroke," Fran said. "She was dehydrated. They're giving her IV fluids and they said she's doing better."

He picked up her chart and looked at it. Fran wondered if he actually understood the stuff that was written there, or if he was just doing it to feel more in control. Even if it was the latter, she wasn't judging. There was no worse feeling, Fran had come to realize, than not being in control when it came to your child.

"How did this happen?" he asked.

"I have no idea. She seemed fine . . . and then all at once . . ."

Nigel put a hand on her shoulder. "Babies can go downhill fast."

"I should have had the air-conditioning on. I should have been keeping a closer eye on her—"

"It's not your fault, Fran."

But she wasn't so sure. If she hadn't had an affair, Nigel wouldn't have gone away. She wouldn't have been distracted. She would have spent more time ensuring her baby had adequate fluids.

Fran started to cry. Nigel dropped into the seat beside her.

"Thank you for coming." She was sobbing. "Honestly, I don't know what I would have done—"

"Shh. It's all right."

A hospital staff member shuffled in. She checked the IV fluid and took her temperature. Fran deduced that she was a nurse. "Her temperature has come down a bit; that's good. And we've got a lot of fluids into her."

"Will she be okay?" Fran asked.

"Heatstroke is always serious in such a young baby." She opened Ava's diaper and glanced inside (checking her urine output, someone had explained earlier). "But she's doing all the things we like to see, which is very encouraging."

Fran wondered if they taught medical staff how to reassure people while *not* answering a direct question. Fran understood why they did it, but as a lawyer, it irritated her. As a mother, it infuriated her. The staff member must have seen her frustration because she added: "The doctor will be in to tell you more in a minute."

And she left the room. Fran felt Nigel's arm go around her

and she rested her head on his comforting shoulder. "I'm sorry," she said. "I'm so, so sorry."

"I told you, it wasn't your f—"

"I'm sorry for being unfaithful. I'm sorry I didn't support you better through your depression."

"You did support me."

"I should have done more. I should have worked harder."

Rosie jolted in Fran's lap. They both looked down at her, but she just snuggled against Fran's tummy and closed her eyes again.

"I got a call from your mother," Nigel said, "to apologize for everything you'd put me through."

Fran's gaze bounced up to Nigel's. "You did *not*."

"She said she was deeply disappointed in you. She said she didn't raise a daughter who had affairs or illegitimate children. But she urged me to stay with you. She said that—"

"—that marriage was hard, but you had to work harder?"

"Yes."

She watched Nigel's face. He'd never liked her mother. Fran had always defended her to him, saying *she means well,* and *she's a product of her upbringing.*

"Did she say that high achievers don't get divorced?"

"More or less."

"And what did you say?"

"I told her that contrary to her opinion, high achievers regularly analyze complex problems and make judgment calls based on the evidence they have and the probable outcomes."

Fran stifled a smile. It was such a Nigel response she couldn't help but love it. But it also made her nervous. Nigel had spent the last few days analyzing their relationship. What would his judgment call be?

"So," she said. "What have you deduced in this case?"

Before he could respond the doctor walked into the room and they both rose to their feet.

62

ESSIE

Ben answered the door. It wasn't the way Essie had planned it, but then again, she'd changed her mind approximately 5,687 times in the past week. Isabelle had also offered to answer the door—which wasn't a ridiculous idea since it was her father and brother out there—but once she'd heard the knock, Essie had grabbed her arm and held her firm.

It was all confirmed now. Essie and Isabelle had both had cheek swabs done which proved they were indeed biological sisters. Essie could just about get her head around that part, but now she had other family members to meet. Family members who were currently at her door.

"Hello! I'm Ben," she heard Ben say in a loud, overfriendly voice that gave away the fact that he was nervous too. Mia stood behind his legs, shyly.

"I'm Graham, and this is my son Freddy," came a booming, grandfatherly voice. Essie couldn't see them from where she sat but she pictured them shaking hands.

"Nice to meet you," Ben said. "This is Mia."

"Well, well," said the voice. "Aren't you beautiful!"

Essie stood as a profile view of her father came into view. He was tall, with thick gray hair and a paunchy belly. Beside him was a man who looked very much like him, except his hair was mostly black and his stomach was flat. Both of them looked at Mia with an expression Essie could only describe as wonder. Then the younger man looked around the room, his gaze landing on Essie.

He gasped. "Dad . . ."

The old man followed his son's gaze. They had the same face, Essie noticed, father and son. The same jaw, the same chin. The same eyes, pale blue, starting to mist over in unison. If Barbara was here, Essie mused, she'd be racing around, making more tea than anyone could drink. She'd be warm and friendly and she'd whisk the children away so everyone could catch up properly. But of course, Barbara would *never* be here. Even if she wasn't in the hospital. She was the woman who'd stolen her.

Essie had gotten the call this morning. Barbara had woken up after a week of being unconscious. She had a broken hip, three fractured ribs, and a partially collapsed lung, and while secondary brain injury was still a possibility, she was showing no signs of brain swelling or bleeding. The police said it was lucky she hadn't been pulled underneath the tram. If not for that, she likely wouldn't have made it. Essie had wanted to go to the hospital immediately after she'd heard her mother was conscious. She'd wanted to go with the same ferocity as she'd wanted to stay away. Part of her, she realized, was afraid to see her mother. Afraid to ask the questions she needed to ask. Afraid of hearing the answers to those questions.

It was Ben, in the end, who'd helped her decide. (*Your father and brother are on their way,* he'd said. *They've waited a long time to see you. Don't make them wait any longer.*)

"Sophie," her father whispered.

Essie made herself smile. She walked over and held out a stiff hand to him. "I'm Esther," she said. "It's nice to meet you."

Her father looked at her hand for a moment. Then he scanned her face, from right to left, top to bottom, as if memorizing it. Maybe he was. He touched the ends of her hair, turning it over in his hand. Finally he pulled her into a hug.

"Hello, honey," he said to Isabelle over Essie's shoulder. He kept one arm around Essie and put the other around Isabelle. Then he smiled warmly down at them both. "I never thought I'd see this day. My two daughters."

Essie recalled that her father had another two daughters. Four, in total. She felt irrationally glad that he'd forgotten them in this moment, and she suspected, judging from Isabelle's face, that she was glad too.

He wiped a tear from the corner of his eye. "I just wish your mother was here."

"I'm Fred," the other man—her brother—said. He hugged her too, but only quickly, then he pulled away again for another look at her. "I'm sorry. I just can't get over how much you look like Mum. I wish she was here."

"I do too," Essie said, though it wasn't her biological mother she was thinking about.

63

BARBARA

Barbara let the words spin around in her head. Postpartum psychosis. Post-traumatic stress disorder. These were all words the psychiatrists had used to describe Barbara's psychotic episodes— this one and the one thirty-two years ago when she'd stolen Essie from the hospital. No one was really sure which diagnosis best fit Barbara's experience—these things were rarely clear-cut, they said. In short, the trauma of her stillbirth had caused her to block out her baby's death, and Isabelle's confrontation had brought it back. She knew she would never in her right mind have stolen a baby. She had believed Essie was hers. Even now, knowing the truth, it was hard to believe Essie *wasn't* hers.

The hospital had taken a cheek swab from Barbara while she was unconscious, and obviously one had been taken from Essie and Isabelle as well because she'd been told they had conclusive evidence:

Essie could not be her daughter. Barbara's reaction, possibly because of the antipsychotic drugs she'd be given, had been anticlimactic. She didn't gasp or scream or beg for another result. She was too bewildered to do any of those things. But the idea that Essie wasn't hers didn't compute. It was as though she'd been told her right arm actually belonged to another person.

Barbara had been in and out of sleep since regaining consciousness. But during her every waking minute, she thought about Essie. So when there was a knock at the door, Barbara's heart leapt. As gently as she could, she swiveled her head so she was facing the door. But it wasn't Essie standing there.

It was Isabelle.

"I just want to talk to you," Isabelle said.

Barbara had expected the visit. Perhaps not quite so soon, but she'd expected it. For some reason, perhaps the medication, she felt oddly numb. "I suppose you want to tell me what you think of me. Go ahead. I'm sure you've got plenty to say."

"I thought I *would* have plenty to say. But as it turns out . . . I don't."

They watched each other, sizing each other up. Isabelle looked like Essie, Barbara realized. Had she always? Or was she projecting it now that she knew the truth? Certainly, looking at her now, it seemed impossible that Barbara hadn't noticed the moment Isabelle arrived in Pleasant Court.

"Have you seen Essie?" Barbara asked.

"Yes."

"Is she all right?"

Isabelle gave a wide-eyed shrug that demonstrated the ridiculousness of the question, and Barbara felt foolish. Of course she wasn't all right. How did anyone process the fact that their mother wasn't their mother? That they were kidnapped as a baby?

Isabelle stood across the room, still in the doorway. She seemed to have run out of things to say, and Barbara didn't know what to say to her. There was no apology or explanation that wouldn't feel useless and inadequate. "I'm on some quite strong medication so I'm not sure that I can do this justice, but for what it's worth, I am sorry for the trauma I caused you and your family."

Isabelle shrugged again. The last time Barbara had seen her she'd had so much to say, but today she seemed lost. Or perhaps *torn* was a better word. It was as if she had no idea what she'd come here for.

"Obviously it's not enough but . . . maybe . . . photo albums from when Essie was a child? Or mementos? I still have every one of her baby teeth. And videos of her ballet concerts! Actually, I have videos of most of her birthdays—"

"You were obviously a good mother, Barbara."

Barbara blinked in surprise. "Well," she said, "I don't know—"

"You were. Essie told me you were."

Isabelle swayed back and forth on the spot. It had been a full-on few days for her, clearly. Barbara wished she were feeling better, so she could make the girl a cup of tea and give her a biscuit.

"How are *you* doing?" Barbara asked.

Isabelle tossed the question around for a few moments. "I'm . . . happy to have my sister back."

"And your family. How are they?"

"They're shocked. Overwhelmed. My dad and my brother are in Melbourne now, actually."

"They are?" Barbara was about to ask why, but of course, she was being dim-witted. *Of course* they were in Melbourne. They were coming to see Essie.

Isabelle still hadn't moved from the doorway. "I want to ask you something, Barbara."

Barbara steeled herself. Here it came.

"What *did* you know?"

Barbara exhaled. "I didn't know anything."

Isabelle watched her with a gaze that wasn't angry or even judgmental. She was assessing her, wondering whether she could be trusted.

"Maybe," Isabelle said.

Barbara opened her mouth to respond but by the time she did Isabelle had already walked out the door.

64

ISABELLE

"Jules?"

Isabelle slammed the front door. She'd had to concentrate on not speeding home from the hospital. It wasn't that she wanted to get away so much as she suddenly—desperately—wanted to get home.

"In here," he called.

Isabelle had expected to feel angry after seeing Barbara, but she didn't. She didn't believe that Barbara knew *nothing*, but she also wasn't sure Barbara was the monster she'd drawn in her mind for years either. The fact was, nothing about finding Sophie had been the way she had expected—least of all, the way she felt now. *Free.*

And determined.

Jules was at the dining table, bent over his computer, but when she entered the room he glanced up. "Hey."

"Hey," she said. "You like coffee, right? Good coffee, I mean. Pretentious coffee. Deconstructed lattes, that sort of thing."

Julian sat back in his chair, stretching his arms above his head. "Who doesn't love a pretentious coffee?"

"And art. And live music, you *love* live music."

He opened his mouth.

"And little laneways with secret doorways leading to wonderful restaurants? Winters that are actually cold? The Great Ocean Road?"

He crossed his arms and waited for her to finish.

"So you know what I was thinking on the way home? You and I aren't Sydney people! I mean, right? We don't care about sunshine or surfing. Our skin burns in the shade."

"Sooo?"

"*Sooo . . .*" She pushed Jules's chair back and sat in his lap. "Sydney is wasted on us. We're *Melbourne* people, don't you think? I think we should move here."

"Uh . . . I have a job, remember?" he said in a *you've lost your mind* voice.

"There are schools in Melbourne. *Needy* schools. Students that need a teacher like you."

She felt a whisper of worry. On the way home from the hospital, during a brief moment of insanity, it had all fit together so perfectly. She and Jules would move to Melbourne, live near her sister and nieces, and live happily ever after. But she'd already asked so much of Jules. She'd abandoned him to go in search of her sister. He'd traveled out here to make sure she was all right, and he'd supported her through the past few weeks. The man had to draw the line somewhere.

"You don't want to live in Melbourne," she said.

It wasn't the end of the world, Isabelle told herself. They'd be able to make it work. She had her *sister* back, that was the important thing. She couldn't expect every puzzle piece of her life to click together just because she wanted it to. All her life she'd lived with a piece of her puzzle missing, and maybe that was just the way life was. Maybe, instead of focusing on the piece she didn't have, she should focus on the pieces she *did* have.

Jules rearranged her on his lap. He cocked his head and let out a long, slow sigh. "I didn't say I didn't want to live in Melbourne."

Isabelle zeroed in on his face, holding her breath.

"I just think that maybe we should go for a deconstructed latte and talk about it."

65

BARBARA

Barbara was feeling a little better. She'd had a visit from Lois, which had lifted her spirits. Lois was utterly convinced that Barbara was the victim in all this, finding out that her daughter wasn't hers after all these years. Everyone needed a friend like Lois. The doctors had told her that she'd stay in the hospital until her physical injuries were under control and then she'd be transferred to Summit Oaks' psychiatric program, the place Essie had been staying.

I didn't know anything. That's what she'd said to Isabelle. But it wasn't entirely true, was it? There *had* been things, little things she'd tried to justify over the years—things that didn't quite add up. Things like . . . why didn't she remember those first moments after Essie was born? Why was Essie so big and healthy when she was born premature? Why did she have auburn hair? And perhaps, now that she thought of it, there were other things too. Like the fact that the name Sophie Heatherington rang a bell. That she'd decided to leave Sydney the day she'd been released from the hospital, and never went back, even to visit friends or family. The fact that from the moment Isabelle had arrived in Pleasant Court, she'd had a bad feeling.

Was it true that she didn't know? Or was it that she didn't *want* to know?

"Mum?"

Barbara glanced toward the door and her heart leapt. It was Essie. She stepped inside uncertainly. "Were you sleeping?"

"No. I was wide awake."

Essie put her purse on the chair in the corner, then came to Barbara's bedside. There was a look of wary affection in her face. "How are you feeling?"

"Oh, you know," Barbara said, sitting up. "Like I've been hit by a tram."

Essie didn't smile.

"I'm glad you're here, honey." Barbara put out a hand and squeezed her forearm. "I worried you wouldn't come."

Essie kept her eyes down and forward. "Of course. You're my . . ."

Essie's gaze bounced up. *You're my mum.* That's what she was going to say. Instead she said: "How did this happen?"

"Well," Barbara said, "they think it was postpartum psychosis, and post-traumatic stress from losing my . . . my other baby and—"

"*I know* what the doctors said." Essie's voice wobbled with restrained emotion. "But I'm asking you. How did this happen?"

Barbara lifted her hands, and then let them fall back against the bed. "I can't answer that. Really, honey, I don't know."

"But how can that be true? *How?* There must have been a part of you that knew. I feel like . . . if Mia or Polly weren't mine . . . I'd know."

"I *did* know." Barbara's voice broke. "I *knew*! I knew you were mine. I knew with every ounce of my body. And then I found out you weren't."

Barbara burst into loud, desperate tears. She curved over onto herself. After a moment, she felt Essie's hand on her back. "All right. All right. I'm sorry."

"You . . . you are my whole life, Essie." Tears racked her body.

"I know. It's okay, Mum. I know."

Barbara cried until she couldn't keep her eyes open any longer, and the nicest part was, after she finally succumbed and drifted off, Essie's hand remained on her back.

66

ANGE

Ange had a paintbrush in her hand when the doorbell rang. She was on the back porch, muddying up a canvas with big streaks of color that clashed. She'd had the idea this morning—why not paint something? It felt remarkably indulgent. Beside her on a large piece of newspaper lay several household utensils—a spatula, a butter knife, a sponge—which she was using to create texture. Once, not so long ago, she'd have taken a picture of the utensils all lined up and posted it on Instagram (#colors; #creating; #art), but she didn't do that today. This little piece of herself wasn't for show. This was something that was just for her.

Ollie had come out half an hour earlier, looking appalled. "What is *that*?" he'd said, curling his lip.

"A painting."

"Why?"

"I used to paint when I was younger," she said brightly. "Why not now?"

He'd wandered off muttering: "Am I the only sane one in this house?"

Perhaps he was. Certainly the painting wasn't any good. The colors had run together, making everything look brown and unappealing. But Ange was enjoying it. As it turned out, Lucas wasn't the only one who could create adventures or fun in her life. She could be spontaneous too. Not once since Lucas had left had she watched a rerun of *Oprah*. Several times over the past few weeks she'd taken the boys out on an adventure. The first one (to the movies) had admittedly not been totally inspired, but it had been raining and she was just starting off. Last night she'd decided that on her next scheduled weekend with the boys she'd drive them to the airport and board the first flight they could get on. Oh yes, her adventures were going to be good. Maybe even better than Lucas's.

The boys seemed to be taking the split well so far, but Ange knew there'd be bumps along the way. Ollie, in particular, had become fond of the phrase "at Dad's house we . . ." Lucas had found himself an apartment in Black Rock, the next suburb, so he was still close by, and their custody arrangement had been working well. Lucas had the boys every other weekend, as well as Wednesday nights. He'd introduced the boys to their sister, which they seemed to have taken in their stride—though when Ollie had asked if Charlie could come and play at their house, Ange had just about choked on her chardonnay. She was going to be the cool, easygoing mum, but even *she* had her limits.

The doorbell rang again, and Ange remembered she was the

only one home. Ollie had just been picked up by a friend's mother to go to karate and Will had gone to the movies with Candace. Before he left, Ange had made a point of having a long talk with him about respecting women. He'd rolled his eyes and looked horrified, but Ange was determined to make sure he got the message—if not from his father, then from her.

She put her brush down on the newspaper, wiped her hands on a cloth, and headed for the door. It was Fran, Essie, and Isabelle, and all of the kids.

"Hello, you lot."

"Did you forget you invited us over?" Fran said.

"Actually, I did. But come on in."

Gone were the days when Ange meticulously prepared for visitors, shopping and cleaning and tidying everything within an inch of its life. Part of it was that Lucas had always done most of the tidying, but a bigger part was that she liked a little mess around the place now. The less perfect things were, she was finding, the more likely they were to be real.

Everyone spilled inside, and the kids beelined for a basket of toys that was on its side with its contents tipping out. The toys were virtually always strewn across the floor now, and between Essie's kids and Fran's, there was always someone playing on her floor. (Often, when he thought no one was looking, Ollie even riffled through the toy basket himself, playing with a figurine or a car. She loved watching those last little moments of childhood. Soon enough they will have drifted away and he'll be interested in girls.) It was nice, living in a house that people felt like they could pop into. It was, she realized, what she'd envisioned when they'd moved into Pleasant Court.

"I have nothing to offer you," Ange said, headed for the kitchen. "Actually . . . I have grapes and . . . popcorn and . . . toast. And coffee."

"Perfect," Fran said, joining her in the kitchen. "I'll make the toast."

Ange still had her share of doubts about asking Lucas to leave. Sometimes it was all she could do to stop herself from picking up the phone and begging him to come back to her. Before long, she knew, he'd find someone else and then she wouldn't have a choice in the matter. (*You just have to hang on until then*, Fran had told her the other day. And to her surprise, Ange had laughed.)

Ange and Fran arranged a plate of grapes, toast, and popcorn and headed into the living room where Essie and Isabelle were talking quietly. They looked up when Ange and Fran walked in, and Ange noticed, grinning from ear to ear.

"What?" Ange and Fran said in unison.

Isabelle sat forward. "I'm pregnant."

67

FRAN

Fran woke while it was still dark. It was quiet, but she had a sense that something had woken her. She reached for the monitor, listening for Ava. But she just heard silence. Ava had been home for a couple of weeks now, but Fran still found herself racing in there several times a night, just to watch her breathe. It was chilly and she pulled the blanket up around her shoulders and closed her eyes again. Fran wasn't sure when it had stopped being hot. It always seemed like the warm nights dragged on and on, and then suddenly, when it did finally turn cold, everyone was aghast and furious, as though autumn was a cruel trick that had been played on them.

It had been a funny few weeks. It felt like the street had changed somehow. Now when she walked out of her house and saw one of the neighbors, she went over and said hello—even if it was early in the morning. It seemed impossible to her now that they had all been going through their own private torture while living right next door to each other. She and Nigel had been slowly rebuilding their relationship and were speaking to each other with a sort of nervous politeness that felt incongruent with the fact that they'd been married nearly ten years—but it was actually quite lovely. People who bothered to be nervous and polite were people who wanted their marriage to work.

She remembered the conversation they'd had at the hospital.

"I can get past the affair," he'd said after the doctor had given them the same information as the nurse had. That Ava was responding well to treatment and that she would, most likely, be fine to go home in a few days.

"And Ava?" Fran had asked, welling up. "Did you want to get a pater—"

He'd flicked his gaze to the crib, where she lay. "I don't need a paternity test," he said. "She's mine."

Fran opened her eyes. The sky outside was starting to lighten . . . she couldn't go back to sleep now. She thought about going for a run, but the chill made her feel lazy. She'd been too lazy to run for a couple of weeks now, ever since Ava was sick. Once they got back into the swing of things, she might start running again. Or she might not.

She rolled over. Nigel's side of the bed was empty, and the bedroom door was ajar. She grabbed her robe and wandered through the quiet house, finding Nigel in Ava's room.

"Was she crying?" she whispered.

"No."

Fran joined him beside the crib and they both looked down at her. She looked different like this, slack with sleep. She was swaddled tightly, her arms stuck to her sides and her plump head peeking out at the top, like an ice cream in a cone. Her eyelashes lay, fat and dark, on her cheeks.

"She's mine," Nigel whispered. "I looked at her chart in the hospital. Her blood group is O negative."

Fran remembered the trivia night. *O negative is quite rare.*

She and Nigel were both O negative.

Rosie was O negative.

Nigel's gaze had moved off Ava, and onto Fran.

"It wouldn't have mattered to me," he said.

"But she's yours? She's actually yours?"

"There is a statistically significant probability that that is the case," he answered, shifting his gaze back to Ava. "And that's good enough for me."

68

ESSIE

Six months later . . .

Essie lay on the couch with Mia, watching *The Little Mermaid* for the 7,896th time. Ben sat on the other end of the couch with Essie's feet in his lap. Ben had been spending a lot more time watching movies with them lately. He'd dropped down to part-time hours and hired a manager to take care of a lot of his duties at The Shed, though he still took a lot of classes, which had always been his favorite part anyway.

"I'm Ariel," Mia said. "Because we have the same hair. You are King Triton, Daddy. Polly is Flounder." She looked at Essie uncertainly. "You are . . . um, Sebastian."

It was a game they always played when they watched movies.

Mia inevitably ended up with the most beautiful, heroic character and Essie ended up being a crab.

"What about Gran?" Essie asked. "Who is she?"

Mia went quiet.

Essie was grateful, at least, that she didn't say Ursula, the vile sea witch that stole Ariel's voice but she was sad that Barbara didn't get a role in this game anymore. Barbara had spent five months as an inpatient in Summit Oaks, as had been ordered by the court. Due to her mental condition, she had been found not guilty of the kidnapping charge brought by the state, and sentencing had been helped greatly by Essie convincing her father—Graham—to speak in Barbara's defense. During her time at Summit Oaks, Essie had visited her twice a week, with Mia and Polly in tow, and while Mia was happy to go, she hadn't fully regained her trust in Barbara after their odd car trip to Albury. She never talked about what happened that day, she just mentioned at random times that her Gran was at the hospital with unusual significance.

When Barbara was released a month ago, she'd moved into a smaller house in Hampton, just a five-minute drive from Pleasant Court. Still close, but not quite as close—which was an accurate appraisal of their relationship too. Barbara was still around, but not as much as she used to be, and they'd all decided that she shouldn't spend unsupervised time with the girls anymore but Essie knew she was struggling with her new role—was she a mother and grandmother? A friend?—and it was made all the more awkward when Mia would mention her biological grandfather, "Papa," who'd been coming to visit nearly every weekend since they'd found her. But they all had adjusting to do. There'd probably be a lot more adjusting to come.

As the credits started to run, there was a brief knock at the door, and Isabelle strolled in.

"Hi, Izzy," they called.

They'd gotten used to this level of comfort around each other over the past months. Isabelle waddled inside and lowered herself onto the other end of the couch. Jules had secured a job at a high school in Melbourne, and they were renting an apartment in Collingwood. After Isabelle's baby was born, Essie was going to go and stay in their spare room and help her with the baby, and she couldn't wait.

Mia crawled out of Essie's embrace and beelined for Isabelle.

"Hello, baby," Mia whispered to Isabelle's tummy.

"Hello, big cousin," Ben said in a baby voice.

Mia looked up. "That was you, Daddy."

"No, it wasn't," he said, indignant. "It was the baby."

Mia giggled, and so did Ben and Isabelle. Essie found herself looking over to the kitchen to share a smile with Barbara, but of course, she wasn't there.

69

BARBARA

The moment Barbara's phone beeped, she felt a pulse of excitement. A text message from Essie. She sat upright in her chair and balanced her knitting on the armrest.

For goodness' sake, Barbara, she told herself. *Calm down.*

It wasn't as if text messages from Essie were rare. Essie texted her several times a week—a chubby-cheeked picture of Polly covered in spaghetti Bolognese or a quick note that Mia had put her face under the water at her swimming lesson and graduated to the Daisy Dolphin class. What *was* sad was the way that Barbara lived for these messages, given her hatred of them only a year ago. She thought of how superior she'd been, insisting she preferred the humble phone call. The problem with the humble phone call, she realized now, was that you couldn't look back at it again and again when you were feeling lonely. You couldn't get out your phone and glance at a phone call in the middle of the night when you couldn't sleep. Oh, yes, Barbara was a convert to text messages. Text messages were often now the highlight of her day.

She put on her glasses and glanced down at the screen. It was a picture of Isabelle and Julian in a hospital room, sent by Essie. Isabelle held a newborn bundled in pale pink blankets. Beneath the picture was the caption: *Sophie Elizabeth*. Barbara exhaled. It felt like they had been waiting a long time for this day.

Another picture came through, this time of Mia proudly holding the baby with a disinterested-looking Polly by her side. Barbara chuckled. She looked at the blanket she'd been knitting—cream wool with a crocheted edge. She'd knitted one each for Mia and Polly when they were born and they had both become their "security blankets" (something Essie had been quite pleased about because, she said, Barbara could simply knit another one if they happened to lose them). Knitting the blanket for Isabelle's baby had given Barbara something to do each evening while she watched television, even if she wasn't sure she'd ever give it to her. She just couldn't decide if it would be appropriate . . . or entirely inappropriate.

These past nine months hadn't been easy. Despite the fact that Essie said she wanted to keep Barbara in her life, their relationship had changed irrevocably. Now, instead of arriving at her house and letting herself in with her key, she prearranged visits and then everyone sat around making self-conscious conversation—as though she was the finicky great-aunt, rather than a close family member. Her yearning for the girls was the worst part. Barbara positively *ached* for Mia and Polly—for their sweet, soft heads and chubby hands, for the quiet huff of their breath as they slept. She ached for the way they used to run to her for comfort, for the privilege of being the one to take care of them.

Lois had tried to help. She'd joined Barbara and herself with a walking group and a book club. Barbara enjoyed them both, but they weren't the same as being part of a family, which was, after all, what she'd always wanted. She remembered meeting John, all those years ago. She'd known he wasn't the greatest catch in the world, but all around her, people were getting married, becoming pregnant, having babies. Creating their own families. She had wanted to create her own family too. That's what she had done. And now, it was gone.

A car door slammed outside, followed by quick, light footsteps pattering up the path. She heard the high-pitched chatter of little children and Barbara's spine straightened.

"Hello!" called a little voice. "Gran?"

Barbara peered out the window. Mia stood on her front step while Polly toddled behind her on wobbly legs. It had been less than a week since she'd seen them last. But how long had it been since they'd just turned up on her doorstep unannounced?

She got up and opened the door. Polly peered up at her, over-balancing in the process and falling onto her bottom. Mia wore a raincoat, though there was no sign of rain. All of this, and so much more, caused Barbara's throat to thicken. "Well," she said. "This is a lovely surprise."

Essie hurried up the path. "We were just driving past, on our way home from the hospital and we thought we'd stop by."

The girls tumbled inside without waiting for an invitation. Barbara stood back to make room for Essie to do the same.

"I hope it's all right to just drop in like this? I mean, you weren't busy, were—"

"Of course it's all right. It's *perfectly* all right." Barbara heard a note of emotion in her voice, so she smiled widely to compensate. She wasn't going to guilt Essie into visiting her more often. As far as she was concerned, a pity visit was worse than no visit at all.

Polly had already found a basket of toys and was hurling items out like there was treasure at the bottom.

"Polly!" Essie said. "Don't make a mess."

"Make as much mess as you like, Polly." Barbara shut the door.

Mia was hovering at the door with them, Barbara noticed. Essie had told Barbara that Mia didn't remember the day they'd run off to Albury anymore. *Kids' memories are short,* she'd said. Barbara wasn't so sure. The funny thing was, she wasn't sure if she wanted Mia to forget. If she had forgotten that day, it might mean she'd forgotten everything that came before then. How close they'd been. How she used to sleep over at Barbara's house, bake cakes with her, fall asleep in her arms. Barbara thought she'd rather Mia remember one mistake, even a scary mistake, than forget all of that.

Barbara felt a tug on her shirtsleeve.

"What is it, Mia?" Barbara asked her.

She pulled Barbara down by the arm, until Barbara's ear was level with her mouth. "Have you got cookies?" she whispered.

"As a matter of fact, I have some Tim Tams in the pantry. Shall I get—"

But Mia was already hurtling toward the kitchen. She didn't know her way around this place like she had known Barbara's house on Pleasant Court, but the wonderful thing about kids was that they didn't hold back out of politeness. And if there was one thing Barbara was sick of, it was politeness. Barbara heard the sound of chair legs scraping against floorboards and then little knees knocking against them. Finally she heard the great crash of the biscuit tin against the floorboards.

"I guess she found them," Essie said.

"I guess she did."

They smiled at each other.

"You got my message then?" Essie said eventually. "Isabelle had her baby."

"Yes." Barbara walked toward the lounge room and Essie followed her. "A little girl. It's wonderful." She sat down, cleared her throat. "So they called her Sophie?"

"Yes. I think they debated it for a while . . . They weren't sure if it was a good idea or not because the name was attached to so many unhappy memories."

"Because there's already a Sophie Heatherington," Barbara said carefully.

"Yes . . . though, I really feel much more like an Essie Walker."

Barbara felt her chest tighten. She'd been working with a psychiatrist for nine months now. During that time fragments of the day she took Essie had started returning to her. The doctor saying her baby had died. The moment she saw Essie in her bassinet and felt certain she was her baby. Picking her up and carrying her out to the taxi. It was important, the doctor said, to remember, so she could deal with the trauma and move past it. But Barbara tried not to dwell on those memories unless she was in a therapy session. What she had done was just too unthinkable to face.

"It must be strange having such a big family now," she said to Essie. "A brother and sister, a father. Two half sisters. And now Mia and Polly have a cousin . . ."

"I know. It *is* strange."

"I'm sorry your mum isn't alive to see you again." Barbara picked up a cushion, fluffed it. She couldn't look Essie in the eye. "And to see those beautiful girls of yours."

An argument erupted between the girls and Polly came clomping into the room wearing one plastic high heel shoe. Barbara couldn't believe that she managed to remain upright in it. Polly had biscuit crumbs all over her hands and face and she dropped her face directly into Essie's lap. Mia appeared a second later, also covered in biscuits, holding the other shoe. She started to rage that she'd had the "clip-clop shoes" first and now Polly had taken one, and you couldn't share shoes because you needed two and anyway Polly was too little to wear clip-clop shoes anyway, right, Mummy?

Essie looked at her desperately. Her face was so achingly trusting, Barbara thought she might burst into tears.

"Right, who wants to bake a cake?" Barbara said,.

By the time Polly lifted her face from Essie's skirt, Mia was already racing to the kitchen to "get things out." As Polly scampered after her, Barbara grabbed the abandoned shoes and stuffed them under a cushion.

Essie flopped back against the couch. "Clearly there's a requirement for a grandmother in this large family of mine." Her tone was casual but she was watching her a little too intently. "I'm taking applications if you know anyone who might be interested?"

"Gran!" Mia called from the kitchen. "Hurry uuuuuuuup!"

"Coming," Barbara replied. She winked at Essie and then hurried into the kitchen to bake with her granddaughters.

Essie / Ben (lift →)
Mia, Polly
barbs - Essies Mom

Fran → lawyer / Nigel — departed
not sure
on baby Rosie, Ava
cady → realtor / photographer
Ange / Lucas (~~worked~~) had affair
(Will, Ollie
→ delivered Ollie noone there

Fran - runner 2nd kid might
had affair - not be Nigels

Angie - husband caught be
having affair - found
I phone
- 2nd child might have come
about by a lie

Isabelle = new neighbor

Melbourne + Sydney

1. The novel opens with quite a dramatic scene: Essie, a new mother, forgets her baby in the park and panics as soon as she realizes what she's done. How do you think this chapter sets the tone for the rest of the novel?

2. What was your initial impression of Isabelle, and more specifically the interactions between Isabelle and Essie? Were you as suspicious of her motives as Ange and some of the other residents of the neighborhood? Why or why not?

3. Throughout the novel, Essie struggles to balance taking care of her children, taking care of herself, and maintaining a healthy marriage. How do you see this balancing act playing out in your own life, or the life of someone close to you? How do you think this struggle shapes the experiences of women in particular?

4. The story moves between the present time and the story of an unnamed narrator in the past. How do you think this structure affected your reading experience? Did you begin to suspect who the unnamed narrator was, or were you completely surprised?

5. Fran and Ange use running and social media, respectively, as a way to cope with the stressful situations in their lives. Do you think that Isabelle became Essie's coping mechanism? Or did she have something else? Are the coping mechanisms the women use healthy or unhealthy, in your opinion?

6. At the core of *The Family Next Door* are questions about the bonds of the family you are born to versus the family you choose for yourself. Do you have strong familial bonds in your own life, whether biological or not, and how do they

St. Martin's Griffin

affect the choices you make? Can you see any of
your own relationships reflected in the novel?

7. On page 193, Leonie says to Ange, "If you tell
   yourself enough that life is perfect . . . somehow, it
   is." Ange disagrees, thinking, "Or maybe you end up
   living a perfect-looking lie." Which of them do you
   agree with, and why? Do you believe in the power
   of positive thinking to create change in your life?

8. In *The Family Next Door*, Essie experiences something
   called genetic sexual attraction, or a sexual attraction
   one experiences with a family member they have
   never met. Had you heard of this prior to reading
   the novel? What did you think of Essie's reaction
   to finding out about her biological family?

9. Do you think that the events of the novel led to a
   lasting change in Essie's neighborhood, or only a
   temporary one? Do you think the women will be
   closer now, after their respective familial dramas,
   or will they still feel distant from each other?

Read on for a sneak peek at
Sally Hepworth's next novel

The Mother-in-Law

Available April 2019

I
———

Lucy

I am folding laundry at my dining room table when the police car
pulls up. There's no fanfare—no sirens or flashing lights—yet that
little niggle starts in the pit of my stomach, Mother Nature's warning that all is not well. It's getting dark out, early evening, and the
neighbors' porch lights are starting to come on. It's *dinnertime*.
Police don't arrive on your doorstep at dinnertime unless something
is wrong.

I glance through the archway to the living room where my sloth-
ful children are stretched across different pieces of furniture, angled
toward their respective devices. Alive. Unharmed. In good health
apart from, perhaps, a mild screen addiction. Seven-year-old Archie is watching a family play Wii games on the big iPad; four-
year-old Harriet is watching little girls in America unwrap toys on
the little iPad. Even two-year-old Edie is staring, slack-jawed, at

the television. I feel some measure of comfort that my family is all under this roof. At least most of them are. *Dad*, I think suddenly. *Oh no, please not Dad.*

I look back at the police car. The headlights illuminate a light mist of rain.

At least it's not the children, a guilty little voice in my head whispers. *At least it isn't Ollie.* Ollie is on the back deck, grilling burgers. Safe. He came home from work early today, not feeling well apparently, though he doesn't seem particularly unwell. In any case, he's alive and I'm wholeheartedly grateful for that.

The rain has picked up a little now, turning the mist into distinct, precise raindrops. The police kill the engine, but don't get out right away. I ball up a pair of Ollie's socks and place them on top of his pile and then reach for another pair. I should stand up, go to the door, but my hands continue to fold on autopilot, as if by continuing to act normal the police car will cease to exist and all will be right in the world again. But it doesn't work. Instead, a uniformed policeman emerges from the driver's seat.

"Muuuuum!" Harriet calls. "Edie is watching the TV!"

Two weeks ago, a prominent news journalist had spoken out publicly about her "revulsion" that children under the age of three were exposed to TV, actually going so far as to call it "child abuse." Like most Australian mothers, I'd been incensed about this and followed with the predictable diatribe of, "What would she know? She probably has a team of nannies and hasn't looked after her children for a day in her life!" before swiftly instating the "no screens for Edie rule," which lasted until twenty minutes ago when I was on the phone with the energy company, and Edie decided to try the old "Mum, muuuum, MUUUUUM . . ." trick until I relented, popping on an episode of *The Wiggles* and retreating to the bedroom to finish my phone call.

"It's all right, Harriet," I say, my eyes still on the window.

Harriet's cross little face appears in front of me, her dark brown hair and thick fringe swishing around her face like a mop. "But you SAID . . ."

"Never mind what I said. A few minutes won't hurt."

The cop looks to be midtwenties, thirty at a push. His police hat is in his hand but he wedges it under one arm to tug at the front of his too-tight trousers. A short, rotund policewoman of a similar age gets out of the passenger side, her hat firmly on her head. They come around the car and start up the path side by side. They are definitely coming to our place. *Nettie,* I think suddenly. *It's about Nettie.*

It's possible. Ollie's sister has certainly had her share of health issues lately. Or maybe it's Patrick? Or is it something else entirely?

The fact is, part of me knows it's not Nettie or Patrick, or Dad. It's funny sometimes what you just *know.*

"Burgers are up."

The fly screen door scrapes open and Ollie appears at the back door holding a plate of meat. The girls flock to him and he snaps his "crocodile tongs" while they jump up and down, squealing loudly enough to nearly drown out the knock at the door.

Nearly.

"Was that the door?" Ollie raises an eyebrow, curious rather than concerned. In fact, he looks animated. *An unexpected guest on a week-night! Who could it be?*

Ollie is the social one of the two of us, the one that volunteers on the Parents and Friends' committee at the kids' school because "it's a good way to meet people," who hangs over the back fence to say hi to the neighbors if he hears them talking in the garden, who approaches people who look vaguely familiar and tries to figure out if they know each other. A people person. To Ollie, an unexpected knock on the door during the week signals excitement rather than doom.

But, of course, he hasn't seen the cop car.

Edie tears down the corridor. "I'll get it, I'll get it."

"Hold on a minute, Edie-bug," Ollie says, looking for somewhere to put down the tray of burgers. He isn't fast enough though because by the time he finds some counter space, Edie has already tossed open the door.

"Poleeth!" she says, awed.

This, of course, is the part where I should run after her, intercept the police at the door and apologize, but my feet are concreted to the floor. Luckily, Ollie is already jogging up behind Edie, ruffling her hair playfully.

"G'day," he says to the cops. He glances over his shoulder back into the house, his mind caught up in the action of a few seconds ago, perhaps wondering if he remembered to turn off the gas canister or checking that he'd placed the burger plate securely on the counter. It's the classic, unassuming behavior of someone about to get bad news. I actually feel like I am watching us all on a TV show—the handsome clueless dad, the cute toddler. The regular suburban family who are about to have their lives turned inside out . . . ruined forever.

"What can I do for you?" Ollie says finally, turning his attention back to the cops.

"I'm Sr. Constable Arthur," I hear a woman say, though I can't see her from my vantage point, "and this is Constable Perkins. Are you Oliver Goodwin?"

"I am." Ollie smiles down at Edie, even throws her a wink. It's enough to convince me that I'm being overly dramatic. Even if there's bad news, it may not be that bad. It may not even be *our* bad news. Perhaps one of the neighbors was burgled? Police always *canvassed the area* after something like that, didn't they?

Suddenly I look forward to that moment in a few minutes' time when I know that everything's fine. I think about how Ollie and I will laugh about how paranoid I was. *You won't believe what I thought,* I'll say to him, and he'll roll his eyes and smile. *Always worrying,* he'll say. *How do you ever get anything done with all that worrying?*

But when I edge forward a few paces, I see that my worrying isn't unnecessary. I see it in the somberness of the policeman's expression, in the downward turn of the corners of his mouth.

The policewoman glances at Edie, then back at Ollie. "Is there somewhere we can talk . . . privately?"

The first traces of uncertainty appear on Ollie's face. His shoulders stiffen and he stands a little bit taller. Perhaps unconsciously, he pushes Edie back from the door, behind him, shielding her from something.

"Edie-bug, would you like me to put on *The Wiggles*?" I say, stepping forward finally.

Edie shakes her head resolutely, her gaze not shifting from the police. Her soft round face is alight with interest; her chunky, wobbly legs are planted with improbable firmness.

"Come on, honey," I try again, sweeping a hand over her pale gold hair. "How about an ice cream?"

This is more of a dilemma for Edie. She glances at me, watching for a long moment, assessing whether I can be trusted. Finally I shout for Archie to get out the Paddle Pops and she scampers off down the hallway.

"Come in," Ollie says to the police, and they do, sending me a quick, polite smile. A *sorry* smile. A smile that pierces my heart, unpicks me a little. *It's not the neighbors,* that smile says. This bad news is yours.

There aren't a lot of private communal areas in our house so Ollie guides the police to the dining room and pulls out a couple of chairs. I follow, pushing my newly folded laundry into a basket. The piles collapse into each other like tumbling buildings. The police sit on the chairs, Ollie balances on the arm of the sofa, and I remain sharply upright, stiff. Bracing.

"Firstly I need to confirm that you are relatives of Diana Goodwin—"

"Yes," Ollie says, "she's my mother."

"Then I'm very sorry to inform you," the policewoman starts, and I close my eyes because I already know what she is going to say.

My mother-in-law is dead.

2

Lucy

Ten years ago . . .

Someone once told me that you have two families in your life—the one you are born into and the one you choose. But that's not entirely true, is it? Yes, you may get to choose your partner, but you don't, for instance, choose your children. You don't choose your brothers- or sisters-in-law, you don't choose your partner's spinster aunt with the drinking problem, or cousin with the revolving door of girlfriends who don't speak English. More importantly, you don't choose your mother-in-law. The cackling mercenaries of fate determine it all.

"Hello?" Ollie calls. "Anybody home?"

I stand in the yawning foyer of the Goodwins' home and pan around at the marble extending out in every direction. A winding staircase sweeps from the basement up to the first floor beneath a magnificent crystal chandelier. I feel like I've stepped into the pages of a *Hello!* magazine spread, the ones with the ridiculous photos of celebrities sprawling on ornate furniture, and on grassy knolls in riding boots with golden retrievers at their feet. I've always pictured that this is what the inside of Buckingham Palace must look like, or if not Buckingham, at least one of the smaller palaces—St. James or Windsor.

I try to catch Ollie's eye, to . . . what? Admonish him? Cheer? Quite frankly I'm not sure but it's moot since he's already charging into the house, announcing our arrival. To say I'm unprepared for this is the most glorious of understatements. When Ollie had suggested I come to his parents' house for dinner I'd been picturing lasagna and salad in a quaint, blond-brick bungalow, the kind of home I'd grown up in. I'd pictured an adoring mother, clasping a photo album of sepia-colored baby photos, and a brusquely proud but socially awkward father, clasping a can of beer and a cautious smile. Instead, artwork and sculptures were uplit and gleaming, and the parents, socially awkward or otherwise, are nowhere to be seen.

"Ollie!" I catch Ollie's elbow and am about to whisper furiously when a plump ruddy-faced man rushes through a large arched doorway at the back of the house, clutching a glass of red wine.

"Dad!" Ollie cries. "There you are!"

"Well, well. Look who the cat dragged in."

Tom Goodwin is the very opposite of his tall, dark-haired son. Short, overweight, and unstylish, he's wearing a red-checked shirt tucked into chinos that are belted below his substantial paunch. He throws his arms around his son, and Ollie thumps his old man on the back.

"You must be Lucy," Tom says, after releasing Ollie. He takes my hand and pumps it heartily, letting out a low whistle. "My word. Well done, son."

"It's nice to meet you, Mr. Goodwin." I smile.

"Tom! Call me Tom." He smiles at me like he's won the Easter raffle, then he appears to remember himself. "Diana! Diana, where are you? They're here!"

After a moment or two Ollie's mother emerges from the back of the house. She's wearing a white shirt and navy slacks and brushing nonexistent crumbs from the front of her shirt. I suddenly wonder about my outfit choice, a full-skirted 1950s red and white polka-dot dress that had belonged to my mother. I thought it would be charming but now it just seems outlandish and stupid, especially given Ollie's mum's plain and demure attire.

"I'm sorry," she says, from several paces away. "I didn't hear the bell."

"This is Lucy," Tom says.

Diana extends her hand. As I reach for it, I notice that she is almost a full head taller that her husband, despite her flat shoes, and she is thin as a street post, apart from a slight middle-aged thickening at the waist. She has silver hair cut into an elegant, chin-length bob, a straight Roman nose, and unlike Tom, bears a strong resemblance to her son.

I also notice that her handshake is cold.

"It's nice to meet you, Mrs. Goodwin," I say, dropping her hand to offer the bunch of flowers I'm carrying. I'd insisted on stopping at the florist on the way, even though Ollie had said, "Flowers aren't really her thing."

"Flowers are every woman's thing," I'd replied with a roll of my eyes. But as I take in her lack of jewelry, her unpainted nails and sensible flat shoes, I start to get the feeling that I'm wrong.

"Hello, Mum," Ollie says, pulling his mother in a bear hug, which she accepts, if not quite embraces. I know, from many conversations with Ollie, that he adores his mother. He practically bursts with pride as he talks about the charity she runs single-handedly for refugees in Australia, many of them pregnant or with small children. *Of course* she would think flowers were trivial, I realize suddenly. I'm an idiot. Perhaps I should have brought baby clothes, or maternity supplies?

"All right, Ollie," she says after a moment or two, when he doesn't let her go. She pulls herself upright. "I haven't even had a chance to say hello properly to Lucy!"

"Why don't we head to the lounge for some drinks and we can all get to know each other better," Tom says, and we all turn toward the back of the house. That's when I notice a face peeking around the corner.

"Nettie!" Ollie cries.

If there is a lack of resemblance between Ollie and Tom, there is no doubt Antoinette is Tom's daughter. She has his ruddy cheeks and stockiness, while at the same time being endearingly pretty. Stylish too, in a grey woolen dress and black suede boots. According to Ollie, his younger sister is married, childless, and some sort of executive at a marketing company who is often asked to speak at conferences about women and the glass ceiling. At thirty-two years old, only two years older than me, I'll admit, I'd found this impressive and a little intimidating, but it is all swept under the rug when she greets me with an enormous bear hug. The Goodwins, it appears, are huggers.

All of them, perhaps, except Diana.

"I've heard so much about you," she says. She links her arm with mine and I am engulfed in a cloud of expensive-smelling perfume. "Come and meet my husband, Patrick."

Nettie drags me through an arched doorway, past what looks like an elevator—*an elevator!* As we walk we pass framed artwork and floral arrangements, and photos of family holidays on the ski slopes and at the beach. There is one photo of Tom, Diana, Nettie, and Ollie on camels in the desert with a pyramid in the background, all of them holding hands and raising their hands skyward.

Growing up, I used to go to the beach town of Portarlington for holidays, less than an hour's drive from my house.

We stop in a room that is roughly the size of my apartment, filled with sofas and armchairs, huge, expensive-looking rugs, and heavy wooden side tables. A gigantic man rises from an armchair.

"Patrick," he says. His handshake is clammy but he looks apologetic so I pretend not to notice.

"Lucy. Nice to meet you."

I'm not sure what I expected for Nettie—perhaps someone small, sharp, eager to please, like her. At six feet three inches, I thought Ollie was tall, but Patrick is positively mountain-like—six seven at least. Apart from his height, he reminds me a little of Tom, in his plaid shirt and chinos, his round face and eager smile. He has a knitted sweater around his shoulders, preppy-style.

With all greetings out of the way, Ollie, Tom and Patrick sink into the large couch and Diana and Nettie wander off toward a drinks station. I hesitate a moment, then fall into step beside the women.

"You sit down, Lucy," Diana directs me.

"Oh, I'm happy to help—"

But Diana raises her hand like a stop sign. "Please," she says. "Just sit."

Diana is obviously trying to be polite, but I can't help but feel a little rejected. She isn't to know, of course, that I'd fantasized about bumping elbows with her in the kitchen, perhaps even facing a little salad crisis together that I could overcome by whipping up a makeshift dressing (a salad crisis was about all my culinary capabilities could stretch to). She isn't to know that I'd imagined nestling up to her as she took me through photo albums, family trees, and long-winded stories that Ollie would groan about. She doesn't know I'd planned to spend the entire evening by her side, and by the time we went home, she'd be as enamored with me as I'd be with her.

Instead, I sat.

"So, you and Ollie work together?" Tom asks me, as I planted myself next to Ollie on the sofa.

"We do," I say. "Have done for three years."

"Three years?" Tom feigns shock. "Took your time, didn't you, mate?"

"It was a slow burn," Ollie says.

Ollie had been the classic, solid guy from work. The one always available to listen to my most terrible dating stories and offer a sympathetic shoulder. Ollie, unlike the powerful, take-charge assholes that I tended to date, was cheerful, unassuming and consistently good guy. Most importantly, he adored me. It had taken me a while to realize it, but being adored was much nicer than being messed around by charismatic bastards.

"He isn't your boss, is he?" Tom twinkles. It's horrendously sexist, but it's hard to be annoyed with Tom.

"Tom!" Diana chides, but it's clear she finds it hard to be annoyed with him too. She's back now with drinks, and she purses her lips in the manner of a mother trying to discipline her very cute, disobedient toddler. She hands me a glass of red wine and sits on the other side of Ollie.

"We're peers," I tell Tom. "I recruit for the technical positions, Ollie does support staff. We work closely together."

Very closely lately. It started, oddly enough, in a dream. A bizarre, meandering dream that started at my great-aunt Gwen's barbeque and ended at the house where my best friend from primary school lived, but she wasn't a little girl anymore, she was an old lady. But somewhere in the middle, Ollie was there. And just like my best friend from primary school, he was different. Sexier. The next day, at work, I sent him an email saying he'd been in my dream the night before. The expected "What was I doing?" banter followed, with an undercurrent. Ollie's office was right next door to mine, but we'd always sent each other emails from the next office—witty commentary about our shared boss's Donald Trump hair, suspicious behavior at the office Christmas party, requests for sushi orders for lunch. But that day, it was different. By the end of the day my heart was skipping a beat when his name appeared in my in-box.

For a while I'd kept my head about it. It was a rendezvous, a tryst . . . not a relationship and certainly not *the* relationship. But when I noticed him giving money to the drunk at the train station every morning (even after the drunk abused him and accused him of stealing his booze); when he'd spotted a lost little boy at the shopping center and immediately lifted him up over his head and asked if he could see his mum anywhere; when he began to occupy more and more of my thoughts, a realization came: this is it. He's the one.

I tell Ollie's family the story (minus the dream), my arms

spinning around me as I talk quickly and without a pause, as I tend to do when I get nervous. Tom is positively enraptured at the storytelling, patting his son on the back at intervals as I talk.

"So tell me about . . . all of you," I say, when I've run out of steam.

"Nettie is the finance manager at MartinHoldsworth," Tom says, proud as punch. "Runs a whole department."

"And what about you, Patrick?" I ask.

"I run a bookkeeping business," Patrick says. "It's small now, but we'll expand with time."

"So tell me about your parents, Lucy," Diana jumps in. "What do they do?"

"My dad was a university professor. Retired now. And my mother's passed away. Breast cancer." It's been seventeen years, so talking about it is uncomfortable rather than upsetting. Mostly the discomfort is for other people, who, upon hearing this news, have to figure out something to say.

"I'm sorry to hear that," Tom says, his booming voice bringing a palpable steadiness to the room.

"I lost my own mother a few years back," Patrick says. "You never get over it."

"You never do," I agree, feeling a sudden kinship with Patrick. "But to answer your question, Diana, my mum was a stay-at-home mother. And before that, a primary schoolteacher."

I always feel proud to tell people she was a teacher. Since her death, countless people have told me what a wonderful teacher she was, how she would have done anything for her students. It seems a waste that she never went back to it, even after I started school myself.

"Why bother having a child, if you're not going to stick around and enjoy her?" she used to say, which is kind of funny since she wasn't able to stick around and enjoy me anyway, dying when I was thirteen.

"Her name was . . ." I start at the same time as Diana stands. We all stop talking and follow her with our eyes. For the first time, I understand the term *matriarch*, and the power of being one.

"Right then," she says. "I think dinner will be ready, if everyone would like to move to the table."

And with that, the conversation about my mother seems to be over.

We have roast lamb for dinner. Diana prepares and serves it up herself. Given the size of their house I almost expected caterers to show up, but this part of the evening, at least, is comfortable and familiar.

"I was so impressed to hear about your charity," I say, once Diana is finally sitting rather than serving. "Ollie is so proud of you, he talks about it to anyone who'll listen."

Diana smiles vaguely in my direction, reaching for the cauliflower cheese. "Does he?"

"You'd better believe it. I'd love to hear more about it."

Diana spoons some cauliflower onto her plate, focusing intently on the transaction as if she were performing surgery. "Oh? What would you like to hear?"

"Well . . ." I feel under the spotlight suddenly. "I guess . . . what gave you the idea to start it? How did it get off the ground?"

Diana shrugs. "I just saw the need. It's not rocket science, collecting baby goods."

"She's humble." Tom pushes more lamb onto his fork, still

chewing what's in his mouth. He shoves the forkful into his mouth and keeps talking. "It's her Catholic upbringing."

"How did you two meet?" I ask, realizing that Ollie has never told me this.

"They met at the movies," Nettie says. "Dad saw Mum across the foyer and sparks flew."

Tom and Diana exchange a glance. There is affection in their gaze but something else too, something I can't quite place.

"What can I say? I knew right away that she was the one. Diana wasn't like anyone else that I knew. She was . . . smarter. More interesting. Out of my league, I thought."

"Mum came from a well-to-do family," Nettie explains. "Middle class, Catholic. Dad was a country boy, no connections, no money. Nothing but the shirt on his back."

I take a moment to undo the unconscious conclusion I'd come to the moment I walked into the house—that Diana had married Tom for his money. It's a sexist thought, but not a ridiculous conclusion to come to, seeing the disparity in their looks. The fact that she'd married him for love raises Diana a few notches in my opinion.

"And how about you, Diana," I ask. "Did you just know?"

"Course she did!" Tom says, framing his face in his hands. "How could you not, seeing this face?"

Everyone laughs.

"Actually I've been trying to tell him I'm not interested for thirty-five years but he just keeps speaking over the top of me," Diana says wryly. She and Tom exchange a smile.

After her earlier formality, it's nice to see this side of her. I allow myself to hope that once we've spent some more time together, she'll let me into this inner sanctum of hers. Maybe one day I'll even start helping her with her charity? Diana might not be the easiest nut to crack, but I'd get there. Before long, we would be the best of friends.

I was thirteen when my mother, Joy, died. Mum was aptly named—always having fun, never taking herself too seriously. She wore kerchiefs and dangly earrings, and she sang loudly in the car when the radio played a song she liked. At my birthday parties, she came in fancy dress, even though none of the other adults did, and she had a pair of tap shoes that she liked to wear from time to time, even though she'd never learned how to tap.

That was the kind of person my mother was.

The only time I saw Mum dress in black—without so much as a headband or wiglet or adornment—was when she attended a conference or dinner with Dad. Dad is the polar opposite of Mum—conservative, serious, gentle. The only time Mum reined in her personality, in fact, was for Dad. When Dad decided to switch tenures midway through his academic career—something tricky and likely to undermine his career and our livelihood—she supported him without question. "Dad's job is to look after us, our job is to look after him."

Dad never recovered after she died. Apparently statistics said that most men remarry within three years of a previous relationship ending, but twenty years on, Dad is still happily single. *Your mother was my life partner*, he always says, *and a life partner is for life*.

Dad hired a housekeeper after Mum died, to cook and clean and shop for us. Maria was probably fifty, but with her black hair flecked with gray that was rolled into a coil she may as well have been a hundred. She wore skirts and pantyhose and low-heeled court shoes, and floral aprons she sewed herself. Her own children were grown and the grandchildren hadn't showed up yet. She came from twelve noon until six P.M. every day. I don't know what Maria's official role was insofar as I was concerned, but she was always there when I got home from school and it seemed like it was the best part of her day. It was the best part of my day too. She'd empty my bag and rinse out my lunchboxes and chop up fruit and cheese on a plate for my afternoon tea—things Mum wouldn't have done in a blind fit. With hindsight, some may have felt smothered by Maria.

I simply felt mothered.

Once, when I had the flu, Maria came for the whole day. She pottered around, checking on me periodically, bringing me water or tea or a cool cloth for my forehead. A couple of times, when I was dozing and heard her enter the room, I'd let out a little moan, just to hear Maria fussing. She'd kiss my forehead and bring me water. She even fed me soup with a spoon.

It was, hand on heart, one of the best days of my life.

Maria left when I turned eighteen. She'd had her first grandchild by then, as well as an aging dog with glaucoma, and besides, I was nearly grown so there wasn't much for her to do anymore. After that, Dad got a regular cleaner, and started doing his grocery shopping on his way home from work. Maria kept in touch with birthday gifts and Christmas cards, but eventually her life got filled up with her own family. And that's when I realized. I needed *my own* family. A husband, some children, an old blind dog. Most importantly, I needed a Maria. Someone to share recipes, to give wisdom, and to drown me in waves of maternal love. Someone who wouldn't leave and go back to her own family because I *was* her family.

I didn't have a mother anymore. But one day, perhaps, I'd have a mother-in-law.